THE KILLING FROST

THE KILLING FROST

.....an american tragedy

Richard J. May

Indy**Publish**

THE KILLING FROST .....an american tragedy

Published in the United States by IndyPublish.com
1487 Chain Bridge Road
Suite 304
McLean, VA 22101

ISBN 1-58827-060-2 (Paperback)
ISBN 1-58827-061-0 (Gemstar Rocket eBook)

Introduction

I spent most of my adult life in northeast Ohio, in and around the Akron area. My occupation was that of a police officer, though I now believe that I have always had a book inside me just waiting to be published. Eventually I strove to obtain my PhD in Criminal Justice from the University of Oklahoma and later at Kennedy-Western University in California, and I am still in the process of that monumental task. I thoroughly enjoyed my second career as a criminologist, but at present, I am retired, and using my time to complete various writing projects and the research which goes along with them.

As a graduate student in the Public Administration Department at the University of Akron, following my retirement from the Akron Police Department, one of my required courses was Historical Preservation Planning. It was one of the last requirements which stood between me and my Master's degree, and I looked forward to it with about as much enthusiasm as a street cop relishes a domestic violence call.

One of the requirements for the course was a research paper on one of several topics selected by the professor. I chose to write on historical restoration, which was a no-brainer for several reasons. First of all, I already had a historical restoration in mind. Secondly, the other topics were bland and uninteresting. Thirdly, the historical restoration that I had in mind would be easy to research, since it lay only about 50 miles from where I was living at the time.

In perfect candor, I suppose that I could be called a "closet historian" because of my affinity for the subject of history, though I knew an academic career in history would be doomed because of my poor memory for dates and names. (Several of my good friends who teach History will never let me live it down after they learn this.)

Much of my interest in history has evolved from my interest in genealogy, and I am proud that my own American roots may be traced back to 1605. My original American ancestor, able seaman James May, was a member of Captain John Smith's crew which founded the First Virginia Company. Some of the descendants of James May later migrated to Ashe County, North Carolina, where my great-grandparents were born. Later, great-grandfather Nathaniel May married Cynthia Dickson, a full-blooded Cherokee woman who had been adopted by a nearby Christian family. I was surprised to learn that President William Clinton and I share the same seventh great grandfather, Benjamin May.

I was extremely pleased and quite proud to learn of my Indian heritage, and it sparked an interest in the Indian culture which has never waned. I consider myself to be a Cherokee. One of the many pleasures that I now have from living in southwest Oklahoma is because I lived in an area of the beautiful Wichita Mountains which is heavily populated with the wonderful Kiowa people. Many of my neighbors were Kiowas, and the headquarters for the Comanche and the Apache tribes, as well as the Kiowa, are centered nearby to my former home in Mountain Village. Many of the present day descendants of the Delaware Indians of this manuscript currently reside in Anadarko, Oklahoma, about 40 miles north of Mountain Village.

The topic of my graduate research paper in historical restoration was Schoenbrunn Village, a Moravian mission which became the first civilized settlement in the state of Ohio. I first learned of Schoenbrunn sometime around 1970, and I can't remember how I came to know of it. But on one clear, warm, spring weekend, I drove my wife and two small sons south on Interstate 77 to the New Philadelphia exit in Tuscarawas County. Just a few miles east of the city of New Philadelphia, off State Route 259, is Schoenbrunn Village, and the history of the area is almost too much for a body to take. It is very near the same feeling I got the first time I saw Washington, DC and the nation's capitol, and the myriad of other historical sites and monuments.

Schoenbrunn (meaning "beautiful spring" in German) is the place of the beginning of the history of what is now the state of Ohio, and the site of one story that has remained largely untold to the American people, the story of the massacre of 96 converted-Christian Delaware Indians. The present village is a historical restoration of the first permanent settlement in the state, and it is situated an easy and beautiful drive just south of the bustling urban centers of Canton, Akron, and Cleveland to the north.

In the lush green and rolling hills of Tuscarawas County, the Ohio Historical Society acquired the nearly three acres of land believed to be the site of the original village in 1923. Preliminary excavations uncovered enough artifacts to convince the Society that the locale was genuine, and work on the restored village soon began. By 1928, several cabins and the church and schoolhouse had been rebuilt. The restored village at Schoenbrunn is truly humbling to behold. It consists of nearly twenty simply constructed log cabins situated about a central church and schoolhouse. Examples of eighteenth century life are everywhere. Wool-spinning, agriculture, religion, education, and home life are accurately represented by tools, artifacts and antiques of the era. Many of the cabins are furnished with items which illustrate the almost spartan existence of those who went before. The "streets" of the village are now expanses of soft green grass crisscrossed by pathways, which lead the visitor to any of several period displays. Authentically costumed volunteers reenact many of the early frontier customs and tasks in live action while tourists watch, cameras click and camcorders whir.

On the north side of the village is the cemetery, called "God's Acre" by the Moravians, and the modest tombstones there give ample evidence of some of the hardships endured by those who helped build Schoenbrunn. Those buried there have headstones bearing only their first name and perhaps their age. The short life enjoyed by the earliest settlers of the Ohio territory is apparent by the number of youths and young adults who now lie in a somber collection of simple historical memories.

There is a wonderfully quaint visitor's center, complete with displays, books, souvenirs and refreshments. The village is managed and maintained by the Ohio Historical Society and there is a minimal admission fee to the grounds. Generous free parking is available and there are also accommodations for the handicapped, except for restrooms. Although none of the village proper is paved, a wheelchair can navigate the crude but smooth pathways with some difficulty.

In the 1970s, each summer, there was a marvelous pageant at a nearby amphitheater called "Trumpet In the Land," and the events of eighteenth century Tuscarawas County were re-enacted by volunteer actors and performers in the community. Now, special candlelight tours are held on the second Saturday of the month from June to October at pleasant intervals of thirty minutes. Children's Day, held annually in June, offers events of eighteenth century Schoenbrunn, such as butter-churning, candle-dipping, spelling bees and games of the era, but it is not just for the kids, but the entire family. On a selected Saturday each August, visitors can sample authentic German and Native American foods prepared over open fires, just as the early settlers did, in the 18th Century Foods Fair, and monies raised by the event support the Schoenbrunn Volunteer Association Fund. A Moravian Love Feast is held each Christmas at Schoenbrunn, earlier in December, on a Saturday, in which visitors join in the singing of holiday hymns and sampling of Moravian sugar cakes. Authentic Moravian music is provided by a brass ensemble choir.

Schoenbrunn Village is open Memorial Day weekend to Labor Day from 9:30 a.m. to 5 p.m. Monday through Saturday, and from noon to 5 p.m. on Sundays. After Labor Day, through October, it is open 9:30 a.m. to 5 p.m. Saturdays, and noon to 5 p.m. on Sundays. School groups are welcome by appointment April and May and September and October. The site is closed November to March each year. Although approximately 25,000 visitors a year tour the grounds, most are "repeaters," who first toured the site as a school child. Too few know of Schoenbrunn Village or the many stories concerning the birth of the state of Ohio. Many of my closest friends have neither visited nor even heard of the place. It remains one of Ohio's best kept secrets. I hope that this work inspires many more to see and learn some of the things that I have learned about the area and its history.

For some reason, I either did not know of or remember the tragedy that occurred in the Tuscarawas region until I began my graduate level research of the restored village. One of the most useful and informative pieces on Schoenbrunn that I uncovered during my research was an article written by Earl P. Olmstead for the August/September 1991 edition of *Timeline*, the magazine of the Ohio Historical Society. Olmstead's article, entitled *A Day of Shame*, is an historical account of the events preceding and surrounding the tragedy, but it reveals little about the human emotion of those involved. I would like to thank Mr. Olmstead for inspiring the desire in me to tell a slightly more intimate version of his story.

The scene of the actual tragedy took place about ten miles to the south, in a subsequent Moravian settlement, known as Gnadenhutten. My own historical bent, coupled with my Cherokee heritage evoked in me a response that could only be answered by telling the human side of the historical events that took place more than two hundred years ago in the Tuscarawas River Valley, and I vowed to myself that someday, I would write such a story. In researching my project, I also visited the site of the beginnings of the Moravian Church, in Herrnhut, Germany, near the Czechoslovakian border. The landscape has obviously changed considerably since the early 1700s, but the trip was a wonderful experience and gave me valuable insight into some of the travails of the founders of the Moravian movement. I experienced goosebumps as I stood there in Bohemia, visualizing the early Moravian pioneers gazing upon the same natural vistas.

"The Killing Frost" is not just a book about a massacre of a large number of innocent Indians. It is an intense historical novel involving the poignant dialogue of those who experienced the excitement of establishing the first white settlement in the state of Ohio, of unfortunate, suffering people who were caught in the middle of the Revolutionary War, and of the immense personal struggles of some of these individuals which have been largely untold.

I was most fortunate to have the cooperation of officials of the Moravian Church, headquartered in Bethlehem, Pennsylvania. Among the materials sent at my request, was an unpublished manuscript, *Spiritual Life in Schoenbrunn Village: A study of the religious life of the first Moravian Indian Mission in Ohio*, and written by the Reverend Doctor Albert H. Frank, Assistant Archivist of the Moravian Church Archives. The piece was read by Rev. Dr. Frank at the annual Vesper of the Moravian Historical Society, in Nazareth, Pennsylvania, on October 12, 1989.

Rev. Dr. Frank's work contained an endnote which very nearly escaped my attention, despite my experience at poring over similar minute details. It pertains to the crux of the problems encountered by Reverend David Zeisberger and the others who established Ohio's first civilized settlement. The footnote reads:

> "[20] A list of Zeisberger's miscellaneous correspondence as found in the Draper collection has been compiled by Earl P. Olmstead of the Tuscarawas County Historical Society showing that much intelligence material passed back and forth between Schoenbrunn and Fort Pitt.
>
> The difference in treatment of events in the diaries and the correspondence may be accounted for in realizing that Zeisberger was aware that the diaries would be read by the Church authorities at Bethlehem who were officially committed to neutrality during the American Revolution. His apparent pro-colonial position, similar to that of Georg Neisser at York, PA, would have met with disapproval and could have jeopardized the future of the work in Ohio. Similar results would have followed if the authorities knew the pressures under which the village actually existed and the diaries were written with selective care to insure continuation of the missions in Ohio. Zeisberger was actually playing both ends against the middle with the village being that middle."

It is obvious that in addition to the problems inherent in establishing a religious mission in an uncharted and uncivilized territory, David Zeisberger, and those who assisted him, were literally and actually caught between the two sides of the Revolutionary War. The British, from their stronghold at Detroit, were successful at enlisting the aid of most of the Indian tribes west of Pennsylvania — including some of the very Indians (the Delaware) that the Moravians were seeking to convert. The colonial forces in the area, centered at Fort Pitt, were simply fed up with being attacked by Indians and saw even the Christianized Delaware as a threat to their existence on the western frontier. Ironically, most of the goods which had to be purchased or traded for by members of the Moravian mission were only available from those within or near Fort Pitt. In order to continue to trade at the fort, the Moravians were expected to resist British influence in the Ohio territory and pass along information of British and /or Indian movements in the area. At the same time, the British, well aware of the need of the Moravians to trade at Fort Pitt, conceded the fact, but with the caveat that no other assistance be given the colonials. A precarious position for the Moravians to be sure, especially with the announced position of the Moravian Church.

The Moravian Church officials in Bethlehem, Pennsylvania, issued a strict official stance of neutrality in the war to its missionaries. If Bethlehem were to learn of the tremendous pressures being exerted upon the missionaries in the Ohio territory by both sides, the Church would have undoubtedly recalled and canceled Zeisberger's duties to his missions. David Zeisberger and his people were faced with seemingly impossible conflict on nearly a daily basis, and the story of the successes of the Moravian experience in Ohio territory despite the opposition, danger and violence is the true essence of **"The Killing Frost."** I am profoundly indebted to Rev. Dr. Frank and the Moravian Church for their assistance in supplying material, for preliminary editing, and for their overall generous support. Without it, this book would never have been possible.

Revelations of mistreatment of a minority group is not new. The enslavement of black Africans in our own history, the annihilation of the Jews during Hitler's rein of terror in Europe, and the recent Serbian ethnic cleansing of Muslim-Croats in eastern Europe are tragedies that are well known and extremely regrettable. Not nearly so well known, however, is the tragedy that occurred at Gnadenhutten, perhaps the first documented example of the wide-spread or large-scale savage mistreatment of Indians by the whites in this country. The subsequent destruction and relegation of the entire Indian culture to the status of second class citizen or worse is a mantle of shame to be worn by many. This work on the Indians and their suffering in the Ohio Territory is intended as a tribute to not only those Indians who perished at Gnadenhutten, but to all American Indians everywhere, whose suffering and deprivation is one of the saddest legacies of this or any nation.

March, 1782

Thomas and Jacob, both aged 10, had somehow survived the horror of the vicious attack. Before them now lay the task of telling those back at the lake about what had occurred, and they knew that they were a long, long way from *those* friendly faces. The weather was brutal and unyielding, and their journey would be monumental. Icy, swirling March winds at times became razor sharp blades which seemed to slice away at their tender skin. Days would be extremely difficult for them, and nights — well, they didn't even want to think about the nights which lay ahead. They were not even thinking about how many nights stood between them and the lake — they only knew that they must hurry onward.

They were not properly clothed for any kind of trip at all; especially not a trip in this harsh, punishing weather. They wore only light clothing. Fragments really, in Thomas's case. Neither had had the luxury or the opportunity to choose more suitable garments. Survival instincts and a chilling loneliness compelled them to flee from the grisly scene northward now, knowing that in that direction there was someone who cared, but behind them, only pure evil and terror. Since leaving the carnage behind, each had experienced a brief doubt as to whether or not they were doing the right thing by fleeing. Their families were back there, somewhere, but they didn't even want to think of what had happened to the others. After pausing to look behind them but once, their frightened eyes met momentarily and they instinctively knew that they had only one option, and that was to go on, to get far away from what had happened. They already knew that there were no other survivors.

Despite the fact that they had made the long trip north on only one previous occasion, their Indian instincts for survival in the wilderness would somehow carry them. Adrenaline alone propelled them to run like the wind through the thin forest which made up the rolling hillside just north of their former camp. Though their sides ached with each breath, they did not stop to rest for the first two days. They were too scared to be tired, so they simply ran on and on. From daylight to darkness they ran and slower, to be sure, but still constantly moving, and into daylight and approaching darkness again. They had not even stopped long enough to plan their path. They just ran.

The cold gray sky which showed hesitantly between stands of starkly bare trees and brush seemed to be mocking their attempts to reach the others. Or to simply survive. The foreboding terrain was a challenge for grown, healthy young men in the best of condition during optimal weather conditions. Only their fear of what they had endured and the desperate urge to survive and warn the others kept them going.

As the second nightfall neared, Thomas, who was taking the lead, slowed to a walk and then slowly ground to a halt as he, for the first time, felt the uphill grade begin to tax his young but bitterly abused body. Jacob, continuing to power on with his head down, ran into the other boy, nearly knocking him off his feet. It was only then that they finally made the unspoken choice to stop. They had not said more than a handful of words to each other to this point, and now they virtually collapsed in each other's arms in sheer exhaustion. As the urgency of escape now began to subside slightly, they began to slowly talk about what had happened. They found it extremely difficult. When they began to discuss their families who had perished, both experienced tears welling up in their eyes, and words and sentences simply stuck in their youthful throats. Although they could not dwell on the horror behind them, inherently they did know that they had to go on. Their physical and emotional conditions not withstanding, they vowed to each other to make it to the northern camp, to tell the others of what they had seen.....and of what they had endured.

A day or two later, in a small, clear pool of unfrozen water in a slow moving stream, Thomas stared for the first time, and for what seemed an eternity, at the wounds on the head and shoulder of a small figure that he could not even recognize as being himself. A huge gash lay encrusted with thick dark blood, clotting slowly alongside a large mis-shapened bump on the front of his head. The dark reflection failed to reveal that the boy's forehead was an ugly colorful mixture of yellow, green, and blue bruises which abutted a reddened swelling near his hairline. He could not see the large, hairless bloody spot which covered much of the top of his head. The throbbing pain in the region of the wound was a constant reminder to him of the dreadful circumstances of the attack. His left shoulder was swollen to nearly twice its normal size. He had experienced a constant, stabbing pain in the area midway between the outer shoulder and his neck, and he had no way of knowing that his shoulder blade had been smashed in two separate fractures. His left arm hung limply and uselessly from the injured shoulder. He wondered if he would ever regain the use of the arm. Right now, the outlook did not look good.

The physical injuries were permanently disfiguring to Thomas, and though it had been several days — could it be that it had been this long already? — he was still in a great deal of pain. Jacob, though relatively uninjured, was a frail little boy, scared and simply worn out. Both by now had suffered swollen and bloody feet, for in the beginning, in their helter skelter flight away from the disaster, they had ignored sharp rocks, thorns and twigs as they fled. Their pace became much slower now, but determined none the less. There was still fear and uncertainty which impelled them northward.

Drawing on each other's assistance and courage all along the way, they had bravely traveled nearly the entire two hundred or so miles of the grueling journey to join the rest of their people. Little of the route was through open country. In fact, aside from a few stretches of graveled creek bed here and there, most of the way was through dense, nearly impassable underbrush. Occasionally a faint but distinct deer trail would ease them through the dense thicket. But the memory of the ordeal was fresh enough in their minds to make them continue to hurry at a breath-taking pace, no matter the terrain. Jacob's side ached almost constantly as they moved through the woodlands, but he did not complain. Instead, he wondered to himself how Thomas had managed to stay alive. He could see that Thomas was in much more pain, but Thomas did not complain either.

Slowing considerably on a long, upward incline, Thomas turned suddenly and said to Jacob, "Do you think that I will always look so scary, Jacob?" The question caught Jacob off guard and he did not know what to say, so he pretended he did not hear what was asked. But the same question had entered Jacob's thoughts further back toward the village. When Thomas stopped and firmly repeated the question, Jacob was forced to answer. "I really don't think so," he said, but the answer was tinged with more hope than reassurance. "Remember the dog who got caught in the bear trap? The men had to cut off his leg, and he looked pretty bad then too, but after he got used to it, it turned out okay," he added.

"Thanks a lot, Jacob!" said Thomas, who was by now looking at his own dangling left arm and continuing to wonder if it would ever again be useful to him. "No, no, I mean....." interjected Jacob, but Thomas had already turned and continued his hurried pace. "Wait, Thomas," he cried after the other boy, who did not stop. Talking to Thomas's back as they briskly climbed upward, he said the only thing he could think of to make things better, "I wish it had been me instead of you." Thomas stopped abruptly in his tracks and turned once more to face the boy behind him, saying, "Now that's stupid. But, thanks." Even this hollow bit of kindness was warmly received by the injured boy. "Come on, let's get going," he said as he resumed their torturous climb. The two never talked about the subject again.

The bitter cold winds whipped them unmercifully as they continued to make their way in the direction of their people. From time to time, during their frenzied flight, they slipped and fell on icy patches, and small but tender patches of skin were ripped from their fragile limbs. By now, each looked as though he had engaged in a wrestling match with a wild cat. And each appeared to have lost. The days were cold for them, but the nights were nearly unbearable. Gradually they became too exhausted to travel at night, and as the sun would begin to slip from their sight, each evening they found themselves looking in vain for some kind of shelter. They usually huddled closely in each other's arms in a small natural pocket out of the cutting path of the wind, trying desperately to cover themselves with piles of damp, cold leaves. The thought of starting a fire had barely occurred to them, so frightened were they of the terror behind them. Without discussing the possibility of a fire, they seemed to know that a fire might reveal their location to their attackers. They simply stopped when it became too dark to go on, and they began each new day with the slightest bit of daylight. Their food intake consisted mainly of small edible roots which they were able to dig from the ground with their small and bloody hands. Jacob did most of the foraging for the morsels, as Thomas's limp left hand was of little use to him.

On one particularly dark and ominous day as they made their way through a small stand of bright green pine trees, a large covey of Grouse flushed unexpectedly and flew practically into their faces, nearly scaring the boys out of their skin. The birds, no doubt, were as frightened as Thomas and Jacob, but it caught the boys totally off guard, and gave their systems an unwelcome shock. Both boys lost their color and breath momentarily as the birds flapped their wings wildly in an amazing natural display of fleeing movement and noise. Instinctively, the boys had turned immediately and begun to run away from the surprising clamor. It was Jacob, however, who first realized what had occurred, and he reassuringly called back Thomas, who had quickly broadened the distance between them. Thomas also realized what had caused their shock at precisely the time that Jacob had called his name. Although it was an event which would have made them laugh in other times, the memory of what they were running from was all too real, and the two merely readjusted their route to the north again. There were no smiles on this day or for many days to yet to come.

It was not the last time that the pair of survivors would be scared out of their wits. About three days from reaching their destination, the boys were surprised by a small Shawnee hunting party as they slept fitfully by a trickling stream. Although they were not enemies of the Shawnee, the boys were still frightened by awakening to the presence of the strangers peering at them. Thomas let out a loud yelp upon awakening face to face with the Shawnee leader, who was intent on getting a closer look at the boy's wound, and it startled the brave enough that he reflexively jumped back a step or two. The other men let out a howl of laughter as their leader almost lost his feet in recoiling from the startled boy's reaction. The boys shivered violently in the early March air as they quickly realized that they were the object of the Shawnee inspection. Their initial reaction was that the men who had caused their terrible ordeal had followed and tracked them down, and for a split-second, the two boys fully expected to die. But the Shawnee meant them no harm and knew that the boys were in trouble, for they were much to young to be alone in this land, and Thomas's wounds evoked a sympathetic response from the hunters. It was immediately obvious to the men that the boys were not at all prepared for camping out in the woodlands at this time of year. The hunters also knew that the boys were Indians, probably Delaware, because they spoke only English, and the men knew that this was because of the missionary called David.

The Shawnee also knew of David, and though they did not subscribe to his beliefs, came to trust him, as he had been fair and honest in his dealings with all the Indians he encountered. At first the Shawnee tried to persuade the boys to accompany them to their village, but Thomas and Jacob were quite emphatic in insisting that they were going all the way to the lake. With a great deal of compassion after hearing their story, the hunters gave the boys a blanket and some pemmican scraps, and then disappeared over a small hill. The two frightened boys, barely talking throughout the balance of their journey, continued northward, and now at an even more hurried pace.

As Thomas chewed hungrily on the jerky, he thought of the Shawnee who had given them the meat. Although himself a Delaware, like other boys his age, Thomas was still impressed by the sight of Indians who had not been converted. He was proud to be an Indian, but also thankful that he and the others were now considered to be "civilized." "How could this be?" he thought, "How could the civilized people do this to me and the rest of our people?" The comparison of the white men's savagery to the kindness of the fearsome Shawnee who had just left them, completely baffled the boy, and his eyes glazed once again with tears as he walked. He knew, however, that Jacob could not see his hurt, and he was glad of that.

The pain in Thomas's head continued to throb and seemed to match the rhythm of each of his steps. Though he was aware of the symmetry, try as he could, he could not change it. He changed his pace from time to time, skipping a step or two, but the staccato beat of the pain lingered persistently until it once more matched his cadence. He also attempted to hum some of the hymns that David had taught them, thinking that it would alleviate the pain, but the throb only intensified, and he stopped humming. He did, however, find great comfort in constantly reciting the words of the hymns as he hurried through the woods. Unknown to Thomas, Jacob had been doing the same thing for several days. It was a genuine tribute to their Christian upbringing that the words of their religion, as taught by the

Moravians, were sustaining them as they continued along on their torturous journey.

From every high ground since they began their trip, they peered north, trying to see the waters of Lake Erie. Each new plateau before them offered them hope that their ordeal would soon end, but one after another, their spirits continued to be dampened. In a final clearing just ahead, they felt certain that the lake would at last be visible, and their unending optimism caused them to hurry their pace. And they were not disappointed again. At last, from a high, rocky ridge, they could now see the lake, and they knew that their journey would soon be over. They would finally be with their people. And in just a few hours, the boys were met by familiar faces, but the faces were not smiling. Thomas's wounds were severe enough to bring an immediate and pronounced startle reaction to all he encountered.

The people who first met them were indeed aghast at the sight of the two bedraggled and injured boys. They wept openly and held the boys close to them. Thomas tried to tell them what had happened, but they quieted him and told him to wait until David was there to hear. It was as if the adults instinctively knew of the terrible incident that had occurred. Perhaps not who was involved, but certainly *what* had befallen the boys. Jacob, now surrounded by those he knew, was once more a little boy, and he too, wept. Exhausted and in terrible anguish, Jacob sobbed and clung to a woman who had once lived nearby his family. A man from this small group left them and ran toward the lake, and they knew that he would summon David. After washing and bandaging Thomas's wounds and the blistered and bloody feet of both boys, the people watched silently and sadly as these two young survivors shivered in the early spring gusts which blew in from the lake. Everyone knew that there was a tale of terror waiting to be told, and they would soon hear it, as David was now approaching.

David Zeisberger was their leader. Not only because he was their spiritual and religious leader, but because they admired and respected his strength and resolve. Throughout his own recent ordeals, David had courageously withstood the torment of all those opposed to him and his beliefs. He had forsaken a life of relative comfort in the east to come to the wilderness of the Ohio country to live and work with the Delaware. In fact, he was as much now a Delaware as the rest of the people were now "civilized." David *was* one of them and he suffered with them. In fact, he suffered more than most of the others.

David greeted the boys with a hug and quieted their tears with his reassuring manner. Thomas was curled within his right arm, while Jacob nestled snugly to his left. Then he said, "Thomas. Jacob. How good to see that you are safe and have rejoined us. Tell us, now, of what has befallen you and what of the rest of the party that returned to our villages in the south?" David stared at Thomas's ugly wounds as his right arm encircled the frightened boy. Thomas winced in pain from his damaged shoulder and David gently relaxed his grip. After a few seconds, as Jacob again began to sob quietly, Thomas said, "The militiamen came to our villages as we were gathering food and they did this to us. They're all gone — all of our people." Jacob sobbed more noticeably, and David tightened his hug at the same time. Tears and quiet sobs were everywhere among the people that had gathered to hear the news. Thomas continued, "They put all of us in houses and would not let us leave. The men were put in one house, and the women and children in another. The next morning, they led us from the houses one by one, and....." his voiced became so quiet that everyone strained to hear. "Go on, my child," urged David, who by now was fighting to hold back tears and found it very difficult to speak. Summoning up his courage, Thomas continued. "They killed everyone. They just took the large wooden cooper's mallet and smashed everyone's head with it," he said, wiping his tears as he went on. "When they thought everyone was dead, they scalped almost everyone. That is what happened to me, Reverend. Only I tricked them into thinking I was dead. When they struck me with the hammer, I fell to the ground and pretended to be dead. I must have fallen asleep, because the next thing that I can recall is that I awoke in great pain and covered with blood. I looked around and the militiamen were gone and all of our people were dead and scattered all around. Nearly everyone had been scalped. Jacob came slowly out of woods and he told me that he had hidden there to escape the Americans." Jacob nodded his endorsement of Thomas's story and Thomas continued. "We looked around for any of the others still alive, but there was no one. They were all gone. Dead."

Those who had gathered round to hear the boys' tale were sickened by the revelation of the deaths of so many of their flock. The sight of a young boy like Thomas, having been scalped and hacked with a tomahawk or skinning knife made many of the older people retch and turn away as the extent of the tragedy unfolded. David stretched free of the boys and then re-extended his free right arm to the boy and Thomas entered the curl and was drawn close to the man. "How do you know they were militiamen, Thomas?" asked David.

At this point, Jacob volunteered to speak, and David turned to look at him. "When the men first arrived in our villages, they began taking prisoners, and my mother and brother and I were placed in one cabin while my father and the other men were placed in another. My mother listened through cracks in the walls and heard them talking. When they came for us, Mama pushed me through a small hole in the wall and told me to run. I was hiding in the underbrush across the river, and I saw what happened. I could also hear them talking and laughing. When they had finished killing everyone, their leader said, "We must leave now to get back to Fort Pitt." One of the men there called him Colonel Williamson. When they left, they went east, toward Fort Pitt," said the boy, who was now crying after

19

his painful recollection of the massacre. David hugged him even tighter then.

"That would be Colonel David Williamson," thought David, who had remembered the name from his many years of correspondence with the colonial Commander at Fort Pitt, Colonel Daniel Brodhead. David had heard enough to be convinced that the massacre was truly the work of the militiamen, but he could not understand why. The people at Fort Pitt knew that he and his flock of converted Delaware clearly favored the Americans over the British, although they were declared neutral. Why had this terrible thing happened? In the next few minutes, he would eventually learn from young Jacob more of what his mother had seen and heard just before the first of the flock had been killed, Colonel Williamson had put the fate of the hostages to a vote. Apparently, it had not been a unanimous vote as to the outcome, and by his mother, Leta's estimate, at least sixteen of the men had voted against the eventual deed. These men were allowed to return to Fort Pitt and were not present when the killing began. As Williamson's men contemplated their next moves, the hostages spent their remaining hours or minutes of life praying and singing hymns taught them by David.

Agony, sorrow and guilt now swelled within the body of this white man who snugged the two young survivors to him in a grip that was so powerful that it almost hurt Thomas's shoulder again. Realizing this, David relaxed his arms and allowed the boys the freedom to move, and they both moved — even closer to him. Staring almost abstractly at the earth before him, David silently searched his mind and heart for what to do and what to say. The people around him were silent also. No one moved, and there was only a hushed, muffled sob from some of those who had lost close relatives in the massacre. All had lost close friends. All were awaiting words of reassurance from David.

Finally, with a voice which began cracked with emotion, but which soon swelled to the timbre of a man of God accustomed to addressing his flock, David said, "Let us offer a prayer for our dear brothers and sisters who have gone on before us." He dropped to one knee and with head bowed, faced those who had gathered. None of them could see the flood of tears which obscured his vision, but stopped just short of forming droplets. With a very heavy heart, he continued to stare at the ground as all the others also sank to their knees. In the trees nearby, birds sang merrily as they always do on an early Spring morning. But on this day, their harbinger furnished but an eerie contrast to the grief that was now shared by so many.

"Our Father," David began, "please accept the collective and individual souls of our dear brothers and sisters who were so suddenly delivered to Thy kingdom from this troubled land of plenty. Judge not, too harshly, those who were lost but now are found." As he spoke initially from his heart, he also slowly pulled his well-worn and ever-present Bible from his coat pocket. His weathered fingers pushed randomly into the pages as if guided by a will of their own. Glancing at the place in the Book which had been found by his fingers, he read from Romans, Chapter 8, "What then shall we say to this? If God is for us, who is against us? He who did not spare His own Son but gave him up for us all, will He not also give us all things with Him? Who shall bring any charge against God's elect? It is God who justifies; who is to condemn? Is it Christ Jesus, who died, yes, who was raised from the dead, who is at the right hand of God, who indeed intercedes for us? Who shall separate us from the love of Christ? Shall tribulation, or distress, or persecution, or famine, or nakedness, or peril, or sword?.....No, in all these things we are more than conquerors through him who loved us."

As he closed the Book, David also thought of what he could say on behalf of those who had caused the deaths of so many of his followers, and with only the slightest delay, continued, "And Father, judge not, too harshly the mean spirited actions of those misdirected souls who have wrought this sorrow and devastation upon Thy children. Look upon them as lost sheep, who have been led astray from Thy flock, but will someday surely return. Forgive them now, as Thou hast forgiven all others for their sins. Watch over and guide them so that they might one day serve in Thy heavenly army. And Father, watch over these two children who have witnessed their terrible actions. Infuse their young souls with forgiveness, love and understanding. Leave no room for the hatred and revenge that occupy mere mortals." David hugged both boys close once more, and said, "Amen." And the people gathered in the small clearing by the lake also said, in unison, and very softly, "Amen."

David turned toward the lake and began to walk slowly, and as he did, he released Thomas and Jacob, who quickly were surrounded by those who sought specific information about loved ones and friends who had been slain at the former village. Without turning, David said loud enough for all to hear, "Feed, bathe and clothe them and allow them to rest. We have not suffered nearly as much as they have." A small group of women then shepherded the two boys toward a crude cabin in obedience to David's remarks.

The chilly morning breeze blew directly into David's face as he peered vacantly out into the dark gray waters of Lake Erie, but the shock of learning of the massacre had already numbed him beyond further feeling. He felt and looked much older than his 60 years. A short man, with a stout physique before the recent problems, he had developed a pronounced, sad-appearing, slumping of the shoulders which would persist until the day he died. Hair that had once been almost bright orange in color was now almost solid white. Only the coarse, curly texture would hint of its former color. He had faced much adversity in his life, but none as devastating as the present situation. He knew that there were those within his flock who had been wavering near the point of losing their adopted Christian faith long before the massacre to the south.

He also knew that the Council of Elders in Bethlehem would be particularly disturbed to learn of the latest tragedy to strike members or converts of the missions in the Ohio Territory. He was well aware of their mounting concerns, and following so closely the recent trial in Detroit, it did not bode well at all. He knew that his own effectiveness and leadership would surely be called into question by the Council, if they had not already done so. His immediate attention must be given to the surviving members, however. Bethlehem could wait. He thought of all the adversities that his congregation had met and overcome. But this? This was something which was almost inconceivable.

He wondered, almost aloud, what new trials and tribulations would test him and his Delaware followers. And would he be able to hold his now decimated flock together? His faith in God and his devotion and dedication to the Indians had always shone through in the past, and now he found himself doubting. Doubting whether or not the people would finally lose faith in him, doubting whether he had done his absolute best for the Delaware. Doubting if he had truly done his best service for God. Had he been the best that the Moravian Church could offer to the uncivilized people of the Ohio Territory?

He began to search his memory for proof of his worth. He needed reassurance from his own subconscious that he had done his best, and that all that had happened to the Delaware was not directly the result of his own personal actions. His stubborn Teutonic manner sometimes made him appear slightly arrogant, but there was not the slightest hint of that on this day. At this particular moment, he felt deeply responsible and was consumed with guilt, and his posture and movements revealed his inner most thoughts. To David, the future of his long and dedicated career as a Moravian missionary seemed nearly as murky as the waters of the icy lake before him.

In a brief, nearly temporal panic, he found himself unable to focus on just one of his many positive accomplishments. Events of the recent past that should have been crystal clear to him evaded his grasp and his focus. Where was the memory of Detroit, so recent in time? What had precipitated the mission's move to Lake Erie? Questions that should have been easy for him were nothing more than gigantic gaps of irretrievable blankness. His mind began to skip wildly backward in time in great, huge leaps as he sought frantically to remember events. Any events. Brief, blurred glimpses of his recent past eventually gave way to longer flashes of memories several years old, but these were vague and elusive also. Regressing even further, longer, clearer images of simpler times as distant as his childhood in far away Europe finally slowed in this dizzying procession. At last, his recall slowed to the point that he was able to concentrate on a time from far away and long ago. He began to think of happier, carefree days of his childhood.

David Zeisberger had been born in the Kingdom of Bohemia, a place which would eventually come to be known as Czechoslovakia, in 1721. He remembered little of his life there, however, because at the age of six, his family had been forced to flee their homeland for the sanctity of Saxony to escape the persecution of the Roman Catholic Counter-Reformation which swept much of central Europe at that time. The Zeisbergers had been living in an area of Bohemia inhabited by many of the communal Christians known as Moravians. Owing to their intense Moravian dedication, the Zeisberger family resisted the efforts of any enforced secular beliefs. And like many of the earliest immigrants to the New World, the search for religious freedom would eventually bring the Zeisbergers to America.

In the eleven years that David Zeisberger lived in Saxony, his family had fully embraced all of the teachings of the Moravians — in fact, to the extent that his parents decided to become missionaries for the church. Their first assignments were in Savannah, Georgia, and after they became settled in the New World, David and two sisters and a brother sailed to join them. The year was 1738 when David Zeisberger first set foot upon the North American continent, where the first Moravians had already been for three years.

By now the Zeisberger family, in its entirety, was totally committed to serving the needs of the Moravian Church, especially young David. While in Georgia, David became acquainted with many different people. Savannah was a thriving seaport and he was exposed to many of the peoples of not only Europe, but the rest of the world, who chose the Georgia port as a doorway to an exciting new life. Backwoods trappers, hunters and traders were among the regulars in the marketplaces of Savannah, and missionaries from a host of other churches and varying nationalities passed through the city also. Most intriguing to David, however, were the Indians who lived just beyond the furthest homesites in Savannah, the Cherokee and the Creeks. He also had some contact with the more distant and somewhat less hospitable Choctaw.

From his earliest contact with the Indians of the area, David not only was intrigued because they were of a different culture, but because they seemed as interested in him as he was in them. He admired the simplicity of their lives and their fascination with the whites from Europe and the black men from Africa who, by now, had begun to arrive regularly as slaves in shiploads. David also admired the utter oneness that the Indian seemed to have with nature and all its aspects. Their unwavering belief in the Great Spirit delighted him thoroughly. It was a kind of spirituality to which he could easily identify. He found that he began to seek out the Indians, and he enjoyed their company much more than anyone else's — including his own family. His family could see, almost from the time that

David arrived in America, that his destiny lay with the Indians. His religious beliefs would determine his lifestyle, his career, and his fate, but it was David's personal choice to dedicate his life to converting the Indians of North America to the Moravian faith. He knew that he would one day live, and probably even die, with the Indians.

As he stood there, gazing out in the direction of the lake, his mind settled on a time just outside Savannah, when he and Nathan, a young Indian man had conversation about each other's future. On that occasion, Nathan had invited David to join his family in a Cherokee tradition of storytelling around the campfire. David learned much from watching and listening to the Cherokee on that night. He watched the faces of all those around the dancing flames, as first one story and then another of Cherokee courage and bravery was retold. He marveled at the simplicity of the lives of these people. David could not help but make a comparison of the Indians to the lifestyle of the people from Christ's era. Nathan, noting the far away look in David's eyes, said to him, "David, do our stories put you to sleep, or do you long to be somewhere else?" Almost embarrassed by his noticeable lapse in attention, David replied, "Oh, no, my friend. I was just thinking of a similar event from long, long ago. I am really enjoying my time with your people."

Nathan then explained to David that most of the storytellers were the elders of the local tribesmen, and that each time the stories were told, a tiny bit of the tale changed. When the audience of young Cherokee giggled or smiled in disbelief, the storyteller would quickly get back to the fearsome deed so as to restore dignity to the affair. As the Cherokee, like other Indians, had no written history, the fireside stories were the only means of passing along accounts of what had happened long before. David nodded his understanding to Nathan, and said, "In my church, we do much the same. Except the stories that we tell never change, because they have been written in a great book. The stories that are told are the same that you have heard when you came to our religious service." Nathan then nodded his own understanding to David. David continued, "That which is being done here tonight is what I would like to spend my life doing — except I want to tell our Lord's story to all the other tribes."

David had already witnessed the conversion to Christianity by Nathan and several of his kinsmen. He was pleased that so many of the Cherokee had chosen to follow Christ. It was the thing that inspired so many missionaries to choose and continue this often dangerous work throughout their lives. David was, by then, as committed to becoming a missionary as any elder in his church. He considered this time, this night with the Indians, as extremely valuable to his knowledge of the true purpose of missionary work. Nathan, too, understood David. Indians already knew of the Great Spirit and that all the wonders in the world emanated from Him, but it was not until the white man came to his land that the Indian learned the specifics of Christianity. It was truly amazing to many of the Indians that the white men already knew about the Great Spirit. It was, to them, as if the whites had gained special access to Him, and they were awed at their ability, especially the missionaries, to know so much of the Indians' spirituality. Now that Nathan and many of his tribe were Christians, they all seemed eager to share their new religious beliefs with all who would listen. To an Indian like Nathan, accepting Christianity was a virtual destiny. To a missionary, the Indian represented God's ultimate challenge, and what was required was to learn the Indians' language, their lifestyle, and communicate the word of God. All missionaries inherently believed that God's message was good enough to convince anyone, as long as the proper language could be found.

And communicating with the Indians was not a problem for young David. He had grown up with the Czech dialect of the Balto-Slavic language as his native tongue, and mastered the Gothic dialect of Germanic during the Zeisberger's stay in Saxony. Upon arriving in America, he quickly learned English, and his fascination with the Indians also led him to learn Macro-Siouian, the language of the Cherokee, Creeks, Choctaw and Chickasaw. During his lifetime, David Zeisberger would also become fluent in the dialect of the Delaware, Cree, Iroquois, and Mohican, all of the Algonquian language. That he was unable to lose his strong Germanic accent as he spoke the various Indian dialects gave a very distinct and strangely unnatural quality to the tone of his voice.

After only two years in Savannah, the Zeisberger family quite naturally began to migrate northward to Pennsylvania, a state in which many Germans and eastern European immigrants had settled. The move to Pennsylvania by the Zeisbergers was carefully planned. It had been done in order to establish links with other immigrants like them, and it brought them closer to the center of their spirituality, for the Moravian Church in America was largely centered in the area of what was to eventually become Bethlehem, Pennsylvania.

The Moravian Church was born as Unitas Fratrum (or the Church of the United Brethren) sometime in the early fifteenth century in Europe largely as a result of the work and beliefs of a Bohemian martyr named Jan Hus. Until the early eighteenth century, the religion was tolerated by various European monarchs primarily because the religion had been quietly obedient and respectful and because the acknowledged membership was small and virtually inconsequential. When the Catholic Church began to purge eastern Europe of other faiths, the Brethren were forced to seek refuge outside their homelands. This resulted in a move to Herrnhut, Saxony in 1722, where Count Nikolaus Ludwig von Zinzendorf, a sympathetic and benevolent aristocrat donated a portion of his huge estate to the Brethren, largely to keep them within the Lutheran state church. In Saxony, the Moravian Brethren flourished, and the circumstances of their exile led to a communal type of Christianity (later identified as Pietism) which cultivated a religion of the heart and an intimate personal relationship with the Savior. Count von Zinzendorf, realizing that the Moravians represented the oldest and purest of all Protestant religions, soon abandoned his Lutheran ties, and embraced the religion and put his wealth and prestige fully in support of their efforts.

In 1741, the Count visited America on a dual mission. He was scouting for a larger quantity of land which would accommodate the growing congregation which was by now, nearly too large for the plot that they had occupied on von Zinzendorf's estate in Saxony. Word of the vast, unclaimed, beautiful and bountiful regions of virgin lands in the New World had also reached the village of Herrnhut. Many of the congregation were certain that a rosy future possibly awaited them in this strange new land called America. Also, by now, the Count had truly been caught up in the fervor of Protestant religion himself, and had become a devout member of the Moravians, as the sect had now begun to be known. He earnestly yearned to see the growth of the religion spread to many of the uncivilized regions of the world, and the American cordiality to exiled religions was, even then, well documented. Moravian missions were also active in the West Indies, Latin America, and Africa.

Aside from handfuls of French Jesuit missionaries who had scattered mostly in the Canadian and Ohio territories nearly two hundred years earlier, this new land had been virtually free of organized religious incursions. Most of the other religions lacked the fervor and zeal of the Moravians in seeking new souls, as they were too busy enjoying the new freedom of practicing their formerly persecuted beliefs. The task of adjusting to the rigors of a largely wild and uncivilized new land also accounted for the scarcity of missionary ideology. However, the Count felt that many of the Germanic peoples now settled in America could be converted to the Moravian faith and then persuaded to go forth across this wild, new continent and convert and claim the souls of the native inhabitants.

Those missionaries that had preceded the Moravians were relatively harsh in their ways and unsympathetic, ignorant or simply intolerant of the Indians' culture and needs. They often attempted to impose their own particular brand of religion on the Indians through a domineering monitoring style which, to many Indians and a few outside that missionary effort, seemed too slave-like. Though there were sizable numbers of such Indian converts, there was a noticeable absence of pronounced happiness among them.

The Moravians chose to adopt a different attitude toward their Indian converts to Christianity, and this was evident in their goals. They sought to deliver a message of belief to only those who seemed genuinely interested and capable of understanding. There would be no wholesale or coerced conversions to the Moravian faith. They were as interested in one single soul of a potential convert as a hundred, while other religions had usually sought to convert entire tribes or villages. The Moravians also targeted, specifically, those Indians who had not been influenced by the teachings of missionaries of other faiths. Neither were the Moravians interested in acquiring Indian lands and goods. They were not merchants or traders, merely devout Christians who wished to spread the word of God. They chose not to interfere in Indian politics, either inter- or intra-tribal. In fact, wherever the Moravians settled, they were more than content to live apart from the cultural and political machinations around them, whether civilized or uncivilized. They simply sought to avoid controversy and confrontation of all forms. Of the various religious missions operating in America, the Moravians were, by far, the least obtrusive in native and colonial affairs.

The first Moravians had come to America in 1734. The prospects of the their firm entrenchment in America seemed challenging, realistic and exciting. Following Count von Zinzendorf's journey of 1741, the headquarters of the Moravian Church was officially established in Bethlehem, and missionaries were soon being trained there. By 1745, Moravian missions had been started in and near other Pennsylvania communities and into the Mohican lands to the north, in what would later become New York state. Among the new missionaries who were being readied for service in the field was David Zeisberger.

For more than twenty five years, Zeisberger worked in the various Moravian missions and outposts in the Pennsylvania and New York area, honing his already considerable Indian language skills in dealings with the Mohicans, Iroquois and Delaware tribes. Eager to go further and further west into the great American wilderness, Zeisberger petitioned his elders for permission to lead a mission into the Ohio Territory, which marked what seemed to be the edge of America to people like the Moravians. But the Moravians were strict in their ways, requiring great expanses of apprenticeship of their missionaries before one was given his own mission. Especially a mission into the wilds of Ohio.

Whites had settled as far west as Detroit to the north and in colonial Pennsylvania to near the present day city of Pittsburgh, but the only whites who had earlier ventured into Ohio Territory were the few French Jesuit missionaries of two centuries before, and a small number of hardy and adventurous trappers and traders — many of whom had never been heard from again. Not that the land or the Indians were particularly dangerous, but simply because much could happen to a person alone in the wilderness at that time.

Biding his time until one day when he would be permitted to build his own mission in the wild and intriguing Ohio Territory, David was content to learn his life's work alongside many of the Moravian Church's most ardent missionaries and teachers in Pennsylvania. In central Pennsylvania in 1765, just south of the present day city of New Castle, and under the watchful tutelage of his Moravian elders, David began his first mission at Friedenshutten. At Friedenshutten, he was to meet his lifelong friend and assistant, 22 year old John Heckewelder.

John Gottlieb Ernestus Heckewelder, like David, was a lifelong Moravian, and also like David, was not married. A handsome man of average height with a thin build, Heckewelder had a smile which looked as though it had frozen on his face. It was always present. Unlike David, John's ancestors had not originated in Bohemia, but had come from Northern Germany. John, himself, had been born in Bedford, England — and was almost 22 years younger than David. John's wavy dark blonde hair was as much a novelty to the Indians as the curly red mane of David. The two men hit it off instantly, and worked long and diligently with a number of Indians from the various tribes in the area. Among the many Indian friends that David and John met while at Friedenshutten, was Chief Netawatwes of the Delaware Indians. It was also at Friedenshutten, in late 1771, that he would meet the woman who would eventually become his wife.

Adam Lecron was a young assistant missionary assigned to Friedenshutten as one of David or John's replacements. Though David had seen Adam at one of the Moravian assemblies in Bethlehem, he had never been introduced. Nor had he ever met or seen Adam's wife, Susan Lecron. Adam was in his late 30s, of middle European heritage, but born near Philadelphia. A skilled speaker, Adam was a darkly complected man of medium height. Susan, a tall, slim woman with red hair and muted freckles, was also born in the new world — just west of Plymouth, Massachusetts, and although it was not apparent to the eye, she was nearly ten years older than her husband.

Upon meeting the Lecrons, David had been impressed with the couple's friendly demeanor. He also admired their shared devotion to their church duties. They liked his enthusiasm for his faith, his spirit of adventure, and listening to stories of his many and exciting experiences. In the months before he left for that assignment, David and the Lecrons became very close. His departure would be a sad day for each of them, and David promised to write immediately and often, and they agreed to do the same. It would be more than eight years before David would see either of the Lecrons face to face. And although Susan Lecron would eventually capture his heart, David was now thoroughly dedicated to the task of preparing for his life's work.

In early 1772, at the age of 51, David Zeisberger was finally given the assignment that he had always wanted. It was to be in the Muskingum River valley, deep in Ohio Territory, and it was at the express invitation of Chief Netawatwes, who had spoken to the Moravian elders. From the point of embarkation, near the mission of Friedensstadt on the Beaver River in western Pennsylvania, near the present Ohio/Pennsylvania border, David and his entourage started west into the Ohio Territory. In addition to John Heckewelder, David would be accompanied by two other Moravian couples, the Schmicks and the Jungmanns, and a contingent of about 25 converted Delaware Indians. The Moravians, Johann Schmick and John Jungmann and their wives, were themselves missionaries-in-training who would help David and John until the elders at Bethlehem felt they were sufficiently prepared to minister on their own.

Before leaving for the Ohio Territory, David met one last time with his mentor at Friedenshutten, Reverend Samuel Eichenlaub, who told him, "David, you are a good man and a wonderful Christian. You believe there is good in all men and you have a knack for finding it. This is what will make you a fine messenger of God for the Moravian Church. I know that you will never lose your faith in your work, but do not lose your faith in mankind, either. You will be severely tested in this new assignment, but you are more capable of succeeding than any man I have ever known. God be with you."

Tears of joy and sadness filled Samuel's eyes at that moment, and the two men knelt and prayed. After each had said what was in his heart, they rose and then shook hands for the final time. David fairly glowed with immense pride, feeling confident that he had been carefully trained and prepared for the newest part of his life's work that he was finally about to undertake. He then turned west and began to walk toward the small group who would accompany him to the beckoning and mysterious lands of the Ohio Territory.

May 3, 1772

The trip to the Ohio Territory was terrifically exciting for the Moravians and their small Delaware escort, but was largely uneventful. The weather was kind to the group, and pleasant temperatures and a cloudless sky enveloped them along the entire journey. The terrain west of Friedensstadt became rugged, but not that difficult to travel. Trails were initially broad and well marked, but gradually narrowed and grew nearly indistinct. Soon, creek beds and animal trails became the route where open expanses ceased to exist.

Along the way, numerous campsites of traders, trappers, and earlier missionaries were encountered and each cast a slight chill of excitement over the missionaries, who readily envisioned themselves in those earlier settings. It was also easy for the Moravians to compare their own immediate mission to those who had gone before. Both David and John frequently found themselves day-dreaming along the trail of what it probably had been like for some of the early French Jesuits, and also envisioning the type of mission settlement that they would eventually build.

Upon arriving in the Muskingum River valley in Ohio Territory, just over a hundred miles due west of Fort Pitt, David Zeisberger surely felt that he had entered the Garden of Eden. He and his followers found an idyllic stream called the Tuscarawas River by the local Indians, a tributary to the larger Muskingum River, which offered clear, cold water, and which teemed with fish and abundant beaver and muskrats. In the lush hardwood forests nearby, game was plentiful. Whitetail deer, and smaller game were seemingly everywhere, and there were also signs of black bear.

Small bands of Shawnee had been conspicuously shadowing David's entourage from the moment that they had entered Ohio Territory, but were certainly not unfriendly. On several occasions, the Shawnee had come right up to the new arrivees and traded for a few small items. The Shawnee seemed mostly curious as to why the obvious Indians among the group were dressed in the clothing of the white man? And why did the Delaware wear their hair short, instead of long, like the Shawnee?

In stark contrast to what many of the trappers and traders had said about the perils of the Ohio Territory, the Indians there seemed amicable enough to the missionaries. Was it because of the influence of Chief Netawatwes, who had extended the invitation to the Moravians, or something else? David surmised, judging by the bountiful nature of the area, that exaggerated tales of danger and strife were merely being spread by the trappers and merchants to keep hoards of colonists from pushing deeper westward into the territory and beyond. "They were probably just keeping this wondrous land all to themselves," David chuckled to himself. He was pleased that he had figured this out through his own instant observations.

In a small clearing on the east bank of the stream, and near a refreshingly cold spring, the missionary party pitched camp in a place that would eventually become the first white settlement in the Ohio Territory. The site was at first selected for its convenience at the time and not necessarily meant to be the location of the main mission, but because of its abundance of ideal qualities, David and the others soon opted to build their dream upon that very spot. They never regretted that decision.

After carefully looking over the immediate area, it was apparent to David, and the others soon concurred, that this was a fine place to establish their homes. With the confidence and enthusiasm of a man long skilled at building villages from the earth up, the plans for the site were drawn up in the clay of a flat clearing by the stream. The new village would not be too unlike most of the other missions that David had been in and around since coming to America, but this one was very special to him. He would design it as he saw fit, and he took a great deal of satisfaction in realizing his responsibilities. Much of his spare time at Friedensstadt before the journey began had been spent in planning this mission settlement.

David and his hardy followers laid out the small village that would be known as Schoenbrunn, which meant "beautiful spring" in German, with as much precision as their limited and simple tools permitted. None of the missionary party had technical surveying experience, but all had participated in the construction of other homes and buildings comprising settlements in other civilized locations back east. They were all eager for the time that their own new village would be referred to by others as "civilization."

The settlement would be built in the form of a tee, with the top of the tee being the main street and running east to west, and the town consisting of some 40 lots, each three rods wide by six rods long. The two streets would be four rods wide. Eventually, Schoenbrunn would grow to become a village of almost 60 houses or cabins. The structures would be of hewn timber. There was also the contingency for a similar but smaller number of Indian huts and lodges to be located within the village. The two most interesting structures to be planned were the church/meeting hall which measured approximately 36 x 40 feet, and a schoolhouse, both of which would be located at the intersection of the two streets. All of the village lots would be fenced in, as would the entire settlement, including the cemetery, known as "God's Acre," which was planned for a nearby plateau, north of the village and near the bottom of the tee.

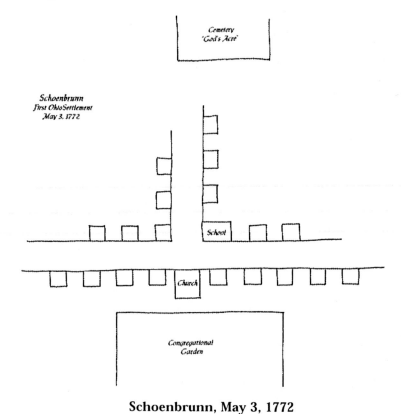

Schoenbrunn, May 3, 1772

The Tuscarawas River was south of and parallel to the planned main street, and the village spring was located to the west end of where the main settlement would be, near the woods. Between the streets and the woods, each personal lot would be tilled and planted, which would provide sustenance for the settlers, supplementing the plentiful game from the surrounding area.

Happily, the Moravians and their handful of Delaware converts began the construction in earnest. In no time at all, many of the centuries-old European techniques of building were being mixed with newer colonial practices in the Ohio Territory wilderness. The Delaware proved to be as industrious as any of the others, and soon worked skillfully with only the minimum of supervision by John or David. In fact, out of respect for their Moravian churchmen, the Delaware attempted to take the heavier, more tedious labor away from the two men. John and David, however, were simply not to be left out of any of the aspects of Schoenbrunn's rise, and they toiled as hard or harder than anyone.

Chief Netawatwes, also anxious to help out with the new construction, sent six of his strongest tribesmen to help out with some of the heavier chores of the settlement, and they were a welcome addition. There were many trees and stumps to be dealt with, and extra muscle was always appreciated. Their presence, however, did little to keep John or David out of the middle of the most grueling work. Of the six men dispatched to the new construction by Netawatwes, five would eventually become Christian converts and occupy homesites within the new village, along with their families. The sixth, a stubborn man called Rilulyan, had trouble abstaining from the use of alcohol and was never serious about seeking conversion. He was, however, extremely well-liked by all who knew him and eventually moved his family to the extreme edge of the village, where he assisted those at Schoenbrunn in various projects for many years.

When, at last, all the timber and stumps had been cleared from the necessary areas, the two streets were laid out in the pre-designed tee. At the top of the tee stood the center of the village, and the center of the universe, as far as David Zeisberger and his Delaware converts were concerned. It was the site of their "Gemeinen Saal," or their church. It would be the largest structure in the new village, serving not only their spiritual needs, but also their civic needs, and it would also house the few personal effects of, and be the future home for the Reverend David Zeisberger. From the front door of the structure, one would eventually be able to look up a slightly inclining street to see the near boundary of "God's Acre."

Directly to the rear of the church plot was the Tuscarawas River. Between the church and the river would be the area reserved for the "Gemeinen Garden" or community garden, where vegetables would be raised to feed the small commune. Since it was already late in the planting season, the community garden got the most attention. Workers hurriedly plowed and planted so that crops could be harvested for the coming winter. The stores of food that had been brought from Friedensstadt would not sustain them beyond the early winter months. Corn, tomatoes, beans, squash, potatoes, pumpkins, and onions would eventually be harvested from the rich, dark, fertile soil adjacent to the river. Wild grape vines grew very near the settlement, as well as fruit-bearing pear, apple, plum, crab apple and cherry trees. Maple trees would provide delicious syrup and tasty maple candy treats each spring for the new settlers. Blackberries, mulberries, raspberries, and strawberries seemed to grow almost everywhere in the beautiful valley which cradled the river.

Across the hard dirt street from the church, the second largest structure in the village, the schoolhouse, would be built. Eventually the schoolhouse would be equipped with rows of coarse wooden benches, fashioned from log halves, and on these the students would sit and do their "ciphering" and other schoolwork on crude slates.

Before the summer was over, most of the permanent features were in place in the village of Schoenbrunn. The two main streets were already showing signs of being well-traveled, and on each side of the streets, the new homes and sheds emitted a smell of freshly cut timber. Vast expanses of untreated wood slabs on the sides of the structures glistened smartly in the direct sunlight. In the fields, a beautiful crop was beginning to give the promise of a later than normal, but adequate harvest. Much of the attention paid the new garden was left to the women and children, who eagerly attended to their tasks while the men went about the business of clearing and building.

Even the children were busily engaged in the construction. Large, flat stones were carried by them from the river's edge to each of the new houses and buildings, to be used as hearths and for steps at the entrances. They were also used to mark off the entrance to the cemetery, which sadly, became the final resting place that very first summer of a tiny baby girl, stillborn to one of the young Delaware couples. David presided over the service for the baby, and for many of the Delaware, especially those who were as yet unconverted, it was their first experience with a Christian burial. It would not be the last.

In the early years at Schoenbrunn, things went relatively smooth for David and the others. Life was good in this new and beautiful territory. David and John, as well as Johann Schmick and John Jungmann, and both their wives, got along exceedingly well with the Christianized Delaware, because their willingness to share was evident. The Indians were pleased that all the Moravians would work side by side with them in the fields, and with any of the physical tasks they encountered. The fact that the Moravians gave so much of themselves to their Indian brethren was not lost upon the Delaware. All of the European Moravians virtually surrendered their own lives to accommodate the needs of their followers. Even on those rare occasions when David would, of necessity, return to Bethlehem on church business, he never tarried — never once wasting a moment that could be spent back in his beloved Schoenbrunn.

To many outside the faith, the Moravian way was exceptionally harsh and disciplined, but David had no trouble convincing the Delaware of its benefits, because they loved and trusted him completely. In return, the Indians were willing to make ample concessions in order to remain a member of the village in good standing. David originally divided his followers into five groups or classes: those who were candidates for baptism, those having been baptized, those who were candidates for communion, those that received communion, and the visitors, newcomers, or those like

Rilulyan who had been allowed to enter the village and become residents.

In most missions of other faiths, everyone who desired could be baptized, simply by asking and subsequently joining the church. Under David's guidance, the Moravians at Schoenbrunn operated slightly differently. Baptism and communion were steps in the conversion process that had to be earned, and each newly attained class or status was a position of honor. To be eligible for baptism, and the first step in the civilization process, one had to give up many of one's previous Delaware practices, and many found this exceedingly difficult. David drew up a list of nearly twenty rules and regulations, which were regularly read in village meetings, church services, and in school.

In addition, the rules were posted on the door of the church and the schoolhouse:

1. *We will know no other God but the one only true God, who made us and all creatures, and came into this world in order to save sinners; to Him alone we will pray.*

2. *We will rest from work on the Lord's Day, and attend public service.*

3. *We will honor father and mother, and when they grow old and needy we will do for them what we can.*

4. *No person shall give leave to dwell with us until our teachers [missionaries] have given their consent and the helpers [native assistants] have examined him.*

5. *We will have nothing to do with thieves, murderers, whoremongers, adulterers, or drunkards.*

6. *We will not take part in dances, sacrifices, heathenish festivals or games.*

7. *We will use no tshapiet, or witchcraft, when hunting.*

8. *We will renounce and abhor all tricks, lies and deceits of Satan.*

9. *We will be obedient to our teachers and to the helpers who are appointed to preserve order in our*

meetings in the towns and fields.

10. *We will not be idle, nor scold, nor beat one another, nor tell lies.*

11. *Whoever injures the property of his neighbor shall make restitution.*

12. *A man shall have but one wife — shall love her and provide for her and his children. A woman shall have but one husband, be obedient to him, care for her children, and be cleanly in all things.*

13. *We will not admit rum or any other intoxicating liquors into our towns. If strangers or traders bring intoxicating liquor, the helpers shall take it from them and not restore it until the owners are ready to leave the place.*

14. *No one shall contract debts with traders, or receive goods to sell for traders, unless the helpers give their consent.*

15. *Whoever goes hunting, or on a journey, shall inform the minister or stewards.*

16. *Young persons shall not marry without the consent of their parents and the minister.*

17. *Whenever the stewards or helpers appoint a time to make fences or perform other work for the public good, we will assist and do as we are bid.*

18. *Whenever corn is needed to entertain strangers, or sugar for Love Feasts, we will freely contribute from our stores.*

19. *We will not go to war, and will not buy anything of warriors taken in war.*
    [This last statute was adopted at a later time, during the Revolutionary War.]

All of the children, boys and girls, attended the school and were very proud to do so — and their parents were equally proud of them. Since there were no textbooks for the nearly one hundred students of the new school, David and his assistant, John Heckewelder, set about the laborious project of writing their own textbooks. Before they completed the textbooks, David and John taught classes to all of the children, at varying times, in either English, Algonquian-Lenape, or German. The textbooks would be predominantly in David's native German.

Among the things prohibited by the rules were alcohol consumption, gambling, dancing, witchcraft, face-painting, Indian clothing, Indian medicinal practices, traditional Indian celebrations, and of course, long hair for men. A difficult transition for the men was that in the mission, men and women alike would tend to the crops in the fields, whereas, in the native tradition, this would have been exclusively the work of the women. Many a converted male suffered the insults of passing warriors who taunted and jeered them in the fields for doing women's work. It was one of the hardest aspects of Christianity for the Delaware to accept. Hunting was allowed, but hunting with bow and arrow was frowned upon because it was too close to the former ways, and since no firearms were allowed in the village, trapping became the mode of obtaining smaller animals. Deer and larger game were still hunted in the traditional manner, although the hunting weapons were not openly displayed in the individual households. In later years, guns would eventually be used by the members for hunting.

In starting the mission at Schoenbrunn, Zeisberger and his Moravian associates also established organized education in their schoolhouse. Reverend Zeisberger, himself, wrote the textbook, which was published later — in 1776 — in Philadelphia. The book was composed of a mixture of prayers, rules, spelling lessons, and the Ten Commandments. Attendance in the school building rose to as many as 100, and the students were instructed in spelling, reading, singing, hygiene, and ciphering.

The church building, which functioned as Zeisberger's residence as well, was also a very busy structure. As many as 300 members would pack the chapel on occasion, although it was never used strictly for services on the Sabbath. It also functioned as a sort of town hall. "Gottes Acker," the first village cemetery at Schoenbrunn eventually held nearly 50 graves, and they were all converted Delaware tribespeople.

Much of what occurred at Schoenbrunn was meticulously chronicled in diaries by each of the missionaries, and although David was a stickler for detail, who had no problem reminding a back-slider of his or her transgressions, he was, for the most part, a very compassionate man who overlooked many minor violations by his flock. His gentle, yet firm admonitions were soon followed by a warm smile and a handshake or a hug. Just about the only thing that he never wavered upon was the required regimen for moving through the various classes or groups. Moravian baptism was not a gift — it had to be earned, and only about a third of the entire Indian population of the village had *earned* baptism, and these were only the very best of the village — those who spoke with authority and were respected by both their fellow converts and the white men who led them.

Because the village was open to all comers, there was a fairly steady stream of non-Christian Indians who visited with their converted brothers and sisters and David encouraged this — as long as none of the rules were broken. He saw all of the visitors as potential converts. Visitors could wear their traditional garb but could not wear war paint or carry weapons while they stayed in the village, and smoking and drinking were strictly *verboten*.

Before one could earn baptism, a certain humility and grace had to be displayed by the potential convert and David scrutinized everyone carefully. Although most baptisms took place after a few months in the village, it was not unusual for some to wait as long as a year.

One such man, who begrudgingly gave up his Indian ways was a man known as Glikhikan, a formidable captain of the Wolf clan, who would eventually be given the Christian name of Isaac. David and Glikhikan had met while David was still posted in western Pennsylvania in the early spring of 1770, and they had gradually developed a long, and lasting respect for each other. Glikhikan had achieved some renown within the Moravian missions because of his respect for the Christians and the fact that he quietly persevered on behalf of the Moravians in numerous disputes with other Indian leaders and tribes. It was a given that Glikhikan, because of his affinity for David and the other Moravians, would one day become a Christian convert. The only question was *when?*

Once he decided to seek Christian salvation, Glikhikan, instantly became Isaac, and had no trouble with most of David's rules, but was adamant about keeping his long hair, which nearly reached his waist. Isaac's obstinance was based largely on some of David's own teachings. Specifically, Isaac was (as were most all of the members) extremely fond of the story of Samson and Delilah, and he questioned David as to why he, Isaac, had to cut his hair, when Samson had met such a poor fate following the loss of his locks. Isaac asked David, following a Sunday service, "Reverend Brother David, why must we cut our hair when today you spoke of Samson and what befell him?"

A gentle smile took over David's face, and placing a hand on Isaac's shoulder, he said, "Samson was a very unique man whom God granted special strength through his hair. He used Samson and the story of what befell him to teach all of us here, today, a lesson about faith. Samson lost that faith and fell victim to the worldly ways of Delilah, who was a pawn for the devil and the heathen Philistines. When Samson eventually regrew his hair and destroyed the temple to which he was chained, he was finally acknowledging that faith in God was the only way.

What happened to the Philistines was also an awakening to them of God's power. My friend, you are more like the Philistines than like Samson, though your hair is long, like his. By cutting your hair, you are saying to God that you are surrendering your heathen ways to His love and guidance. It is a sign that you will obey His words. Your strength is not *in* your hair, but in your heart, in the fact that you have at last found God, and are willing to cut your hair to show that you are His. Where Samson surrendered to a mere mortal woman, you are surrendering to the almighty God, and for this, He will smile upon you. You need only look as far as Joshua there, who now wears the short hair. Is he not still as strong as when his hair was as long as your own?"

Isaac looked in the direction in which David was pointing and he saw Joshua in the distance, and Joshua was certainly a fine physical specimen who was generally acknowledged to be the strongest man in the village. Isaac, at last, understood the difference between his own hair and the hair of Samson, and he said to David, "I believe you, Brother David, and I will cut my hair before the sun rises tomorrow. When may I be baptized?" David chuckled at Isaac's willingness to finally comply, and asked, "How long has it been since you first came to me and asked to become a Christian?" Isaac cocked his head to one side and gave the appearance of a man searching his memory for an important fact. He also rubbed his chin to accentuate the fact that he was deep in thought, but an impish smile began creeping across his face. Both men knew for certain that it had been almost a year to the day, and they each laughed as they coyly contemplated the other's next move. David spoke first, "I guess it has been long enough, Isaac. Could you be prepared to be baptized next Sunday?" Squaring his shoulders and yet trying to look as unconcerned as possible, Isaac said simply, "I will try to be prepared." After a warm handshake, Isaac strode confidently in the direction of his cabin. The following Sunday, an Isaac with short hair was baptized at the regular service, as the entire village looked on happily with pride.

Since founding Schoenbrunn, the flock had grown to unbelievable numbers, and it soon became necessary to expand. There would be other missions to grow out of the original Schoenbrunn establishment, and although they would be headed by other missionaries, under instructions from Bethlehem, David would continue to function as Superintendent of the Moravian missions in the Ohio Territory.

In 1773, the mission at Gnadenhutten, about twelve miles down the Tuscarawas was established, and David's longtime assistant, Johann Schmick, was appointed head missionary of that village. Schmick, a former Lutheran minister, who had himself been converted to the Moravian religion, was an accomplished musician, and taught music to many of his converts. His wife, Johanna, had been active in the Moravian religion in her native Norway, and she was the perfect assistant to Johann. Eventually the mission at Gnadenhutten grew to more than 100 converts, and in time, the site would become an important piece in the history of the Moravians in Ohio.

In correspondence with the Church headquarters in Bethlehem, David lobbied for his friend, Adam Lecron to replace Johann Schmick, but learned that Adam had died recently after contracting pneumonia. A letter from Susan to David arrived with the same distressing news as David was preparing to write her of his remorse. David and Susan would continue to correspond for a number of years to follow.

By 1775, both Schoenbrunn and Gnadenhutten had grown to more than 400 members, and it became necessary for the mission to expand once more. This time, David placed another of his married assistants, John Jungmann, in charge of Schoenbrunn, while David and 35 of the original members established the mission of Lichtenau about 20 miles downstream from Gnadenhutten. David was accompanied to the new mission by his trusty right-hand, John Heckewelder. The new village was located about three miles south of the main encampment of the Delaware nation, Goschachgunk (near the present day city of Coshocton, Ohio), over which, David's old friend, Chief Netawatwes reigned.

Both of the newer missions were established in mirror images of the first, at Schoenbrunn, and the rules, customs and practices were the same for all of the villages. True to the wishes of the Moravian Church head-quarters in Bethlehem, the conscientious and dutiful Reverend Zeisberger assumed the role as Superintendent over all of the missions established in the Ohio Territory. All three missions continued to flourish, and life was good for each of the members, despite the gathering clouds of war to the east, which would soon engulf even the Ohio Territory.

July, 1776

After the French and Indian War, the Treaty of 1763 had ceded to England all of Canada and the land from the Appalachians to as far west as the Mississippi River. But there was a new land company based at Fort Pitt, and its presence signaled an ominous change for the Ohio Territory. Slowly at first, and then in a steadily growing stream, settlers had begun pouring into the Ohio River valley with their sights set on lands to the west. Fort Pitt had been planned and started in 1754 by William Trent, of the Ohio Land Company of Virginia, under a grant by the English king, George II, as a jumping off point for many of those planning to move further west. Trent was a trader, intent on encouraging massive westward expansion, and filling his own pockets in the process. But shortly after Trent began construction of the fort, named after the British Prime Minister, William Pitt, it fell almost immediately to French and Indian forces, and the French promptly renamed it Fort Duquesne, after the Governor of New France (Canada). Land speculators had been busy scheming in ways to divide the new territory for more than twenty years and Indians were being pushed further and further west.

Chief Pontiac rallied and united most of the Indians of the territory against the white incursion, but after a stinging defeat at the hands of the British at Bushy Run, near Fort Duquesne, in 1763, the garrison was re-captured from the French and renamed Fort Pitt. To pacify the various tribes which had joined Pontiac against the British, England issued the Proclamation of 1763 which prohibited settlers from claiming lands which held water flowing into the Atlantic Ocean. At the time, it was thought that this provision would prevent much of the anticipated push toward the interior. And to enforce the provisions of the proclamation, England had stationed troops at the former French fort at Detroit. Later, when the American Revolutionary War began, the colonists found themselves flanked to the northwest by this strong, though largely defensive force at Detroit. Seldom did the British forces march en masse from Detroit, as the troops were stationed there primarily to prevent colonial control of Lake Erie. On occasion, small English patrols, accompanied by larger Indian war parties, would scout the south shore of Lake Erie, but there was little actual military activity into the interior of the Ohio Territory.

Since the first volley had been fired by British troops against militiamen at Lexington, Massachusetts, the American colonists were now being pressed by the English on several fronts. And although the interior of the Ohio Territory was strategically located, Zeisberger and his flock were clearly not in harm's way. To be sure, the rare skirmishes in the territory were nothing like the clearly defined battle lines such as were occurring back east, but those people in the Muskingum River Valley were still very well aware of the war.

At first, those farther into the interior, like Zeisberger's flock, knew only of hostility between the British and the colonists. They were not fully aware that in Philadelphia, a full independence from Britain was now sought unanimously by all the colonies. Eventually, word from Fort Pitt arrived that a full-scale war of independence was now being waged against the King's army. Both the colonists and the British wanted the Indians from the Ohio Territory on their side. The British, having experienced the wrath of the Indians during the French and Indian War, were more than willing to avoid more hostilities with the natives again, and enlisted their aid against the colonists, who were aptly portrayed as "the encroaching settlers."

Major Arendt de Peyster, the British Commander of the troops at Detroit, was successful in enlisting the aid of the Shawnees, the Wyandots, and the Mingos, who stood to lose the most to the advancing civilization. In addition, those Indians who sided with the British in the Ohio Territory were among the fiercest warriors, and represented a grave threat to anyone foolish enough to oppose them. Scalplocks of doomed settlers adorned the belts of the Indians who joined the British. There were no Indian scalps among these coup.

The American forces stayed, for the most part, out of the Ohio Territory, marshaling the troops at their western most outpost at Fort Pitt. Occasionally, the militiamen would stage retaliatory raids on the bands of hostiles who were sent by the British on periodic attacks in and around Fort Pitt, but most of the Ohio Territory remained basically free of intense campaigns. David Zeisberger was largely responsible for this quasi-neutrality accorded to the Ohio Territory.

Aside from a few trappers and traders long familiar and friendly to the hostile tribes who were allowed to continue plying their trades, Zeisberger and his small group of converted Christian Delawares represented the only permanent settlements in the entire Ohio Territory. The Moravians and their Delaware converts did not seek great quantities of land, and did not hunt, fish, or trap with the intensity of the other settlers. The mission people were largely content to grow their own crops and raise their own livestock, and were therefore, really no threat to the land, the game, or the Indians and the British, who were extremely tolerant of the missionaries' presence in the territory. Most importantly, however, was the fact that Zeisberger had convinced the non-converted Delaware in the territory to remain neutral.

Through his long friendship with the main Delaware Chieftain, Netawatwes, and also with Chief White Eyes, of the splinter Delaware Turtle Clan, Zeisberger maintained a steady neutrality. Both the British and the colonial militiamen, passing through the peaceful Muskingum River Valley on rare patrols would inquire of the missionaries of the presence or movements of the other forces, and Zeisberger would truthfully answer. The Moravians at each of the three settlements really did not desire to antagonize either side, as they traded occasionally with both. Zeisberger did, however, tend to be slightly pro-colonial due to the history of the English religious suppression, and the fact that the Americans were much more tolerant of the Moravian, as basically they were with all other religions.

In truth, David could probably be characterized as being slightly biased against the British, for during one of his earlier missionary assignments in the Mohawk Valley of New York, he had been wrongly accused of being a French spy and had been briefly imprisoned by the British. From the Pennsylvania headquarters of the Moravian church, at Bethlehem, missionaries had been sent out into the rugged back country of New York, Pennsylvania, and the largely uncharted Ohio Territory. The pioneer Moravian missionary to visit the Ohio Territory was Reverend Christian Frederick Post, whose primary role was to secure the neutrality of the region's Indians during the French and Indian War. However, a hostile Indian uprising later dubbed "Pontiac's Conspiracy" soon interrupted their plans.

From his British cell in New York, Zeisberger was given the choice of remaining in jail or abandoning his mission post and returning to Bethlehem. The choice was an easy one, and after short sojourns at missions at Friedenshutten and Friedensstadt he was awarded his own mission in the Ohio Territory. The man who was named his assistant, John Heckewelder, had also been the chief assistant to Christian Frederick Post, whose short tenure in the Ohio Territory had been terminated quickly and quite unexpectedly by the French and Indian War.

A great deal of David Zeisberger's pro-colonial sentiments could also be traced to his early and enjoyable experiences in this new world which occurred in the colonial settlements of Savannah, Friedenshutten, and Friedensstadt. David often allowed his thoughts to drift back to those happier, simpler times, but now most of his waking moments, and a great deal of his dreams also, were spent in planning ways to keep his congregation out of harm's way. Moravian officials in Bethlehem, Pennsylvania were officially adamant about each of their missions and missionaries remaining neutral, and Zeisberger's diary entries for this period reflect that he obeyed his superiors.

When new tools or other manufactured artifacts were needed, more often than not, David Zeisberger would send a man or two from the village back to Fort Pitt, because it was much closer than Detroit, and it had also been from this area that he and the others had first pushed off into the Ohio Territory. There were still active Moravian settlements near the fort and many old friends remained in that general vicinity. When such trips were made, it was not unusual for Zeisberger to send messages to the American commander which casually mentioned British and/or hostile Indian movements, though they could hardly be called reports or intelligence. In this manner, Zeisberger kept the Moravians *and* the Delawares in the good graces of the Americans and made trading a lot easier. It was *not* something of which those at either Bethlehem or Detroit would be so approving, however.

Later that summer, an English patrol from Detroit arrived at Lichtenau, headed by Lieutenant Jonathan Kent. The six soldiers were joined by eight Wyandot warriors, who were painted and armed, as if ready for battle. The war party marched right up the street toward the church, and David stood waiting to greet them. "Hello Lieutenant," waved David as the approaching unit was in earshot, but the officer did not respond to the minister's greeting, nor to the disarming smile now curling David's lips.

"Patrol.....Ready.....Halt!" barked the commander as his troops stopped their steps smartly in unison just at the front of the entrance to the chapel. "Reverend Zeisberger," spat the officer, as he swung about to face David, who was by now, nearly in front of the column of men, "My men are in need of water and rest. We shall encamp in yon field," pointing to a large open area just beyond the far cabin. "Are there any rebels about?" he asked in a brisk tone, while at the same time looking here and there nervously, as if he fully expected to be ambushed by a squad of colonists. And before even allowing David to answer the question, he said, "We have received word that the militiamen are quite possibly preparing to mount an attack upon Detroit, and have reason to believe that perhaps you know something of those plans."

David simply shrugged, with palms upturned and replied, "To my knowledge, there are no colonists about, and sir, if there are, I know nothing of any such plans, and your suspicions of our knowledge is entirely unwarranted." Quickly, the British officer snapped back, "I meant of your *personal* knowledge!" It was then obvious to David that the Lieutenant was certainly not there for a cordial visit. It had long been whispered in Detroit that not only had Zeisberger and the Delawares been trading with those at Fort Pitt, but that the Moravians had also been passing along strategic information to the militiamen about British or hostile native movements. But never before had David been subjected to what amounted to nearly an outright accusation of aiding the colonists.

Lieutenant Kent was a typical British officer, bound by a blind obedience to the crown and to the military way of life. His manner and his style were as stiff and officious as the bayonets attached to the muskets carried by his men. David knew of Lieutenant Kent, but had never met him. David also, correctly, figured that what was now being delivered was as much the personal message of this young egotistical Englishman as the edict from the high command at Detroit. David chose his words carefully before he began to speak.

"We are a religious community, sir," said David, "and it is our belief that all men are our brothers. We treat all men the same, and favor none over the other, save for Christians over all others. On occasion, we have given water and comfort to small groups of soldiers and militiamen who have passed through our village both this way and that." he said, gesturing toward first the west, and then the east. "We have done nothing more for those men than we shall do for you and your men as you shall encamp among us tonight. It is the will of our Lord that we not join any conflict or fight. Why, surely you know that the Moravians do not even possess weapons. Even the Delaware brothers among us have long ago laid down their arms and have chosen to embrace Christ. We mean no harm to anyone."

As he was speaking, David noticed the Wyandots closely examining the converted Delaware, many of whom by now, were beginning to gather in the village's main intersection. To the other Indians of the region, the Delaware were a strange people. They were Indians, to be sure, because their skin was as dark as even the Shawnee, but they wore white man's clothing, spoke only the white man's language, and strangest of all — their hair was cut almost as short as the white missionaries that they lived among. The more hostile Indians also baited and taunted the Christianized Indians, knowing that the peaceful Delaware no longer hunted, smoked, drank whiskey, or did many of the other things that were long common to other Indians.

David continued, "One of the very reasons that we chose to come to this place in the Ohio Territory is because it offered us a means to avoid those who possess ill will toward either our church or its members. We intend to live in peace and to let those about us also live in peace."

Lieutenant Kent heard David's words, albeit rather obliquely, but did not fully choose to listen. He then walked closer to David, until he was less than an arm's length away, and peering intently into the eyes of the somewhat shorter missionary, said, "Reverend Zeisberger, we know who you are and why you are here. Do not think for one minute that we do not know of the depth of your friendship with the colonists at Fort Pitt. My commander would like you to know that he has a special affinity for you and your followers and he desires that no harm befalls any of you. However, he would also like to impress upon you the fact that the British are the most powerful presence in the northwest territory and will eventually put down the insolent militiamen who dare oppose his majesty, King George. Major de Peyster will guarantee your safety for as long as you choose to remain here. His only request of you is that you and your followers affirm your allegiance to his majesty and agree to pass along any information as to the movements of the militia. Surely this is not asking too much for your continued well being."

Like a father admonishing a know-it-all son, David sighed, and rolled his eyes upward as if to re-emphasize his position to the young lieutenant. Then he tilted his head ever so slightly and fixed his gaze at Kent's eyes and spoke in an almost forlorn voice, "Lieutenant, I understand your message from Major de Peyster and I fully appreciate your concern for us here in the Muskingum region, but I must tell you that it is baseless. First of all, I already serve the most powerful presence in the northwest territory, and you are sadly mistaken if you believe otherwise. Our Lord has protected us and provided for our needs long before we came here, and will continue to guarantee our well being. Secondly, we have already proclaimed our allegiance to the Savior, so we cannot do the same for your commander. Lastly, and once more, I shall tell you that in this war between men in this territory, we shall join neither side. As for now.....you and your men may stay among us for as long as you like, and I shall have some food sent to your camp shortly. Good day, Lieutenant." With that, David turned and strode confidently back into the church.

Kent stood there for a moment, psychologically recoiling as though he had just been splashed across the face with a tin dipper of ice cold water. Then shaking his head, as though in disbelief, he ordered his unit on to the distant clearing, where they would encamp for the night. There was considerably less arrogance in his stride and manner now than when he had initially marched up to David outside the church. In a tone so low that only he could hear himself, Lieutenant Kent muttered a slight oath about the stubbornness of this man.

Later in the evening, after the visitors from Detroit had eaten and were preparing to bed down for the night, two of the Wyandots approached one of the converted Delaware, Levi, who lived in the cabin closest to the clearing where the men were camped. The Wyandots had been put up to approaching Levi, or any of the other Delaware, by Lieutenant Kent, long before the patrol reached Lichtenau that day. The two warriors sought to have the Delaware betray David and the others, and to join them against the colonial settlers and the militiamen. The Wyandot had been drinking, and they offered Levi a swig from their jug of rum, but Levi was not at all tempted, and refused. He was, however, willing to talk to the two visitors, and was very cordial.

Their tone to Levi, though, was anything *but* cordial. After he refused their rum, they began to taunt him about being a slave to the white man, David. They attacked his manhood and insulted his appearance by laughing at his haircut, and the ill-fitting white man's clothing that he wore. "Have you no pride in the fact that you are a Delaware warrior?" asked the more sober of the two Wyandots. "You dress like one of the white prisoners of the British at Fort Detroit. Why have you laid down your tools and weapons of the Indian to live in that white man's cabin there? Do you seek to become the pack animal for the missionaries who rule this place and others like it?" The second Wyandot was by now laughing so hard that he nearly lost his balance, and he said, "The Delaware are like goats. They go and do as the white man tells them and they are afraid to break away from his control."

Although Levi was, indeed, a very devout Christian, who was already forming a careful and logical reply to the two braves, he felt the sting of their insults, but remained calm in spite of it all. "I am a slave to no man, for I have been freed by my Lord, Jesus. I dress the way I choose to dress — no man commands me to dress this way or that. I choose to live the life of a Christian because it is the only way to live. Look at both of you, you decry my lack of freedom, and yet you are led around by the British, who also are white, as though you had a ring in your nose like our oxen in yon pen. You are free to live your life as any Indian in his own lands, and yet you depend on the British to tell you what to do, when to do it, and to supply you with food and rum, not aware that as he gives you the rum, he is also controlling your freedom. If there are goats about disguised as men, I am certain that they wear feathers in their hair and carry British silver in their medicine bags. If you would like to know more about my Lord and how he can set you free, I will be glad to assist you in any way," said Levi.

But the Wyandot had already fallen prey to the demons within the earthen jug and could not understand the analogy and clearly did not wish to be rescued by this strangely appearing Delaware. Then, the most sober of the two spoke, saying, "If you will tell us about the movements and doings of the militiamen, our British friends will pay you handsomely. If you do not wish their rum, fine — it is merely more for us." Both Wyandots then collapsed in each other's arms, laughing hysterically at the odd behavior of Levi, who would be so stupid as to refuse the offer of rum. Collecting himself slightly, the Wyandot then said, "One day soon, you will be forced to join either our side or theirs. We do not want to add Indian scalps to our coup." And he held up his collection of scalps, which numbered four, and were blonde and brown in color, and the lighter of the two was of such texture as to indicate that it, no doubt, came from the head of a very young person, perhaps even a child. "Will you join us?" the Wyandot asked, with an eerie smile on his face.

Clasping his hands in front of him, and wringing them ever so imperceptibly, Levi again reiterated his faith and said, "When David spoke to your Lieutenant earlier, he spoke for all of us. We will join no one in battle. We serve only the Lord. We do not wish to provoke our Wyandot brothers or any of the peoples of other tribes — we seek only to live here quietly." Worried that the drunken Wyandot might not fully understand his simple and logical repudiation, Levi excused himself, said goodnight, and retreated slowly in the direction of his wife, Ruth, who had witnessed the entire scene from the doorway of their small cabin. The more drunken Wyandot was busily gulping down more rum when the other brave tugged it from him, causing much of the precious contents to splash out, and the vessel became slippery and they dropped it, smashing the jug and spilling the rum on the ground. "Poor, dumb Delaware," said one of them, as they staggered back to where their other tribesmen were staying. The sky was clear and stars shone brightly as nightfall came at Lichtenau. By dawn's first light, the British patrol and their Wyandot friends had begun to leave the peaceful village — without saying anything further to any of the residents.

The following October, Netawatwes died after a lingering illness which had sapped much of his strength and vitality. He died an old man, as much broken by the fact that he could not unite his tribe into one people, as he had been ravaged by the sickness itself. He had been the most vocal of all the Delaware in striving to maintain neutrality during the war. He and David had agreed almost wholly that keeping the Delaware out of the war was the best and most important thing that each could do. He was succeeded as chieftain by his naive grandson, Gelelemend, who also favored a neutral position for the Delaware, but lacked any of the tact and diplomacy that his wise grandfather had possessed. Tradition dictated that the Delaware would follow him, to be sure, but Gelelemend had to gradually win their confidence.

Netawatwes, although not a Christian, was accorded a Christian burial by David and his followers, with not one objection from the family of the old warrior. Though long a friend and supporter of the Moravians, the old chief had never fully embraced their religion, but it was obvious to many that he admired their faith. He had even spoken on more than one occasion with David about Christianity, and David forever gently prodded the old man to accept Christ. David also felt that it was only a matter of time until Netawatwes joined the church. However, death had beaten human decision.

At the service for Netawatwes, David asked the Lord to accept the soul of the old chief, and songs of both Christian rejoicing and Delaware mourning filled the still Ohio air on the day of his funeral. He was buried in a simple grave in the village cemetery, alongside many of the same Delaware who had originally come west together with the Moravians. Long after the last mourner had gone, David lingered at the gravesite and was consumed by the thoughts of the consequences of Netawatwes' death. He prayed, silently, that Gelelemend would be a strong and wise leader for the Delaware, and that someday soon, Gelelemend might seek to join the church.

David also prayed that the news of Netawatwes' death would be slow in reaching those at Detroit, because he feared that de Peyster would embark upon a renewed mission to recruit the weaker Gelelemend and the Delaware into service for the British against the militiamen. Netawatwes had been firm with de Peyster on his posture of neutrality, but David could not be absolutely sure about the resolve of the untested Gelelemend. If Detroit were slow in learning of the old chief's death, it might give David enough time to work with Gelelemend in attempting to condition him to resist the British offers. The one thing that David had on his side was the fact that Gelelemend had grown up with the knowledge that his grandfather had respected and trusted David and the other Moravian missionaries. He was somewhat confident that Gelelemend would remain away from not only the British, but the colonist's influence as well.

As for White Eyes, the chief of the Turtle Clan of the Delawares, David was not as certain as to his resolve at remaining neutral. Especially now that Netawatwes was gone. White Eyes had always seemed to be as genuinely honorable as Netawatwes, but the fact that the Turtle Clan had always remained slightly distant from their other brothers always nagged at David. White Eyes, although extremely friendly with the Moravians, never seemed to be completely at ease with some of the ways of the Christians. For one thing, the chief had never been willing to accept those Delaware who now wore their hair in the white man style. Whenever White Eyes neared one of the converted people, he would avoid looking into the person's eyes. It was almost as if White Eyes feared that eye contact would somehow erode his position as chief. There never was open disdain, but there was always an icy atmosphere which seemed to just border on civility. Only the steadying influence of the wise Netawatwes had managed to keep White Eyes totally loyal to *all* the other Delaware, and therefore neutral. As he walked slowly from the cemetery, David made a mental note to call upon White Eyes, and reaffirm the continued neutrality of the Turtle Clan.

Within a month of the death of Netawatwes, the Moravian headquarters in Bethlehem dispatched an assistant to David Zeisberger to help with the missionary villages. The man they sent was William Edwards, a bachelor, and a native of Maryland. David was pleased to see that the church had had the wisdom to send a bachelor to what was more and more beginning to seem like the next volatile front of the war. "Reverend Zeisberger, I am your new assistant, William Edwards," he said extending his hand to David. "So good to meet you Mr. Edwards, but please.....call me David," said the missionary who used both hands to greet the new assistant. "Done.....if you will call me William, sir," replied Edwards. At this, William reached into his bag and produced a number of letters for David and the others in the Ohio Territory from Fort Pitt, Bethlehem, and points east. David was especially pleased to see that William had brought with him a letter from Susan Lecron, as their correspondence had increased. David smiled and placed her letter in his inner pocket, then took the new man on a tour of the village and introduced him to all they encountered.

David liked William immediately. He was impressed by the cleanliness of the man after the trip from the east, and he also liked his easy manner. Edwards was just over forty years old, but had the physique of a much younger man. His thinning brown hair receded sharply into a pronounced widow's peak, and there was a hint of baldness in his crown. "That scalp will never be worn as a coup," thought David, who subconsciously ran his fingers through his own coarse, curly red hair. In addition to his religious training, William was an accomplished musician, who would be warmly welcomed by the Delaware members of the flock, who relished their opportunity to sing the hymns at the services.

As a musician, William had the habit of constantly humming or singing — a trait which was sometimes annoying, but David and the others welcomed him warmly and never complained about the constant litany of melody he emitted. Most likely, it was because David was virtually tone deaf, and could never manage to sing on key. His own singing was an embarrassment to him and the other missionaries had been simply too kind or respectful to speak of it with him. A young Delaware convert had been standing next to David at Sunday service one day and during the singing, she looked at David with all of the innocence of any five year old and whispered to him, "Reverend Zeisberger, why don't you try singing with only your lips.....and not making any sounds?" A small smile instantly engulfed David, who thereafter only mouthed the words. Everybody was happier for it.

By May of 1777, the evidence of war was frighteningly clear to the residents of the Muskingum River valley. Almost incessantly now, patrols and war parties would pass through the territory from first the east and then the west, by the militiamen, and then the British. War parties of Mingos, Shawnee and Wyandot seemed to filter through the area with increasing frequency from all directions, and it was not unusual to see mixed war parties of several tribes. Once, about two miles north of Lichtenau, a calamitous battle was heard, but not seen by the converts and missionaries. Volley after volley of musket retorts were heard for what sounded like an hour or more, and the villagers waited until almost dark for one side or the other to come dragging their dead and wounded in for bandaging or burial. When this never happened, and after it had been perfectly quiet for a long, long time, David and William, accompanied by three of the men of the flock, set out to see to the dead or injured.

Finding the location of the skirmish was not difficult. The crisp smell of black powder from the flintlocks hung heavily in the humid air, barely masking the smell of blood and death. It was William who came across the first tangible proof of a battle, the badly shredded and bloody red tunic of an English soldier, apparently cut off the man in order to attend to his wounds. "David," he yelled, "over here!" For the men had spread out until there were now several yards between them. The others responded to the find along with David. One by one, the men from the village found a scrap or weapon indicating that a fierce fight had taken place, but there were no casualties found. The colonists had long ago taken to removing their wounded and dead from the battlefield because the hostiles who usually accompanied the British would scalp anyone left behind. Word was that de Peyster was giving a shilling for each scalp brought in, and the militiamen were having none of that. The British, due to their strict regimentation, simply removed their casualties as a routine matter of military duty. In this woodland shootout, there were what amounted to buckets of blood everywhere, and the stench of death was ominous, but there were no bodies to be found.

"Let us return to our village," said David, who shuddered slightly at the thought of the violence being so noticeably close to his peaceful flock. On the short trek back to the village, no one said a word, but the fact that they returned much closer together indicated that they each were painfully aware of the frightening nature of war. As they made their way along the Tuscarawas, David pondered his options for reducing the possibility of involvement of his flock in anything like what they had just witnessed a mile or so back. He could either withdraw completely, moving all several hundred of his converts back to the relative safety of Pennsylvania, move his entire flock much further west into territory across the great river, or simply consolidate his flock from the three villages which they now occupied, to one single village — Lichtenau. He prayed for guidance from above, because the decision was not an easy one for him. His immediate instincts were to remove everyone to the safety of one of the closer eastern missions. He was not a quitter, but his concern for the safety of his flock was paramount.

By the time that they had at last reached the village, David had made his decision. He told William and the others with him to gather up all the villagers for an important meeting in the church that evening. "What is it, David?" asked his assistant, as the others set about notifying the remaining villagers. "I have decided that this infernal war is much too close for us to continue on as we have, William. I believe that it is necessary for us to gather all our sheep and move the entire flock to Lichtenau," replied David. "First thing tomorrow morning, you and Joshua must go to Gnadenhutten and alert Johann Schmick and the others to begin the move right away, then go on to Schoenbrunn and let the Jungmanns know that we are waiting. I want everyone safely gathered at Lichtenau by Friday," said David, with a very serious look in his eye. It was now Wednesday. William acknowledged David's orders and then set about notifying the others in the lower end of the village, of the meeting that evening.

51

The church that night was buzzing with excitement. All of those who had seen the bloody battlefield had by now told someone who told someone else until every last person in town was talking of the gore and the war. David entered the church and strode to his familiar position at the pulpit, with both hands gripping the wooden structure tightly on the sides. This was also a signal that he was now ready to speak and the hum of the flock died quickly to total silence. Only the quiet presence of a large moth circling the candlelight above David could be heard. And then he spoke.

"My brothers and sisters," David began, "today several of us saw the sights and smelled the blood of war very near our peaceful village. It is my earnest desire that none of you be as close to battle as we were today. The British and their Indian allies, and the militiamen from Fort Pitt have brought their death and destruction entirely too close for us to live as we have lived in the past, and it is with much regret that I now inform you that we are going to abandon the beautiful garden village of Schoenbrunn, as well as the village at Gnadenhutten, and move everyone in the flock to Lichtenau. I fear that if we do not unite in a single village, that we are certain to be victimized by one side or the other in this dreadful conflict. Brother William, along with Brother Joshua, will leave in the morning to alert the other villages of our plans, and we must prepare for the other villagers to join us. I know that it may be somewhat difficult, but we must all open our homes and our hearts to those villagers who will soon join us here." David closed the meeting with a short prayer and the hasty exit of the people indicated that they were all eager to prepare for the others to move to Lichtenau.

William and Joshua were away on their trip by sunrise, and in the next hour after, the entire village was a virtual beehive of activity as people hurried and scurried here and there preparing for the arrival of the others at Lichtenau. The converted Delaware children were extremely well behaved, and very helpful to their families — especially in times such as these. David often marveled at how mature these fine youngsters seemed, and it was now particularly evident. There was not a wasted minute or movement throughout the entire village, and David swelled with pride as he thought how much these wonderful people were willing to sacrifice to stay together. Not one person had come forward to object to any of the things that he had proposed to them the night before, and everyone was eager to help his or her arriving neighbor. The others would be very weary after the short, but rugged trip to Lichtenau, some thirty miles south of Schoenbrunn.

The entire trip could be covered by canoeing down the Tuscarawas, but there were not nearly enough watercraft for the entire flock at the two distant villages. It was decided that the very old, the very young, and a few who were suffering from various afflictions would journey by the river, while everyone else would merely walk alongside the river, along with their dogs and other animals, including horses, cows, mules, oxen and goats. There were two rafts hastily assembled at Schoenbrunn for the trip, but because of the shallows and narrows of the river in places, their size was somewhat limited.

When the first of the evacuees reached Lichtenau, David immediately noticed that all of those arriving were residents of Schoenbrunn. The Jungmanns and the rest of the Schoenbrunn population had all arrived without incident, but it was nearing dark on Friday and none of the Gnadenhutten flock had yet arrived. William Edwards was among the last to arrive and he reported that Johann Schmick had resolved to remain at Gnadenhutten despite the concerns of the other Moravians. After giving everyone their choice of either leaving or staying, Johann found that all of the approximate one hundred villagers decided to stay in their homes. David was not pleased, but by this time, Johann *did* have a certain autonomy in the mission at Gnadenhutten, and clearly, David understood the people's reluctance to abandon their homes and the land that they had worked. He held no ill will for Schmick or any of those at Gnadenhutten, but his fears for their safety would never subside.

Although there were no direct incidents involving either missionaries or Delaware, David was becoming increasingly concerned about the war posturing of both the colonists and the British. The increased commitment to the British by the other Indians in the territory was also problematic for the missionaries. It would also not be good news to those Moravians in Bethlehem. David knew that in the event of heavy fighting in the area, hostile Indians would most likely turn ugly in their attitudes toward the missionaries and their peaceful Delaware converts. It was possible that even the non-Christian Delaware could be turned against the Moravians and their followers. For this reason, and with the official backing of the Church main, David eventually ordered all the other Moravians and their families to leave the Muskingum region and return to the relative safety of Bethlehem. For although the war in the east was more devastating, there was too much isolation, too many potential enemies and too much danger for the whites to stay in the Ohio Territory. William Edwards had, in this very short period, become completely immersed in the work of the missions, and he also was totally committed to remaining in the Ohio Territory. By the fall of 1777, David and William would be the only remaining Moravian whites remaining in the Ohio Territory.

In a tearful goodbye at the eastern edge of Lichtenau, the five other Moravians, which included the Jungmanns, the Schmicks, and the trusty John Heckewelder, bade their old friend David farewell. The bright and lively autumn colors on the leaves of the trees were a stark contrast to the dark mood of the missions' inhabitants. All of the people of the village gathered to see the sad departure, and there was much hugging and praying. There was not a dry eye within a mile of the village. John extended his hand to David, but David instead chose to give his best friend a bear hug, which brought tears to each man, and John promised to return.

Although David had not meant it to be so, John saw his role in the evacuation as that of a guide, whose task was to simply take the others back east and then return to assist David and the villagers. David felt wholly responsible for the lives of the other Moravians, and he was engulfed in a sense of relief that they would soon be out of harm's way. "Goodbye my brother," said David, as he took John's hand. "No, *not* goodbye, David," he replied. "I am trusting you to keep my cabin tidy until my return." David laughed a hollow laugh and gently shoved the younger man in the direction of the departing party. "Away with you now," he added. It would be a long time, but John Heckewelder would eventually return to help David and William with the business of saving souls in the Ohio Territory.

April, 1778

John Heckewelder made good on his pledge and returned to the Muskingum region, and his return was a joy to everyone. Johann Schmick's former mission at Gnadenhutten numbered over a hundred converts, and there were another three hundred or more Christianized Delaware at Lichtenau. The original village of Schoenbrunn remained empty and unused, but both David and William were both wearing down from attempting to minister to the spiritual needs of so many in the two locales. In addition to the converted Delaware, several families of settlers had migrated to the surrounding area, feeling safety in numbers, and were utilizing the Moravian missions for their religious needs. Many of the settlers worshipped regularly at the Sunday services conducted by David and William. Heckewelder's return was most welcome, and the first thing that he did was to finally convince the Gnadenhutten flock to join their brothers and sisters at Lichtenau.

In the meanwhile, the friendly relations between the non-Christian Delaware at nearby Goschachgunk, and those at the Lichtenau mission had started to deteriorate for reasons which were not clear to either faction. Communications, trade, and simple reciprocal visits simply lessened and lessened to slightly a trickle. The Moravians suspected British meddling in tribal politics, in turn causing the main body of the Delaware Nation to be suspicious of the aspirations of the missionaries. By October of 1778, poor attitudes in the Delaware natives were made even worse by the murder of White Eyes by a colonial militiaman.

Apparently, White Eyes and a group of Delaware hunters were surprised by a scouting party of militiamen, who were on one of their retaliatory raids in the Ohio Territory against the British-inspired hostile

Indians. The point man of the militia's patrol fired almost randomly into the main body at the first sight of the approaching Delaware, and White Eyes died almost instantly of a shot to the heart. The other Delaware managed to escape the ambush and flee to their village, and the militiamen never knew that White Eyes had, in fact, been a friend to the colonists.

The incident concerning White Eyes' death was literally the last straw for many of the Delaware. In utter disgust over the death of his good friend, White Eyes, Captain Pipe, the chief of the Delaware Wolf Clan decided to join with British forces shortly after learning of the ambush. Much to the dismay of those in the Moravian mission and a great number of non-Christian Delaware, Captain Pipe moved his people to the Upper Sandusky region on the south shore of Lake Erie to be closer to British headquarters at Detroit. The slow but steady unraveling of what had been a long and healthy relationship between the Delaware and their Moravian friends was agonizingly obvious to David and the others.

The death of White Eyes and the resultant defection of Captain Pipe to the British side had, by now, completely turned the situation in the Muskingum region into a mixed bag. From the very beginning, it had been the desire of David and the other Moravians to maintain an unwavering neutrality in the war, and they had thus far been able to do just that. But things were rapidly changing in the Ohio Territory, and the Moravians found themselves smack in the middle of it all. The colonial militia had begun to get the better of the British in the mounting number of skirmishes in the area, despite the overwhelming odds against them, and now the militiamen were pushing all the way across and through the Ohio Territory to the Wabash Valley, near the present Indiana-Illinois border. Obviously, the colonists meant to next drive north, and attack the British at Detroit from both the front and the rear.

The successes of the colonists were, to say the least, unsettling to those Delaware who were sympathetic to the British and also to the undeclared and non-Christian Delaware who lived in and around the Moravian mission at Lichtenau. There were small signs that the remaining Delaware were wavering and would join the British, as the rest of their fellow tribesmen had done. The more than 400 Christian Delaware and the handful of white missionaries who were now living at Lichtenau seemed more and more at risk from all sides.

On April 12, 1779, David arranged a meeting with Chief Gelelemend to discuss the war situation. As David approached the lodge of the Chief, the sun had already begun its descent from its highest spring position, and shadows were beginning to grow longer. Despite the fact that many people were apparently moving about the village, he noticed that he was not greeted by the customary group of admiring Delaware. Always in the past, whenever David entered the village at Goschachgunk, he had been greeted at the edge of the village by a smiling and friendly number of

Delaware children who would escort him to the Chief's lodge. All of the people at Goschachgunk knew David on sight, and all were comfortable with him in their midst, but the air of friendly acceptance seemed strangely absent on this occasion. As he strode through the village, hardly anyone paid any attention to him, although he did manage to get a smile and a limp wave from one old man whom he had known since their days in Pennsylvania.

Gelelemend met David a few feet from his lodge, and they exchanged a pleasant hello, but even the friendly spirit of Gelelemend seemed somehow different to David, who had known the newest chief all of his life. "And what brings my Moravian brother to my village on this day?" asked Gelelemend. Wiping the dust from his face with a handkerchief, and clearing even more dust from his throat, David said, "Chief Gelelemend, I come to you this day to speak of the nearness of the warring between the colonists and the British. Have you and your people suffered any casualties from the many battles that have taken place so near to where we are now standing?" Gelelemend motioned for David to sit, in the sparse shade of a nearby tree, and answered him by saying, "No white man's lead have struck our people since the death of White Eyes, but I fear more those balls fired by my Shawnee and Wyandot brothers.....and now the Mingos. The white man's ball that dropped White Eyes was likely meant for a hostile Indian, but I fear that the hostiles may well mean for their shots to be aimed at the peaceful Delaware that are about you now." He motioned with his arm in a sweep that encompassed the entire village.

The chief politely offered David his pipe, knowing full well that Zeisberger had never smoked in the past, and David merely bowed and cocked his head slightly, which Gelelemend took to be a "no." To an Indian, the pipe was as much a part of any serious meeting as the mind set of any of the participants, but the man of God could not countenance its use, even in times such as these. After drawing a full breath of the powerful mixture into his body, Gelelemend continued, "We are the only tribe between the Wabash and Fort Pitt who are not at war against the colonists and we are not popular with most of our Indian neighbors. Nearly every day, a war party from this tribe or that enters our village and attempts to get us to join them against the colonists. When we tell them that we are at war with no man, they laugh at us and tell us to watch out, that the colonists will soon be erecting a new fort at our village's edge, and that.....," but his voiced trailed off abruptly as he took a small puff from the pipe. "And that what?" asked David, after an inordinately long wait for the chief to finish his statement. ".....and that we will soon be wearing our hair in the style of the Moravians," said Gelelemend, who was clearly embarrassed that he had to relay this information to his old friend.

"You are a strong and powerful leader of your people, Gelelemend, do you allow the other tribesmen to speak for you?" asked David, who by now was peering intently into the chief's eyes, trying to see the slightest hint of wavering resolve. "No, my friend," replied Gelelemend, "you know that I am as Netawatwes, my grandfather was, but I fear that my people may be losing faith in me to lead them wisely."

The two men spoke earnestly to each other about their concerns and their dreams for most of the afternoon and when Gelelemend tapped out the residue of his pipe on the earth near him and rose from his sitting position, David knew that their meeting was over. Despite the cordiality and the content of their conversation, David began to have an unsettling feeling about the meeting. He sensed a certain urgency to Gelelemend's words, although the chief certainly had not appeared to intend it. "Goodbye, my friend," said David, and the two men shook hands. As he turned and walked toward the direction of his flock, David attempted to focus on what Gelelemend had said that caused this uneasiness. Was it merely the nearness and the reality of the war, or possibly a subtle message being conveyed by the chief?

The one thing that was clear, however, was that this was the first time that Gelelemend had suggested that any of the non-Christian Delaware had even the slightest notion that the missionaries' presence in the area was possibly a problem. As he pondered the chief's words, David had no way of knowing that he and Gelelemend, whom he had known since birth, would not speak to each other again for almost ten years.

By the time that David had covered the short distance to Lichtenau, he had already dismissed many of his concerns about the relationship of the other non-Christian Delaware to those who were now among his flock and who greeted him warmly upon his return. The Christian amiability of the converted Delaware was a tremendous comfort to him and to all of the other missionaries. The delivery of these many wonderful people would always be considered by the Moravians to be their greatest gift to God.

Over the next several months, however, many things would occur which would alter the status quo of all those living in the Ohio Territory interior. The sightings of both colonists and British troops in the area increased markedly, although no further skirmishes were seen or heard by the Lichtenau residents. Somehow, God seemed to be keeping the battle away from his peaceful children of the Tuscarawas valley. The most obvious occurrence for both the Christians and non-Christians was the slow but steady inclusion of many of the non-Christian Delaware into the war effort. To Zeisberger and the others, it mattered little as to which side the Delaware took. What hurt the most was that they appeared to be deserting their own people. There was, indeed, a delicate balance of peace in the valley, but for how much longer, no one could tell.

By late November, it became much too clear that more and more Delaware were being recruited into the British side of the war. Zeisberger and the other missionaries were more than a little concerned that a full-fledged Delaware commitment to the British would mean big trouble for those at the nearby settlement of Lichtenau and also for the colonists. David and Gelelemend had not spoken since their meeting in April, although they regularly communicated through messengers. Gelelemend's last message, only three days old, had let David and the others know that the Delaware Council of Chiefs, although headed by Gelelemend, were leaning to a total commitment to the British. Though Gelelemend strived for absolute neutrality, it was apparent that many Delaware were succumbing to British influence.

The Delaware village at Goschachgunk was by now, only a shadow of its former self and those at Lichtenau were well aware of the creeping Delaware alliance with the British war effort. David and the other missionaries, at a meeting just before December, now reversed their earlier thinking. They all felt that if the remaining Delaware were to fully commit to the British, it might be extremely dangerous for them because all of the approximate 400 were so close to the main tribal encampment at Goschachgunk. After much discussion, it was agreed that the flock might be better served to separate into three groups and to evacuate the site at Lichtenau.

The first group would depart for a new location, just across the Tuscarawas from the original Moravian village of Schoenbrunn, the second would return to the former village at Gnadenhutten, and the last group would settle a new area, to be called Salem, which was across the river from and just south of Gnadenhutten. The move would be hard for all those involved, but each knew that it was for the best and certainly done with God's grace.

David had chosen the most central location, at Gnadenhutten, as his headquarters, and he was joined there by most of the senior original Indian converts. Isaac and Levi and their families were among those who chose to remain close to their friend and leader. William Edwards, was chosen to lead the people of New Schoenbrunn, as the northern most village was called, and John Heckewelder was designated by Zeisberger to guide the remaining converts at Salem. Each of the settlements contained approximately the same number of people; about 150.

By the spring of 1780, all of the moves had been accomplished and each of the members of the flock had settled in and began planning and working on the coming planting season. The move to areas more distant from Goschachgunk had placed the war a little further away from the peaceful missionaries and their converts and life resumed with perhaps the slightest lessening of tension. To be sure, war parties from each side were still visible, but things were returning to normal and the renewed optimism of the planting season was eagerly anticipated.

The spring that followed was warm and gracious to all of God's children, but it was especially kind to the people of the Tuscarawas valley. The fields were bountiful and many of the families were awaiting births. David, walking among the rows of maize one day, was joined by a young man named Joseph, who asked, "How much longer will these wonderful days go on for us, Father?" David smiled, and answered, "I'm not sure of all of God's plans, Joseph, but I do know that He has smiled on us and will continue to do so as long as we obey Him. We meet regularly with Him, and each of us has devoted our lives to Him. I'm sure that He is taking all of this into consideration." Joseph smiled back at the simplicity of David's answer, and nodded his agreement. "I have people who are at Goschachgunk, and I worry for them. Do you suppose that God will watch over them the same way that He does me?" After inspecting the progress of one particular plant in the row, and without looking up, David said, "I worry for the good people at Goschachgunk also, but I know that God will watch over those who have Him in their hearts, even though they do not openly praise Him as you and I and the others have done. I know many of those at the village feel this way, but are just not able to come forward, as you and the others have done. I pray that they make their choice to do so before the war leaves it mark." Both men then turned and walked toward the cabins which faced the fields.

As they reached the edge of the field, they saw a commotion of a group of people in the area just in front of the schoolhouse. At the center of them was a small war party of Shawnee, which numbered about ten braves. As David and Joseph approached, everyone turned toward the Reverend and David raised his hand in a friendly gesture. The Shawnee were clearly on the side of the British, but also knew of the Moravians' neutrality, and they often stopped in or near the villages of the missionaries for water, food, and for trading. More often than not, the missionaries would hear of the latest British victories, but mostly the peaceful Moravian villages represented a simple, convenient, and peaceful rest stop. On this occasion, the Shawnee were obviously tired, nervous, and slightly the worse for wear following an encounter with colonists about thirty miles to the east. Some were wounded, although none seriously.

David said to their leader, "I see from the wounds of your men that you have just come from battle. May we bandage those for you?" The Shawnee leader managed a polite no, and clearly felt relief that he and his men were now among peaceful, friendly people. "May we rest by the stream there?" he asked, as he nodded toward the Tuscarawas. "Of course, my friend," answered David, who began moving with the Shawnee toward the shadows of two giant sycamore trees at the river bank. The villagers in the group slowly began to dissipate and move on to their respective chores and families. Joseph continued on with David and the Shawnee.

As the tired Shawnee sank to the ground, David bade Joseph to fetch the men some fresh water from a nearby spring and also some food from among the villagers. Then, turning his attention to the visitors once more, he asked, "How close are the British troops? We have not seen many British soldiers in several weeks. Have they returned to Detroit?" In truth, David was doing nothing more than making conversation with the Indian leader. "Major de Peyster and his men are about one day north of us at this time," said the Shawnee leader, who was beginning to chew on a small piece of pemmican from within his belt. "They have met and defeated the militia near Sandusky. We chased a small group of the remaining militia just past your northern village this very morning. See?" he asked, as he held up two freshly taken scalps.

David refused to look at the disgusting scalps, but instead looked into the Shawnee's eyes and said, "I know that you are paid well for your service to the British, but do you not realize that you are surrendering your own lives to do the will of someone else? Someone who will only use you until you are no longer needed?" It was not David's intention to openly talk down the British, but to merely point out the futility and lack of morality in a bloody war. He sat on the river bank and talked to the Shawnee leader until Joseph returned with some bread, fruit, and water for the war party, and he continued to talk while they ate and until long into darkness. He tried to convince the Shawnee to quit the war and to return to their own families. He had recently been successful in convincing a group of Wyandots to go home after they, too, had stopped for a rest in Gnadenhutten.

At New Schoenbrunn, William Edwards had also been able to recently deter a very large band of Shawnee from continuing the war, and Heckewelder had had similar success with some Mingos and Delaware at Salem. On this day, however, this particular party of Shawnee were not buying David's message. They listened, albeit begrudgingly, while they ate the food and drank the water, and they rested through the night. By dawn, they were gone, and David knew that he had failed to hit the mark with his message to these Shawnee warriors. It wasn't much, but the missionaries had done something that they felt was positive in ending the war. At least in the Ohio Territory. It was also something that each instinctively did in his role as an emissary of God.

The following day, a trader from Fort Pitt passed through the village and dropped off a bundle of letters for those in the Muskingum valley. David hurriedly went through the bundle, scanning each for the familiar handwriting of Susan Lecron, and halfway through the stack, he found it. After placing the rest of the letters on a table in his quarters, he put Susan's in his inside pocket and went outside. Looking about here and there, he could see no one walking toward him or the church structure, so he quietly and quickly rounded the corner of the building and hurried toward the bank of the nearby river. He often found himself at the river whenever he wanted to think or to write — especially to Susan Lecron. In his last letter to her, now more than two months ago, David had asked her to marry him. He knew that the letter in his pocket contained her answer to him, and though he was anxious to read it, he knew that it had to be read under precisely the right circumstances. His familiar spot on a large fallen sycamore by the friendly Tuscarawas was that perfect spot.

At the river, he was somewhat annoyed to find that although his favorite meditation spot was free, one of the male converts of the village, Noah, was fishing only about 50 feet away. At first, David considered moving further downstream to seek his solitude, but as he stood by the log, he was relieved to notice that Noah had seen him and was obviously not going to strike up a conversation. Looking behind him one last time, David took out the letter and sat down, as his fingers unfolded the pages.

In the seven years since her husband, Adam, had died, Susan had continued to write David. He had seen her mood, through her letters, move from the sadness at the time of his death, to a long, drawn out loneliness about which pained David to read. Over those seven years, the two had gradually written longer and longer letters, and each seemed to sense each other's low points as well as the joys. Boldly, David had proposed to her in his last letter — offering even to relocate to Friedenshutten if she so desired. It wasn't that he was particularly anxious to leave the Muskingum valley, by any means, but he was now 59 years old, and Susan's letters had certainly found their mark in his heart. He was now ready to assume the responsibility of marriage.

He knew that war would soon be upon those within the Muskingum region, and although he did not wish to place anyone in its path, there was a certain loneliness within him that could only be erased by Susan. His most recent letters to her had detailed all of the perils that were about those in the Ohio Territory. He was particularly careful to paint an accurate picture of the kind of life that those within the territory were now facing and were about to face. His dark and foreboding letters to her had been answered with an obvious concern for David, but there were also hints of something much more from within her. She had, on more than one occasion, asked him to leave the territory and return to the relative safety of the area of Friedenshutten — knowing full well that it was something he would never do. Her last letter had even said that she "ought come to the territory to personally watch out" for him. This one, singular phrase had, in fact, given him the courage to ask for her hand in marriage.

Except for David, John, and William, other members of the mission were married and appeared to be quite happy. David had long admired those women who had unselfishly dedicated their lives to assisting their husbands in the ways of Moravian missionary work. John had even been smitten recently by the eldest daughter of a non-Moravian family who had taken roots nearby the mission at Salem and seemed destined to be one day wed. More than ever before, it now seemed to David that not only was marriage something that would not interfere with his missionary work, but something which could even enhance it. The perils of the nearness of war were the only thing which cast negative thoughts on the prospect of marriage.

With a mountain of anticipation welling up inside him, his eyes eagerly searched for the appropriate words on the parchment, but he needed to look no further than the new, more intimate salutation. The letter read:

"My Darling David,

I received your warm and wonderful letter just this morning, and my desire to let you know of how proud I would be to be your wife nearly overwhelms me! I persuaded Mr. Muller, who was about to depart for Bethlehem with some westbound letters, to sit patiently while I hurriedly replied to your letter. This letter will be necessarily short, but I want, so much, for you to know of my love for you as soon as possible.

I will begin to make plans for our wedding as soon as I learn of when you will arrive in Friedenshutten. I am prepared to come to the mission, with or without the threat of war, for I do not expect you to give up the one thing that has empowered your spirit thus far. Together, we shall work side by side at whatever you choose because that is the proper role for a wife. I shall eagerly await your next letter. Your friend, your partner, your love.....

Susan"

Relieved, and smiling broadly at last — David's body came to life and he nearly fell into the river, so eager was he to tell someone of his plans. He gathered himself and hurried in the direction of Noah, who was, at the time, busily engaged in the process of pulling a rather large catfish to the shore. When David was but a few steps away from the fisherman, Noah turned his head and saw the gigantic smile upon his face. Believing it to be in response to the large fish which was by now thrashing about on the shore, Noah cried out, "I've just landed a big one, Reverend!" With that, David grabbed the man and hugged him, and happily replied, "So have I, Noah. So have I," then hurried off in the direction of the church. Noah looked blankly in the direction of the departing minister, trying to figure out how this was possible, since the Reverend had not had a fishing pole in his hands all the while he sat at the riverside.

In a few days, all the members of each of the missions knew of the imminent plans of their leader to wed. He had immediately written her, saying that he would return to Friedenshutten by July so that they could be married, and the days began to fly by quickly. For a short time, the thoughts of everyone were happily diverted from the nearness of war. It also seemed that David, always cheerful by nature, was now even more so. His smile broadened and his handshakes and hugs were even firmer than in the days before. The mood of the entire community, because of the pending marriage, had noticeably become more upbeat. David set about building a suitable bed for his new wife, because the one that he had been using was only a plain and narrow cot, barely wide enough for one person. He also began building a small set of shelves which would hold his personal clothing and effects, as he had planned to give Susan the small chest of drawers that he had originally brought west with him.

Early on June 22nd, David met with John and William before embarking on his matrimonial journey. There were no regularly scheduled trips back to Bethlehem or Fort Pitt, but trips were made in anticipation of supply shortages or when special needs occurred. It was customary for David to pass on last minute instructions to his assistants, or to hear from them on something or other needed from either of the locations. The trio smiled easily as David contemplated the trip before him. As their gifts to him, John presented David with a walking stick, into which he had carved remarkable likenesses of Christ and the twelve Apostles, while William gave him a wool blanket, which had been woven by members of the congregation according to William's design and instructions. Both John and William genuinely admired and loved David and their hearts were filled with wonderful wishes for him. David's advanced age — he was now 59 — and the religious nature of their work kept the joking and kidding to a respectable level, but the mood was lively and enjoyable all around.

After kneeling for a short prayer session near the entrance to the church, the three men shook hands, exchanged hugs, and then David began his trip. As he stepped almost out of sight on the trail at the edge of the woods, he turned and waved one last time to the two men who were waving their goodbye to him. David was accompanied by the convert, Joseph, who would go only as far as Fort Pitt, and who would return to the Muskingum valley with supplies. Although David was very familiar with the trail, Joseph was a superior woodsman and his presence was a reassurance to the members of the congregation as well as to David.

The trail between the missions and points east was not much of a trail in the beginning. Consisting mostly of open spaces between the trees, there was little evidence of usage by man. As the trail went further and further, there began to be more discernible markings of hoof prints, livestock droppings, and occasionally a human foot print in either direction. A chopped stump to either side occasionally indicated that someone had once attempted to widen the way. The closer to Fort Pitt, bare spots and ruts appeared where ox carts and wagons had passed. After periods of heavy rain, much of the eastern portions of the trail would turn to nearly impassable quagmires. Fortunately for David and Joseph, the weather would do nothing to hinder their journey this time. The empty ox cart which David brought along, would provide relief for a short portion of the journey, but like Joseph, he preferred to walk most of the way.

Upon reaching Fort Pitt, David did not tarry, because his most pressing business was obviously further east. He did stay long enough, however, to say hello to old friends in the vicinity of the colonial stronghold. The mission at Friedensstadt had a number of Moravians with whom he had trained and served in other places. He was as eager to see them as they were him. David was also eager to let them know of his successes at not only converting the Indians to Christianity, but also those whom he had been able to persuade to leave the British and simply return to their villages. Although he had not necessarily intended it, this same information would shortly reach the Commandant at Fort Pitt, and somewhat later, the unhappy ears of British Major de Peyster at Detroit. The innocent conversation of David Zeisberger would be interpreted quite differently by the warring factions.

Although always a site of happy homecomings, at Bethlehem, David stayed only as long as absolutely necessary. He submitted a perfunctory report of mission activities and received the warm wishes of all that he encountered. News of his impending marriage had already reached Church headquarters. He thought that his business was complete, and was about to leave when he was summoned before the Council of Elders. It was not unusual for a mission head to be asked to appear before the Council of Elders. Among its many duties, the Council was responsible for setting Church policy, making assignments worldwide, and settling internal controversies, — to both established congregations and to missions. David felt that his summons probably was to be an official blessing on his marriage, for in his heart, he knew that he had done nothing to fear the Council.

When he entered the large Council room, David was ushered to a seat at the long table, around which the Council members sat. It was not an unfamiliar scene to him. He had sat in precisely the same place more than nine years earlier, when he had been given the Ohio Territory assignment. The members of the Council were not all smiles, however. There was a noticeably somber mood among the ten men already seated. At the urging of the Reverend Chairman, Henrik Muench, he pulled the large, heavy chair away from the table and lowered himself into a sitting position.

"Reverend Zeisberger," started Reverend Chairman Muench, "we would like to take this opportunity to wish you and your intended bride, Mrs. Lecron, a long and happy life in your marriage. You both have been splendid models of Moravian principles, with unquestioned reverence, duty, and virtue." David's smile at the congratulatory message was short-lived, however, as the light mood in the room suddenly became more serious. "However, Reverend Zeisberger," Reverend Chairman Muench continued, "this is not the only reason that you were called to sit before the Council members. We are deeply concerned for you and the other members of your missions in the Ohio Territory because of the nearness of the war. It is well documented that most of your trading has been done with those at the colonial post at Fort Pitt. While we do not, in any way, object to this, we know that this has not escaped the notice of British authority — particularly the post nearest you, at Detroit. The British have marshaled most of the Indian support in the Ohio territory except for those poor creatures that you have brought into the Church's fold. There is every reason that the British should hold you and the others at the missions in contempt, or at least in suspicion. I know, Reverend Zeisberger, that you need not be reminded of the consequences of British suspicions" Every man seated at the table was well aware of David's prior imprisonment in New York, at the hands of the British. Most were nodding their heads slightly.

The Reverend Chairman continued, "In summation, I must remind you, Reverend Zeisberger, that it is the official policy of the Moravian Church to remain wholly and unequivocally neutral in this declared war between the British and the colonials. In short, David," he said as his tone decidedly became more personal, "we do not wish that you do anything to provoke either side. You and the others have done tremendous work in the wilderness to the west. Do nothing to jeopardize these wonderful accomplishments. Leave no doubt among either the British or the colonials that you are a man of God — a living messenger of God's word through this very Church. Your ultimate allegiance is to Him and Him alone, and this must be absolutely clear to everyone. Do you understand and confirm our position?"

In the instance before he replied, David scanned his thoughts for what he would say. The Council's stance on the war had been well known to him and the other missionaries long ago, and David did not wish to even slightly appear as if he were doubting the wisdom of either the Council or the policy. He knew, better than anyone else, that his position in the Ohio Territory was now extremely tenuous. Although he really did want to remain neutral, more than anything else, he wanted to remain in the Muskingum valley. To do so, however, meant that on occasion, he befriend either side, but provoke neither. A most difficult task, especially in light of the Council's pronounced position of neutrality.

David began his answer with a short question, "Is there something that I have done or failed to do which would cause you to call me before this esteemed body on the subject of neutrality?" Not receiving an audible response, he continued, "I have long been aware of the Church's official position on its neutrality and I have followed that policy unerringly. I shall continue to operate the missions in the Ohio territory according to the wishes of the Church and with the utmost concern for those members so near to the conflict. Now, more than ever before, I have even more personal reasons for adhering to that policy. And I thank you for your well wishes."

The Chairman sat more upright in his seat and cleared his throat before speaking again, "David, we are not criticizing you, by any means. You are walking paths that many would never attempt, and we simply fear for your safety. Please....." and there followed a long pause, "keep our message in your thoughts as we have you and the others in our hearts, our thoughts, and our prayers. Now hurry on to Friedenshutten, for you are needed there." A large smile was on his face as he extended his hand to David. David rose and shook the Reverend Chairman's hand first and then those of other members of the Council. Many hugged him with warm embraces before he departed the enclave.

As he left Bethlehem the next morning, David pondered the conversation that had been held in the Council of Elders. He knew that his own subtle bias toward the colonials, had he chosen to disclose it, would have caused a great deal of consternation for everyone concerned. He silently vowed to himself to consciously avoid any situation in which his actions would either cause the Council to question him or bring his secret political nature to the surface. He was certain that the continued existence of the missions in the Ohio Territory depended on this. Though he tried to clear his mind of the dialogue with the Council, he found that it nagged him all the way to Friedenshutten, several days away.

Upon arriving in Friedenshutten, David went directly to Susan Lecron's home. Susan greeted him with a warm embrace and a stiff, unfamiliar kiss which felt strange for each of them. David blushed noticeably and Susan worked at keeping both feet on the ground. They had, after all, only recently revealed their love for one another and expressed the desire to marry. Before that, for nearly nine years, they had been merely good friends, separated by many miles and all the inconveniences of a growing war. Love, which was now growing by quantum leaps within their hearts, had not yet discovered how to respond face to face. It was at once embarrassingly uncomfortable and yet so delicious for each of them! Almost as if on cue, they each took a step backward and laughed lightly at their own awkwardness. Then, as though choreographed, they re-closed the distance between them and embraced once more. Their second kiss was much more natural, softer, and lasted longer. To David, it was simply the first time in his life that he had kissed a woman with passion. For Susan, it was the reawakening of long-stilled fires which had died years earlier with her former husband. When their lips at last separated, they each laughed lightly again, but now for quite a different reason. Dizzy exhilaration filled both their bodies and it was a grand and welcome feeling. Arm in arm, they walked to the bench which sat in the shade beside Susan's small log home.

"I've arranged for Reverend Fromm to marry us on July 4th, if that is all right with you, David," said Susan. "Of course," he muttered weakly. July 4th was but two days away, but at that moment, time meant nothing to David — he only knew that he was definitely in love with the woman who was now holding his hand. She could have said any date and he would have agreed to it. He would have to be reminded of the date on at least two other occasions, so intoxicating were the feelings that now enveloped his entire being. Until early evening they sat and talked outside her home, oblivious to everything else. Finally, Susan suggested that she prepare something for their meal, and they went inside. David looked around the modest cabin and saw that the woman he had chosen was a very good housekeeper. He had remembered her that way and nothing that he now saw betrayed his original observations.

"I still have to find a place to stay tonight, Susan," said David, "so I'll set out after dinner." Both of them knew that it would be no problem for David to find a place among the missionaries for the two nights until they were wed. As she set about preparing their meal, they engaged in more small talk — determined to learn more and more about each other. "Tell me more about your mission, David, darling," she said as she went about her task. He enjoyed hearing her call him "darling," but he did not tell her this. She could tell by his expression and body language that he savored it. On and on, throughout the meal, until David found it necessary to leave for the night, he told her of the Moravian missions in the Ohio Territory. He named and described almost each and every Delaware convert for her, and her rapt attention to detail impressed David even more. They were definitely a match for each other.

Their parting kiss that evening was the sweetest, by far. It left them both aching for more, but in the true spirit of their religious upbringing, neither felt overly tempted to cross the line. Both were content in knowing that soon enough, they would be man and wife. David set out toward the main collection of cabins in Friedenshutten, and Susan watched until his image blended totally into the darkening shadows. To Susan, the day had been the start of her life with David Zeisberger. She was eager to be with him, having already agreed to return to the Ohio Territory with him. David had never been happier. His feet barely touched the earth as he made his way toward the others of the village.

Word of the approaching marriage had spread easily and unfettered throughout the tiny Moravian village of Friedenshutten. Both David and Susan were inundated with the well wishes of old friends. Faces that were very familiar to David from years gone by suddenly appeared, smiling and congratulatory. Very early on the morning of July 3rd, he had checked to insure that Reverend Ernst Fromm had the date and all the particulars correct about the wedding. Next, at Susan's suggestion, he called upon the older brother of Adam Lecron, Seth, and was delighted that Seth and his wife, Martha, had agreed to be their witnesses. In the next several hours, first one and then another inquired as to the health and status of someone in the Muskingum valley. Most of David's time on July 3rd was spent in this way — catching everyone up on the news of those with whom he served.

Nearing dusk, as a light rain began to gently fall in the area, David found himself back at Susan's cabin and once more preparing to share the evening meal with her. Another very warm and satisfying kiss preceded another short but appropriate spell, during which both adults giggled and smiled like playful youth. An then Susan's attention turned to the meal. She had baked fresh bread to go along with a large kettle of vegetable soup and the aroma was magnified by the moisture in the air. David happily inhaled those scents as Susan placed the food upon the table. "I trust that the weather yon will ease before the appointed hour tomorrow," said Susan, as she pulled her chair nearer the table.

"We shall ask God to intervene for us, Susan," replied David, as he bowed his head to say grace. "Our heavenly Father," he began, "we thank You for this wonderful food that we are about to receive. Bless and provide for those who are less fortunate than either of us, and provide a bountiful harvest for all those who work the land. Be especially alert to the needs of those who are aged or ill, and Father....." he paused, "let tomorrow be a day when those who would lift their eyes to You for guidance, be able to do so with a dry brow. Amen." Susan smiled and reached across the small table and patted his hand as a means of thanking him for his thoughtfulness. David merely looked resolutely into her eyes, with a confident dignity that seemed to say simply, "This is my job."

Following the delicious dinner, they spent almost two hours making additional plans. Plans for the wedding, plans for the evening of the wedding, and plans for the several days following the wedding before they would set out together for the Ohio Territory. The only time they lost grip on each other's hands was when one or the other would pat the other's hands. It got darker earlier than usual that day because of the light rain, and David at last stood up and excused himself for the evening. Arm in arm they walked to the door and after a modest and very delicate kiss good night, David made his way to the cabin where he would spend his last night as a bachelor. Before he arrived at the friend's cabin, the moon and stars began to be slowly visible through the thin clouds, causing the light rain to nearly halt, and David glanced upward — a smile smugly fixed upon his face.

The wedding had been set for one o'clock on the afternoon of the 4th, and by the noon hour, there was no trace of the previous evening's rainfall. Except for appearing more lush and green than the days before. It was a splendid omen for the later events of the day. When David arrived at the church, Reverend Fromm greeted him warmly and told him that Susan had already arrived, and was in an adjoining room, preparing herself for the ceremony. True to the customs of the day, David would not see his bride-to-be until she walked up to the altar at precisely the right moment. Seth and Martha soon arrived and Martha excused herself to be of assistance to Susan, while the three men were left to wait the final few minutes together. At exactly one o'clock, Reverend Fromm put his pocketwatch away and looked up to see his wife and Martha Lecron enter the chapel, just ahead of Susan. They each took up a spot to the left of David, leaving just enough space for Susan, who quietly assumed her place in front of Reverend Fromm, lightly brushing her right shoulder with David's left. David glanced nervously in her direction, but only long enough to be certain that it was, indeed, Susan who stood alongside him. He did, however, note that she clasped a small bouquet of lilacs and tiny white flowers in front of her.

"We are gathered today in the house of the Lord," began Reverend Fromm, "to join this man and this woman in holy matrimony. Marriage is a holy sacrament in the Moravian Church and not one to be taken lightly or to be easily discarded. David and Susan have chosen to emulate the actions of our Lord and Savior, Jesus Christ, who chose to marry Himself to His faith in God, the Father. And like our Savior, their faithful union will mirror the other in holiness. In as much as there is no person present who would object to this marriage, do you David, promise to love, honor and cherish Susan for as long as you shall live?" And David proudly said, "I do." Reverend Fromm continued, "And do you Susan, promise to love, honor, and obey David for as long as you shall live?" And Susan replied, "I do." "Do you both promise to live your lives as man and wife forever serving the needs of our Lord?" asked Reverend Fromm. "I do," answered both David and Susan simultaneously.

"What symbol of your devotion to this marriage have you brought to this occasion?" asked Reverend Fromm. "I have this ring," answered David, and he produced a small, simple gold band from his pocket. It had been his mother's. He held it up for Reverend Fromm to see. It was the first time that Susan had seen the ring also. She smiled widely.

"Place the ring upon her finger, David," said the minister, and David complied. With that, Reverend Fromm took David's hands and placed them upon Susan's, then covered both with his own hands. "Let us pray," he said, and the entire wedding party bowed their heads. "Our heavenly Father," he went on, "bless this marriage between David and Susan, keep their hearts and mind pure and ever dedicated to each other and to Your service. For as much as they have pledged their everlasting love for each other within Your house, let no man put this union asunder. Amen. Congratulations to you both."

At the close of the prayer for the new couple, David turned slowly to Susan and encircled her tall frame with his arms, looking all the while deep into her eyes. He kissed her very tenderly and she responded with as much ardor as her strict religious background would permit. It was extremely difficult for each of them to keep their emotions in check in front of their long time friends, but they managed. As they parted slightly after kissing, the other four persons present began to applaud and offer their congratulations. The new couple was totally flushed with the excitement of the moment, and barely were heard to respond with their thanks. Reverend and Mrs. David Zeisberger were ready to begin sharing their lives, and they quietly yearned now, to be alone.

Seth and Martha Lecron exited the chapel first, and were holding the door open for the newlyweds, and Seth gave David a hearty slap on the back as he passed. Both of them gave Susan a warm and tender hug, which confirmed a long and lasting relationship with her former brother-

and sister-in-law, and definitely gave notice that it would always remain so. Both David and Susan had thanked and said goodbye to Marna and Ernst Fromm inside the chapel, because like David, the minister of Friedenshutten also lived at the church, and the Fromms had merely gone home, into the next room.

As they walked the short distance to Susan's home, they were hand in hand, and were stopped and saluted by almost everyone they encountered. The warm and pleasant weather had all but guaranteed the couple this friendly "gauntlet." It mattered little to the couple just wed that they were both of middle-age — the youthful mantle of love had so completely enveloped them and they were reveling in all its glory. Their light and lively pace did nothing to disguise their status as newly weds, and their feelings for each other beamed like sunshine from each of their faces. Though the cabin was but several hundred yards from the church, it seemed much farther.

Alone at last in Susan's cabin, both of them were extraordinarily reserved toward each other, except for a long and truly passionate kiss which took place immediately upon closing the door. David walked about the small cabin as though off in a trance, not wishing his new bride to think him too impetuous in this alien, yet wonderful, state of bliss.

He proceeded to straighten a few items on the mantle, which were already perfectly fine as they were. Susan, also masking her emotions, found herself rearranging the furniture from the new positions into which it had been placed only the day before. Had either been clear-headed enough to realize this sweet dilemma, they probably would have been too flustered to do anything any differently anyway, and the rest of the day continued in this manner.

However, shortly on the heels of a later than usual and light dinner, Susan began to yawn noticeably, despite being as lady-like as possible, and David — no doubt inspired by her actions — stood up several times and stretched, stifling a yawn himself on the last occasion. Finally, at an hour when most of the residents of Friedenshutten were still engaged in conversation or acts of everyday responsibilities, the new Reverend and Mrs. Zeisberger retired for the evening and consummated their marriage.

For Susan, this night, now and forever, terminated what had been a terribly lonely existence for her since the death of Adam. She felt whole again and became instantly optimistic concerning her future. While her busy activities in the church had been most satisfying and occupying, she felt a deep sense of relief at now having David as her husband. Life in the colonial era — especially in those places away from the major cities — was difficult for anyone, not the least certainly a widow in her middle age. Late that night, to emphasize the revived fulfillment which she now felt, she gave her husband a final tender and reassuring hug.

The embrace stirred David, who had not yet been able to fall asleep, and he responded in kind, but even more lightly — unsure if his bride were fully awake. He was now content to lie and ponder this day, and its context in his life. That David had been celibate these many years had certainly not gone unnoticed by Susan, but she was patient and sensitive to the occasion. Though awkward and unpracticed in the ways of lovemaking, David, was a kind and gentle man by nature, and also mature to the point of realizing the complexities of the circumstances. He assumed, quite accurately, that the first night or so might be difficult and unchartable, but he had taken care to see that he was not clumsy. The years that lay before them were promise enough of abundant cherished moments to work at their efforts of passion for and understanding of each other. At last, David was awash with total bliss and contentment as his thoughts became enmeshed in that hazy evolution that precedes dreams, and he drifted into sleep.

Over the next two days, the new couple worked tirelessly at preparing for the return to the Ohio Territory. Susan had already earmarked the pieces of furniture and personal items that she wanted to take. After confirming their value with David, she had been able to set aside those things which were superfluous, and gifted them to her friends nearby or to less fortunate families in the area. The ox cart which David had brought with him was full, to be sure, but not to the point of being unmanageable over the rough and undeveloped trail west. He would walk the entire distance, while Susan could ride for short spells in a place that he devised specifically for her. However, she mostly preferred walking at the side of her husband, and would do so for most of their journey. At last ready for departure, the couple knelt and prayed, as was the custom for those in the Moravian faith before undertaking any journey of more than one day. As they began their trip west, most of the residents in the area turned out to wish them well and to say their good-byes. Susan wept lightly, for she was leaving those friends that had been so close for many years. David understood perfectly, and squeezed her hand gently to acknowledge her trepidation and allay her concern.

For David, the return trip to Gnadenhutten was not nearly as burdensome as the journey east had been. The prize of a new bride as his traveling companion was certainly gratifying, to say the least. Along the way, he and Susan would utilize the nights of camping out in the open to comprehend and appreciate even more of the other. At Fort Pitt, Susan was introduced to many friends and acquaintances of David's, and they greeted her with the cordiality and respect that a minister's wife ought to expect. At Friedensstadt, Susan was surprised to meet a distant cousin of her late husband, as well as some others from within the Moravian Church she had known for quite a long time, but had nearly forgotten. Except for one small incident, the trip would be largely uneventful.

The first night out of Friedensstadt, shortly after lighting the campfire, David looked up and found himself staring straight into the eyes of a Wyandot warrior, not ten paces away. Behind the Wyandot were three others, and none were wearing warpaint. Susan was near the ox cart, busy getting something to use to prepare for the meal, and was unaware of the Indians. Fluent in the Wyandot tongue, David greeted them, "Welcome my brothers, would you share our evening's meal with us?" The leader of the braves, the one nearest to David, replied, "No, we only wanted to learn who was on the trail near us. Your full wagon tells me that you are a settler. Why are you moving your possessions onto our lands?" Before David could answer, the brave nearest the leader said, "I have seen this man before. He is the missionary who lives among the Delaware."

As David was about to acknowledge what the second brave had said, Susan turned around and took two steps toward the fire before she saw the Indians facing her husband. She gave out a pronounced, "Oh my," in apparent alarm, but David quickly assured her that the visitors meant no harm. Then he said to the Indians, "Yes, I am the missionary of the Delaware, and I am returning to my village. This is my new wife, and she has not yet been to my village." David then translated what he had just said for Susan, and both turned to see all of the Wyandot grinning broadly and gesturing. What the Wyandot said to each other about the missionary's new wife was not answered or translated by David, who simply smiled at them as they turned and disappeared into the forest.

Although Susan had met and been around other Indians in the past, it was the first time she had met any Wyandot. A fierce people from the Ohio Territory, the Wyandot she encountered that night had somewhat unnerved her. David put his arms around her to comfort her, and she said softly to him, "I really wasn't frightened, my darling, not with you here to protect me." David replied, "The Wyandot are wonderful people that I have not yet been able to reach, but basically they mean no harm to the Moravians. Their main concern are the encroaching settlers — those who would disturb the lands away from the missions. They know that we mean no harm to them. Did you see how happy they were when they left?" A tiny smile upon his face was concealed as he buried his face in her hair. He could not bring himself to tell her that they had crudely — but innocently — joked of the nuances of a new marriage. The balance of the journey to the mission would be less disconcerting to her, he thought.

The members of the Gnadenhutten congregation were delighted with their minister's new wife. Her friendly, easy manner was immediately evident, and the kindred spirits of the converted Delaware were equally and warmly received by Susan. David took special effort and pleasure to acquaint Susan with those from his flock that he had described to her back at Friedenshutten. Many of the women had prepared special dishes or breads in anticipation of their minister's return, and all sought to meet or greet both the returnees. There was an entire night of celebrating on the day that David and Susan arrived. The schoolhouse was set up for a sumptuous banquet, and everybody was there. William and John were also there, having been summoned by one of David's flock.

John, especially, had something to say to David and the new bride. "David and Susan," he announced, after having been introduced to Susan, "I would like you to meet my wife, Sarah." David was both shocked and very pleased at John's disclosure, and his jaw noticeably dropped open. John continued, "We were married on July 4th," and this second disclosure brought audible gasps to both David and Susan. "What's wrong?" asked John, perplexed that the date of his wedding had evoked such a response. Laughing gently, both David and Susan simultaneously replied, "We got married on July 4th also!" With that, everybody in the foursome began to smile heartily and exchange hugs. "Imagine that — each of us old men married on exactly the same day," David muttered aloud. His amazement was met by even more of a merry response, and everyone partied happily into the night.

Susan Zeisberger would blend perfectly into the role of wife and chief assistant to her minister husband in the missions in the Ohio Territory. She eagerly and earnestly accompanied David on trips to the other mission sites, and was liked and admired by all she encountered. She had been particularly welcomed by Gelelemend, who made a special trip to the Gnadenhutten mission to meet and pay his respects to her. It was the first of many visits by non-Christian Indians to Gnadenhutten.

In the days that followed, war parties from both sides entered the villages of the missionaries, rested, and went on their way. To the colonists, there was simply no way that they could or would be deterred in their fight with the hated British. The Indians who allied with the British were another matter. David and the other missionaries continued to be able to convince more Indians to give up the fight and simply go home. Although the Moravians' attempted to convince all Indian groups to quit the warring, their successes mostly occurred in smaller parties of less than five. To a Christian, however, as in winning a single soul for Christ, each Indian deterred from war represented a major accomplishment.

When a group of militiamen came into Gnadenhutten in the fall of 1780, their young leader, a lieutenant, sought out David and asked him about the possibility of any British troops in the area. He also cautioned David about helping any of the enemy, including any of the various tribesmen who were by now aiding the British cause. David told him that each of the mission settlements were completely neutral, and that they would remain neutral. David also told the lieutenant that he and the others had been able to persuade a number of Indians to give up the war and to return to their own families. This was welcome news to the militia officer, but he exhibited little enthusiasm, and instead warned David again, this time, even more sternly, about assisting any of the enemy. Period.

What David did not know was that word of his successes in persuading various Indians to leave the war had already reached the ears of Colonel Daniel Brodhead, and that this commandant at Fort Pitt was extremely pleased. David also was unaware that word of his persuasive speeches had also reached the ears of Major de Peyster at Detroit, and the British reaction was considerably less well received.

Since the very beginning of the war, the Moravian neutrality had been suspect by the British, and for at least the last several years, de Peyster suspected Zeisberger and his associates of full-blown subversive efforts against the British and their Indian allies. The most recent evidence against Zeisberger had come from the Shawnee war party that had left Gnadenhutten in the previous spring only to meet up with the main body of de Peyster's troops on the south shore of Lake Erie. The Shawnee leader told of Zeisberger's hospitality, and the British commander was pleased. He was not as pleased to learn that Zeisberger had attempted to talk the Shawnee into quitting the British, and he was most interested that this Moravian missionary should have inquired about the position of the main body of British troops.

What really aggravated the British commander was the fact that in recent months, his troops had begun to lose strategic battles to the militiamen when his Indian-backed troops were virtually annihilated by the colonists. He simply could not fathom that the colonists were more dedicated, more determined, and more ferocious in battle than the various tribesmen enlisted in the British cause. He failed to realize, also, that the colonists were fighting a life and death struggle for their right to a free and independent country, while the British were simply putting down an insurrection — far away from their own native soil. More importantly, Major de Peyster simply never took into account that most of the Indians who joined the British did so for simplistic reasons like a ready supply of rum or money that could buy it. Unlike the British or the colonists, there was no deep Indian ideology to the war. The Indian allegiance was totally negotiable.

To the aggravated de Peyster, however, there had to be more concrete reasons for his losses and more and more, the duplicity of Zeisberger and his fellow Moravians came into focus as that reason. de Peyster would never believe that the colonial rebels were possibly being alerted by certain members of his own forces, and it would be a long time before he discovered the true reasons for his losses in the Ohio Territory.

In January of the following year, Major de Peyster dispatched a personal emissary to Goschachgunk to Gelelemend and the other Delaware chieftains in a final and determined effort to get them to finally commit to the British cause. The emissary was courteously received, but once more Gelelemend was able to convince the diminished Delaware to remain neutral. What the emissary was able to do was to stir up enough controversy among many of the dissident Delaware to eventually overcome Gelelemend's resistance.

By March of 1781, the Delaware Council of Chiefs were openly opposing the dictates of Gelelemend and suggesting that the chief be replaced. At the Council meeting, Gelelemend outwardly stood firm in his resolve to remain neutral as members of the Council angrily denounced him and called him cowardly. Inwardly, Gelelemend knew instinctively that his life, as well as the lives of the members of his family were now at risk. He had noticed the glares and angry looks which had punctuated the meeting of the chiefs and he knew, all too well, of the intentions of the others to replace him. That could only be accomplished within the Delaware culture by killing the leader outright, as well as those within his immediate family.

Under cover of darkness, as several other Delaware chiefs indeed plotted his assassination, Gelelemend and his family slipped silently away from Goschachgunk and made their way southward toward the lower Ohio River valley. He had saved his family from certain death, and though he would one day be reunited with David Zeisberger, the once proud chief of all the Delaware, and the son of their greatest leader would never again return to the position of leader of his people.

When the would-be assassins entered Gelelemend's lodge late that night, they were surprised to find that he had fled, and a huge celebration ensued in the open area just outside. The Delaware sang and danced long into the night, and as the remaining chiefs now pledged their full allegiance to the British, the men donned the paints of war, while the women began to assemble their weapons for them.

During the war dance, a handful of the less war-like Delaware, relatives of those encamped further north with the Moravian missionaries, quietly slipped away from Goschachgunk and joined their Christianized Delaware brothers. Though they would not be missed by the now-warring Delaware, they would relate the events of the night to David and his associates.

One of the families who chose to flee to the sanctity of the Moravians was headed by Rondmanund, a slender man in his early 40s, who had long secretly desired to be baptized and join the other Christianized Delaware. He had been torn between his native Delaware culture and that of the others for almost a year. During that time, Rondmanund had seen several of his tribe baptized and welcomed into the Zeisberger flock, including one of his own brothers, now called Joseph. Before slipping away from the shouts of the now-warring Delaware and the energy of the blazing fires, before which they danced, tears welled in his eyes. A proud man, Rondmanund, said nothing to his wife and two young children, but gestured mutely to them with just his eyes and a finger to his lips. The family had already talked of such a move and they were all ready for it. None of them wanted to be a part of the scary fervor which was sweeping all of the Delaware around them.

On the darkened trail, Rondmanund's family hurried along without a sound. The man led the way, carrying his youngest son, while the oldest son and the wife followed within a step of the father. To keep his family together in the darkness, Rondmanund had tied a thin string of hide around his waist, looped it to his walking son, and tied the end to his wife, who carried a precious few of the family possessions. About three feet separated each of those walking the pitch-dark trail. The toddler in his arms shivered noticeably and Rondmanund whispered to him, "We will soon be there, my son. I shall warm you and feed you then. Make no noise." The little boy snuggled closer to his father and squeezed his arm, as if to acknowledge his father's wishes, and the four made their way the almost twenty miles to Gnadenhutten.

David, Susan, and the others received Rondmanund and his family warmly, but the news of Gelelemend's overthrow brought mixed reactions. On the one hand, they were pleased that a good man and his family had avoided death at the hands of the insurgents, but they also thought that they would never see their friend again. They also knew that the decision of the Delaware to join the British was an ill omen for them, although all but three of the missionaries and their converts were Delaware by birth.

Shortly thereafter, news of the Delaware/British alliance reached Fort Pitt, and it was not well received. Colonel Brodhead immediately decided on retaliatory measures against the Delaware and led his men on a raid on Goschachgunk on April 19, 1781. In a surprise night raid against the Delaware, more than thirty Delaware warriors were killed and the entire village was burned to the ground. Fortunately for the Delaware, most had already left the village at Goschachgunk to join the British to the north. Against his better judgment, Brodhead allowed many of his men to take the scalps of the Delaware men who had been slain at Goschachgunk. What the colonial troops left at the village was a grisly sight for the Delaware warriors who would eventually seek revenge upon their return.

On their way back to Fort Pitt, Brodhead's men were in a very spirited mood, following their annihilation of the Delaware, and they traveled the Tuscarawas until they reached the area of Salem. From just outside the Salem mission, many of Brodhead's men openly suggested to their commander that "they should just go on in and kill the rest of those murdering Delawares." To the colonists from Fort Pitt, an Indian was an Indian was an Indian, and it didn't matter where or how they lived. The men were just blood thirsty enough to want to go in and finish all those at each of the three Moravian missions, and to burn all of them to the ground. The scalplocks, still wet on their belts, failed to alert them as to the depths to which they had descended. But good sense somehow prevailed.

Brodhead steadfastly refused to be swayed by his men's adrenaline. He had formed a utilitarian alliance with Zeisberger over the years and the Moravian missionary had never caused him any grief. Brodhead also saw Zeisberger as a future source of intelligence deep in the Ohio Territory, although not much of the dialogue between the two could ever be truly characterized as intelligence. Despite the logical orders of Brodhead to the militiamen who accompanied him, there was a great deal of grumbling under the breath of many of his men, and as they made their way past the last of the three Moravian encampments, the eyes of the men revealed the hatred that each held for all Indians. This deep seated hatred would burn intensely and ominously long within the hearts of too many of Brodhead's men.

Meanwhile, in Detroit, Major de Peyster, because of the colonial attack on the Delaware village of Goschachgunk, was now incensed. As illogical as the connection could be, it somehow firmly convinced him of the treasonous actions of Zeisberger and his flock. As he paced the floor of his quarters at the fort, de Peyster cursed David and the Delaware under his breath. "I should not have allowed them to remain in the Muskingum Valley," he said aloud, as he pounded his fist upon a table in open anger. Visions of Zeisberger, Heckewelder, and the others standing upon a British gallows flashed through the commander's mind. He was that angry.

It had been only four months since Gelelemend's abdication and the subsequent alliance between the Delaware and the British, but de Peyster had been poring over his intelligence reports the entire time. Now, at last, he was sure that the Moravian missionaries had been passing along information to the colonists at Fort Pitt. The information that finally convinced him was a report from one of his own spies who had long been accepted as one of Brodhead's volunteers.

Owen, as he was simply called, had sent a message to de Peyster of how Brodhead had spared the mission villages as the colonists had returned to Fort Pitt, while the rest of the men wanted to go in and wipe out the Indians. To the spy, Owen, what had really happened was that Brodhead had spared those around Zeisberger only because the Moravians were obviously working for the colonists, and this is exactly what he sent to de Peyster. Right or wrong, coupled with the reports of Zeisberger attempting to get bands of Indians to quit the war effort, and the fact that British forces were being out-fought regularly now, de Peyster believed Owen's report. To the British commander, the reports before him were undeniable — Zeisberger *was*, indeed, working for the colonists.

Most of de Peyster's observations about Zeisberger and the Moravians were exaggerated because of what he saw as his tactical position in the overall scheme of the war. British army accounts of the war that reached de Peyster regularly played down the mounting losses to the east, but concentrated mostly on de Peyster's isolated situation to the rear and along the Canadian frontier. In actuality, the bulk of the war simply had not yet reached that far west, and de Peyster's garrison was yet to feel the full force of what other redcoats were experiencing further east. To the ill-informed de Peyster and apparently to the British high command as well, it was as simple as day and night — if the British could gain full control of the Ohio Territory, they could seal off the rear and then mount an offensive which would begin a victory drive to the Atlantic Ocean. And right or wrong, de Peyster blindly focused on Zeisberger and the Moravians as his immediate obstacles in the territory. He should have been looking more closely to home.

To be sure, the evidence against Zeisberger, although largely hearsay, circumstantial, and simply coincidental, was mounting but still lacked the certainty necessary for a conviction on grounds of treason. de Peyster wanted the Moravians — especially David Zeisberger — out of the Muskingum valley, and they soon would be. And then the Major devised a plan to do precisely that. "Yes!" he practically shouted, as he slammed his fist against his desk top again. "I have it!" he thought to himself. "Captain!" he bellowed confidently as he summoned his adjutant in the adjoining office; and his plan was about to be put into effect.

August 20, 1781

Captain Matthew Elliot, adjutant to Major de Peyster at Detroit, six British regulars, and another 250 Wyandot and a few Indian allies from other tribes arrived at Gnadenhutten after a long, hot, and extremely speedy march. Word of the imminent arrival of the troops reached David and the others long before they first appeared on the far side of the river, just northwest of the mission. It was not unusual to see British regulars in the area, not even a detachment with so many Indian allies, and no one in the village was overly alarmed. It was mid-morning, and it was apparent to David that the British were going to camp just across from the main buildings of the mission. In anticipation of their visit to the mission, Susan had large pots of tea prepared, and some of the women of the village were baking biscuits. Two of the families began to break out the butter churns and unopened jars of current and blackberry preserves were readied for the visitors. The Moravians had long been noted for their warm hospitality.

Shortly after encampment, Captain Elliot reached into his bedroll and pulled out a worn leather sheath, the kind which had long been used to protect official messages. He untied the thin leather string which circled the sheath and pulled a crisp parchment page from between the leather protectors. Elliot steadied himself by placing his left foot across the branch of a fallen sycamore, and he peered at the writing on the paper. The document was an order of removal from the area of David Zeisberger and *all* of his associates and followers, whites and Indians alike, and it had been issued and signed by Major de Peyster, acting in his capacity as the King's representative in the area.

Although he had only met Zeisberger on one previous occasion, Elliot had not been particularly impressed by David's warm personal nature nor his obvious reverence for the Lord. He smiled quite smugly to himself as he thought of how he would present and execute the warrant. Convincing David Zeisberger to move his entourage from his beloved Muskingum River Valley was not was not going to be an easy task, and because of the large number of "hostiles" involved, Elliot easily warmed to the task. Perhaps his own command awaited him upon completion of this foray. With a sense of pride and pompousness, Elliot slowly turned and fixed his gaze toward the people who were moving about across the river from him. "Corporal Watkins," he boomed in the direction of his own men, "You and Smithers will accompany me to the mission."

Almost two hours after they had reached the Tuscarawas River, Elliot and the other two waded across the river and marched directly up to David and Susan, who stood waiting outside their own building, which also housed the chapel. "Good afternoon, Captain," said David. Susan nodded her hello. "We have prepared some tea and bread for you and your men. Welcome to the Lord's own village of Gnadenhutten," said David as he extended his hand in friendship. Captain Elliot tipped his hat slightly to salute Susan and shook the missionary's hand weakly and thanked him for the cordial welcome, but he was not smiling, and he could not look directly into the other man's face. With an air of nearly open contempt, Elliot looked everywhere but into the face of the man who had offered him his hand. In the English tradition, Elliot signaled his men to take tea and all of them sat in chairs in the narrow strip of shadow against the wall of the chapel. By now, the group included David, Susan, the three British soldiers, and Isaac and Levi, two of the most senior Delaware converts. Another group of converted Delaware, mostly children, stood awkwardly by, about twenty feet away, and stern looks from David did not immediately cause them to leave. As the warm morning sun bore down upon them, one by one, the onlookers drifted away. Those in the shade were merely having small talk.

Finally, after clearing his throat, Elliot stood and looking directly at David, said, "Reverend, I'm afraid that I've arrived with some rather painful news for you," and he reached into his bright red tunic and removed the stiff parchment warrant. This time Elliot did not take his eyes from David's. It was all that Elliot could do to keep the earlier evil smile from curling his thin, hateful lips. Reading from the paper, "Upon orders from His Royal Majesty's magistrate at Fort Detroit, I am commanded to remove you and the others from the Muskingum River valley, and to relocate you to the south shore of Lake Erie, near the mouth of the Sandusky. Would you like to read the order for yourself, Zeisberger?" asked the officer, who had by now abandoned any pretext of respect for the Moravian missionary. Susan was simply stunned, and sat silently, nearly paralyzed.

Slowly David arose and reached out for the parchment. He was already able to see de Peyster's official seal at the bottom of the document, and there was no doubt in his mind that what he had just heard was true. Elliot's smirking face was proof enough for him. His eyes scanned the document quickly, not seeing every word, but "conspiring with the insurgent colonials" immediately jumped out at him. Even more slowly than he had risen, David now sat again, though Elliot remained standing. Susan was peering into David's face, attempting to learn of his emotions. Isaac and Levi both leaned forward toward David, trying to gauge his response. David almost lost his balance as he groped for his seat behind him while lowering his body into the chair.

Once seated, David made a pronounced effort to read and consider everything in the warrant. He read and reread everything very slowly. Aloud, he read the final paragraph, "An investigation into Moravian actions has begun. If charges of treasonous activities are found to be warranted, those accused will be arrested, and if found guilty of such charges, will be sentenced to death, and said sentence will be carried out at the earliest possible opportunity." "Oh, my," mused David, "Major de Peyster is certainly anxious to put an end to me and my work, isn't he, Captain?" David glanced first at his wife, and then in the direction of the two converts, who each nodded their beliefs. Susan remained motionless.

"Look, Zeisberger," snapped Elliot, "we've known about your efforts on the part of those rebels at Fort Pitt for quite a while now. You were given every opportunity to distance yourself from them, and since you have not, you must now pay the price! There are those at Detroit who feel that you should have been charged long ago." David started to protest his innocence, but by the look on the Captain's almost snarling face, he could see that it would be for naught. Instead, David just shook his head in disbelief and handed the warrant back to Elliot. "You realize, of course, Captain," he began, "that it will take a little time to get everyone ready. You don't mean to say that even the children must go too, do you?" "Everyone!" answered Elliot, as he looked in the direction of the minister's wife, and then added, "I have been instructed by Major de Peyster to allow as much time as reasonable for you and your group to prepare for the trip. My men and I will remain in our camp until you are prepared for the trip. Good day, Reverend. Mrs. Zeisberger!" With that, Elliot did a smart, but abbreviated about-face and marched toward the river with his men.

As soon as the visitors had reached the river, David turned to the convert next to him and each could see the concern in the other's eyes. "Isaac," said David, "go and fetch John Heckewelder. Tell him only what you have just heard, and tell him that it is urgent!" David and Levi slowly stood up as Isaac rose and started to move quickly away. "And Isaac," added David as an afterthought, "be sure avoid the troops across yon river. We don't want the Captain to think that any of us might be escaping." The words brought a slight smile to the face of the Moravian, which let Levi see that if the Reverend was worrying, it most certainly was not apparent. Levi was then given the same instructions in order for William Edwards to be summoned from New Schoenbrunn. It was obvious to David that Elliot believed all the Moravians and converts were at Gnadenhutten, and that de Peyster's intelligence network had failed to notice that the Moravians had separated into three groups. At the moment, he was not sure how he could utilize this fact, but for now, Elliot could go on believing that everyone was at Gnadenhutten.

David, standing alone beside the structure which was his residence, as well as the church, took off his heavy black hat and scratched his head in a manner which clearly indicated that he was indeed perplexed, although he said nothing. Susan now moved very closely to her husband, reaching for his hand for encouragement. Despite his reassuring mannerisms and words to Isaac and Levi, he was, at best, totally uncertain as to what next to do. Uncertain about what to do *after* he prayed, that is, and David and Susan entered the chapel where they could pray to the Lord to show them the way. Outside in the small village, the children played as the men and women worked, and all were unaware of the fate that awaited them. The warm summer weather and the abundant crops were their gifts from God, and nothing else mattered to them at this moment.

It was nightfall before Isaac and John Heckewelder arrived at Gnadenhutten, and almost midnight before Levi returned with William Edwards. Wisely, Sarah Heckewelder had not accompanied her husband. In order not to disturb the British and their group across the river from the main settlement, the men had taken circuitous routes. Elliot had already posted sentries and dispatched scouts in order to be vigilant against incursions by the colonists. It was vital that the men avoid the sentries and scouts, lest the Moravians be fired upon as rebel scouts. William Edwards and Levi had, in fact, very nearly walked right into a Wyandot scout, and had been forced to lie perfectly motionless in the undergrowth for a considerable spell, as the Indian relieved himself but five feet away from them. It was their misfortune to have to approach Gnadenhutten after dark, and from the same general direction from which a militia attack might be undertaken.

Alone in David's quarters, the three missionaries contemplated the fate of the Moravians and their flock in the Muskingum River Valley. Susan, not participating in the conference, dutifully made coffee and tea for the trio. After opening their hushed meeting with a prayer, David said, "Although de Peyster's warrant calls only for our removal to Upper Sandusky, I do not believe that this is the full extent of British action against the Moravian order. Let us examine our options. What can we do about this? We do not have time to seek the advice or approval from Bethlehem."

Neither Edwards or Heckewelder considered an answer to David's rhetorical question, but both scooted forward in their seats with obvious concern as to how it would be answered. "We may simply do as the British command, and go meekly north to their intended home for us," continued David, "But if we do this thing, we are ceasing to do the one thing that each of us has dedicated our lives to doing. While it is true that we would still have our flock with us, our home is here, along the Tuscarawas. We planted the seeds for this congregation and have done God's work, and we have grown in number, vision, and wisdom. Do you not agree, John?" asked David, as he looked directly into Heckewelder's eyes. He also glanced in the direction of his wife, who signaled her approval to what her husband had just said.

"There is no question about our mission in this valley and how it has prospered, David," answered John solemnly, who then looked toward William for confirmation. "Aye, my brothers, but for all the good that we have done, I'm afraid that there are so many who do not see our work with the same enthusiasm," replied William. "But for this cursed war, we should probably live in utter peace and harmony," he added. "Amen, William," said David, and John simply nodded his head in agreement. "The British think we are helping the colonists and there has been little chance of convincing them otherwise. Time and time again, I have given them my word that we in the Tuscarawas region are completely neutral, but they simply do not believe me," said David, with a tone of decided chagrin. "I've no doubt that we would be believed if we were missionaries of the Church of England," replied William sarcastically. The remark brought about audible chuckles from the other two men. "Or even Jesuits," Susan added, and her contribution to the meeting drew an amen from William and nods from David and John.

"No, Susan, I have reason to believe that even the Jesuits are suffering the effects of the war, just as we have," replied David. "As for the Church of the British," he continued, "I'm fairly certain that it is one of the reasons that the war is raging all around us now. The colonists do not want anything to do with a religion that is imposed upon them by the King, or by anyone else." Thinking back to his own childhood and the problems that the Moravian Church had encountered as it began in Europe, David clearly saw a parallel with the present situation. It was also a development to which John could easily relate. "Religious beliefs and practices are so vital to each of us, and so personally inviolable that in our zeal to protect them, we simply cannot help stepping on the rights of someone else. But enough of this philosophy! We must decide on how we are to meet this latest crisis."

"One thing, I believe," continued David, "is that although de Peyster means for the entire flock to be relocated, I do not believe that he means to send Elliot to three separate villages along the river. Did either of you see Elliot's men as they made their way to Gnadenhutten?" Before the other two could each answer no, David looked off into the distant night sky and spoke his thoughts aloud, "I'm not too sure about the route that Elliot took from Detroit. He probably did not go up or down stream, but marched directly to this village." The image of Elliot and his British military efficiency clearly answered David's own question. "Unless I hear otherwise from Captain Elliot, I am not going to do anything about having either or both of you move with us to Sandusky. Oh, to be sure, they know about our other villages, but I'm certain that it is me that they want out of this region, and if it has to be, then that's all that they shall get. Just me and the flock here at Gnadenhutten." It was obvious by his look into Susan's eyes that she would also go with David, wherever that might be. "If Elliot does demand that we all go along, then we shall simply deal with it at that time," he concluded.

"Do we not have any other choices, David?" asked John. "Can we not simply steal away in the middle of the night, leaving Elliot to return to Detroit empty-handed?" he asked. "Where would we go, John?" asked David, in answering the younger man. "Our choices are extremely poor. If we return to Fort Pitt, our fate would likely be no better. To be sure, we whites would be safe, but after what happened to those poor souls at Goschachgunk this Spring, I'm just not willing to subject these Christian children to the wrath of a stirred-up group of colonists that appear to be totally anti-Indian.

If we go north and across Lake Erie into Canada, we risk conflict with the French, the Jesuits, and the Indians that are there. Besides, the relations between France and England are just as bad as that of the American rebels and England. It would only be a matter of time until we were placed in the self same situation in which we find ourselves now. If we decided to move south or west, we would be risking our flock against even more perilous circumstances. There is little known about the agricultural quality of those lands, but there are many stories of the murderous nature of some of the Indians in these two areas. Again..... I'm not willing to put our flock at risk." A quiet, forlorn atmosphere enveloped all of the four people in the room.

David continued, "We must also consider that our food supply is rapidly dwindling and the current crops must be harvested in order for us to survive into next planting season. And though we might well steal away in any direction, I am certain, but we would have precious little to feed on in the course of our escape." All three of the men agreed on this point. "Possibly the best thing for the entire flock would be to go along with Elliot to the south shore of Lake Erie," continued David, "The earth there is splendid for growing, and we could return after this insane war is ended. What do you think, William? John?" Both of the younger men agreed that acceding to de Peyster and Elliot would be the least painful course of action for all concerned. However, they did not look enthusiastically forward to seeing David and the flock be literally driven out of the beautiful Muskingum region that they had long called home.

To confirm what seemed a set plan, David also asked Susan for her thoughts. "I told you a long time ago, darling, that I would join you in everything. If that means moving anywhere, you know that I will support your decision, said Susan." "Aye, David," said John. "Sarah has told me the exact same thing, and I am just grateful that we both have such fine Moravian wives." William offered up a toast to the character of both Susan and Sarah, and soon their three cups clinked softly in the night air.

"Before the cock crows on the morrow, I reason that we had best get some sleep, my brothers," said David, as he and Susan readied places on the floor of their simple home upon which the younger men could bed down. Out of deference to Susan, each turned their backs toward the couple's bed. As he blew out the candle, David gave a pronounced sigh, which was duplicated by each of the other men. Together, in hushed tones, and at David's signal, they recited the Lord's prayer. Several minutes of silence followed really serious conversation and prayer seemed an eternity, but David knew that the others were still awake. In the darkness, and speaking in the direction of the timbered ceiling above him, David said quietly, "I shall call a meeting of the congregation for tomorrow night and inform the flock about what has been visited upon us and of our intentions. You two must do the same at Salem and New Schoenbrunn as soon as you return." From the pallets on the floor, came two assenting sounds, and the three men grudgingly began to yield to fatigue and sleep. Susan nestled closely to David and found a perfect spot for her head in the crook of his arm. Though she was awake to hear the others sounds of sleep, she was awake much later than the others.

Shortly after dawn, everyone was awake and moving about. As John washed his face and hands in the nearby basin, David and William were embracing goodbye, as was the custom with the missionaries. William and John both also hugged Susan, not knowing when they would see each other again. David then hugged John, and after the younger pair had embraced, David led everyone in prayer again. With hands joined and heads bowed, he began, "Oh Lord, guide us all with the wisdom and love that You have always shown us, and protect each of us so that we may continue to let others know of Your love for them. Amen." After three more "Amens," John and William set out for their respective villages.

David went to the window which faced toward the rest of the village and stared for a moment at Isaac's house in hopes of seeing some movement, but there was as yet none. He told Susan that he was checking to see if Isaac were up yet. Then he almost automatically surveyed all of the village that the view from his window permitted. He smiled with satisfaction as his eyes took him from one structure to the next, and from the last structure to the green and bountiful fields which lay just beyond the last tiny cabin in the distance. He felt an immense pride, and rightly so, in all that he gazed upon. His feelings of fulfillment came not from any of the material images before him, but from a spiritual gratification from the knowledge that he was looking at the evidence of a unique culture — a collection of truly civilized human beings who lived in harmony with each other, their environment, their neighbors, and one God. The one God from whom sprang all things possible. The pride welled up inside him and began to seep gently downward from the corners of his eyes, and it was several seconds before David even realized that his vision had become too blurred to see. Then David stiffened and began to refocus his gaze — not at one thing in particular, but with an accompanying clarity which made him feel a little embarrassed for his prideful thoughts. He did all this with his face toward the window, so Susan could not see his anguish, although he knew that she could feel it.

David was such a simple, unassuming man that it was simply not possible for him to attribute any of the Moravian villages' accomplishments to anything that he had done. To him, he was but God's messenger, and he had faithfully delivered every message entrusted to him. Now, the content of the message from de Peyster that he was soon to deliver to the flock brought him instantly back to reality and with a sneeze caused by the bright morning sunlight in his eyes. "Gesundheit, my darling," said Susan, and he straightened himself and stared once more at Isaac's cabin. At last, he saw movement, and he hastened outside to beckon to Isaac to join him.

In the few minutes it took Isaac to reach the Gemeinen Saal, and David and Susan's residence, several other villagers had arisen and were headed into the fields to tend and groom what was destined to be a bumper crop. Almost everyone of them had seen and waved to or spoken a bright good morning greeting to their Reverend. The idyllic atmosphere of Gnadenhutten had not yet been disturbed by those encamped on the opposite banks of the Tuscarawas.

David met Isaac just outside the door to the chapel and placed both hands on his shoulders as he spoke directly into the man's eyes. "Brother Isaac, please inform the members of the flock that there will be a meeting here tonight, just after dusk, and it is vital that all adults attend. We must tell them of de Peyster's plans for us." said David. "Reverend father," asked Isaac, "are we not also going to tell the children?" The innocent tone of Isaac's question brought a smile to David's face, and he embraced Isaac warmly and replied, "We shall leave that to each family, Isaac. To be handled in a manner when and how best served each and every household. Go now, friend." And Isaac dutifully began the task of notifying each of the village's families, which numbered nearly forty. David walked to the edge of the main building and looked across the morning mist of the river and saw that Elliot's camp was stirring also. With but the slightest hint of sarcasm dancing across his thoughts, David wondered if Captain Elliot would bring Gnadenhutten more good news today.

The meeting that evening was held in the Gemeinen Saal and there had already been hushed whispers about what was happening. Both Isaac and Levi had not revealed what they already knew, to anyone — not even their own wives, and the members of the flock were not prone to gossip, but almost everyone expected a meeting which would reveal some kind of bad news. David and the other missionaries had always inspired the converted Delaware to be optimistic, and their adopted Christian beliefs and attitudes also nurtured and encouraged the faith that only the best lay ahead for them. But the presence of the British troops and so many hostile Indians just across the river was definitely an ominous sign.

As was the normal order of business in the chapel, David opened the meeting with a rather generic but heartfelt prayer which gave no hint of what was later to be revealed. His message to the members of the flock was direct and to the point. He called on members of the village to do their individual parts in making the move to the Upper Sandusky as easy and painless as possible. At the end of his news, David asked if there were questions, and some of the flock did have concerns. Young Samuel, 18, had suffered a broken leg just recently during a slate-gathering expedition upstream. Would he, too, have to go? And what of the women now carrying unborn in the village? Mary, wife of Thomas, would give birth at any moment, and there were others. What of them?

David acknowledged each individual hardship and pledged to the group that he would do his best to persuade Captain Elliot to allow special consideration for those requiring it. As a father who reassures his children each night at bedtime, David also urged his congregation to rest easy. "Do not worry, my brothers and sisters," he began, "we shall all endure these sudden and troublesome plans for us." His thoughts at the moment were as much with his own wife as with the other members of his flock. He motioned gently with his outstretched hands, as if to have them remain in their places, but not a soul was about to leave just yet. "We must all remember that we are God's children, and that this is merely another duty for us. We must remain united in our belief in Him and also in our belief in each other. No harm will come to any of us, for God will not forsake us," said David confidently. The smiles on the faces of those before him redoubled his own confidence, and he led them into a warm and inspirational hymn before closing with a long and poignant prayer.

After the last person had left the building, David and Susan readied themselves for bed. From the only window in their simple room, David could see the campfires from across the river. He wondered, almost aloud, if Elliot would give the flock enough time and latitude to do what was needed. He thought of Major de Peyster back at Detroit, and tried to make sense of the commander's orders, but shook his head incredulously, when he could not. He also searched his mind for an analogy to the present situation, and remembered happily that the early Moravian exile from Bohemia and subsequent relocation to Saxony was nearly identical to the situation at hand. "We survived that and became much stronger, and we'll do the same here, too," he said to himself as he smacked his fist into his palm! And with this renewed and uplifted faith, David read from his bible, nearly drifting off to sleep in his chair. He was jarred to reality by Susan, gently tugging the book from his hands and urging him to come to bed.

For the next day or so, none of those in Gnadenhutten saw or heard anything from Elliot. True to his word as an officer, he was giving David and the others ample time to get things in order before the move. Mary's new baby, a boy, was born during this time and both she and the infant were healthy and progressing nicely. Thomas, the father of the new child, named the baby David, after Zeisberger, and the whole village rejoiced.

The next child due was to be born in early October, and David would somehow try to get Major Elliot to wait until a short time after that before commencing the inevitable. More important to the welfare of the entire village, however, were the crops, which were slowly ripening in the fields. David had always silently believed that Elliot would have to wait until harvest, and the fact that he had not seen or heard the British leader led credence to his notions. About him, the men and women of the flock worked diligently in the fields and life went on in the village as if nothing out of the ordinary was in store. Adam and his new wife, Sarah, were still in the midst of building their first cabin, and several of the other families helped. It would be completed in only a day or two more, as Gnadenhutten continued to prosper and grow.

On the morning of August 27th, David peered out of his window as Elliot and another soldier once more waded toward him. By the time the two British reached David's house, he had readied himself to meet with them outside. Susan was preparing to spin yarn and would not join him just now. "Good morning, Captain Elliot," said David, and then to be polite, he included the other soldier, "and good morning to you, also young man." Both men stood rigidly at attention and merely nodded a response to David, giving little evidence that they were appreciating the glory of this particular day. With a somber look on his face, Elliot crisply said, "Reverend Zeisberger, my men and I have been here for a week and we are tiring of this place. We wish to return to our own homes at Detroit. Are your people preparing for the move to the Upper Sandusky?" "Oh, to be sure, Captain," replied David. "We had the birth of a child here only four days ago, and I'm pleased to say....." "I know that you are pleased to say anything and everything, Zeisberger," interrupted Elliot, "but I want you to emphasize to these people here that we will be moving out in three days! On the 30th! Do you understand me?" "Why, of course, I do Captain, but....." and again David was interrupted, as the two men about-faced and returned abruptly to their camp, without awaiting the completion of David's reply. David followed them with his eyes as they retraced their steps, and he thought about the curt message they had just delivered.

There was no doubt that Elliot meant what he said. The stinging tone of the officer left a residue of disbelief in the ears of this peaceful man of God, and David could only imagine how and why one human being could be so callous to another. Looking skyward, as if for a response, David shrugged his shoulders in a gesture of incredulity, and then strolled off toward the fields for a visit with the men there. Along the way, David stopped to check on Mary and his new namesake, and also to call upon the young family who next awaited their own arrival. David and Susan did little to change their routine, despite what Elliot had just told them. Life at Gnadenhutten continued at God's pace.

As the morning of the 30th arrived, David and Susan awoke to find a light rain had begun to fall. David smiled to himself, certain that this was God's answer to his prayer of the previous evening. He had no way of foreseeing what was yet to occur. In the next hour or so, the rain intensified to the point of becoming a heavy downpour. In the distant western skies, flashes of lightning spasmodically tickled the earth and moved slowly toward the village amid long, low rumbling tones from the heavens. Before the morning had ended, a raging thunderstorm of near tornadic proportion had wreaked havoc upon the area. Unbelievably high winds buffeted and rocked the valley, and large trees were uprooted or simply blown over. The Tuscarawas flowed southward with a terrible vengeance at levels which threatened to spill over onto Gnadenhutten.

David strained to look out of his rain-streaked window in the direction of the encampment, but could see little. It almost appeared as if the camp had just vanished overnight, but David simply believed it was because of the poor visibility. He smiled mischievously to himself as he said aloud, "I trust the good Captain and his men are adequately equipped and prepared for the storm." Susan chuckled at her husband's unfamiliar sarcasm. His breath on the pane fogged it to the point of completely obscuring his view, and David sat down on his chair and thumbed contentedly through his bible. He pulled a blanket around his shoulders, thankful that he and Susan had remained warm and dry. None of the Gnadenhutten structures had suffered wind or water damage, although a sizable portion of the crops had been destroyed by the storm, and one cow was either lost or swept away by the river.

On the opposite side of the river, which was considerably lower and less protected, Elliot and his men were literally blown (or washed) backward more than two hundred yards. Although the storm cleared later in the afternoon, the steady rainfall persisted, as did the wrath of the river, which was by now licking the edges of the shelters which housed the thoroughly saturated troops and their Indian compatriots. The men were chilled to the bone and it would be a long while until they managed to dry off. Mud was ankle deep everywhere, and Elliot did not even bother to look in the direction of the church. During the storm, several British horses panicked and broke free, and were scattered over a distance of several miles. It would be three more days before Matthew Elliot would again visit David and Susan, as it took that long for the Tuscarawas to recede to fordable depths. Elliot seethed with a quiet, but obvious fury as he was forced to wait until nature allowed him access to the village just across from him.

On September 3rd, at near 8:00 o'clock in the morning, Captain Elliot banged his fist harshly upon the door of the chapel building and fairly screamed, "Zeisberger! I command you to open this door in the name of the King! Zeis — ber — ger!" Pomoacan, the Wyandot chief who had accompanied Elliot on this day's soiree peered into a nearby window and looked this way and that, as the Englishman tapped his foot impatiently. Another Wyandot brave stood near his chieftain. As Elliot waited, facing the door as if he were a cat about to pounce upon a mouse, David and Susan appeared at the schoolhouse door directly across the narrow sodden street and David called out, "Just a moment, Captain, and I will open that door for you." Spinning quickly, Elliot almost lost his balance with the surprise that David was behind him. "Never mind this damned door, Zeisberger," he barked, "I want you and this miserable group of yours to be ready to leave here in the morning." Elliot walked briskly toward the couple, Pomoacan and the other Indian in tow, as he continued, "I have given you ample time to wrap up your business here and tomorrow at dawn, my men will be here to see that you are fully in compliance with my orders. No more stalling, period!" With that, Elliot's smart about-face brought him into contact with the Indian to his rear, and he snapped, "Get out of my way, you idiot!" Pomoacan grunted slightly and side stepped the Captain, and the three started toward their camp.

As he neared the opposite edge of the street, Elliot suddenly turned and, nearly bumping into Pomoacan again, said, "And Zeisberger, my orders are for *all* your people. That includes those missionaries and Delaware in the other two settlements. Have you even notified them of my orders? Where are they now? I don't see them about." As if on command, Pomoacan looked first to the left and then to the right and shrugged a silent agreement with the Englishman, and the third man imitated the gestures of his chief. Now David became extremely concerned, for it would not be possible to delay the officer before him one minute longer, and he walked from the school toward Elliot and the Wyandot, who waited for him. "Captain Elliot, I did not know that you meant for the other two missions to be included. I must be given time to tell them of this move to the Upper Sandusky, and they must be allowed a little time to prepare, as you have been so generous with us here, at Gnadenhutten," said David, as he clasped his hands in front of him. "Please allow us just a few more days?"

As David was requesting more time, Elliot stood silently staring at his own boots. He did not wish the Moravian to see that his face was contorted with anger and he was nearly to the point of exploding. Susan saw, however, and she would later tell David about the look. Pomoacan then stepped forward and whispered in the Captain's ear, as the other Indian strained to hear, and shortly Elliot raised his head and glared directly into David's eyes. For the longest time, Elliot did not speak, and by the time he did, the scarlet flush of anger had at last vanished. He cleared his throat with a subdued cough, gathered his thoughts, and said, "One week from tomorrow, on September 11th, at dawn, if every Moravian and Delaware in the Ohio territory are not here assembled and ready for the move to the

Sandusky, I swear by the crown that I will allow Pomoacan and his Wyandots to begin executing each and everyone of you miserable scum right here where we stand! And Zeisberger," he added, without a change of his now unemotional delivery, "You and your assistants will be first. I will simply tell Major de Peyster that there was resistance due to arms supplied the Moravians by the rebels, and that will be that. Take notice, Zeisberger — I am considerably beyond caring about what happens to you." And on that ominous warning, Elliot and the two Wyandots retreated to their camp.

By this time several of the flock had gathered in the shadows nearby and had seen and overheard the exchange between the Reverend and the British soldier. Isaac was there to witness the whole thing, but Levi had to be summoned from the fields. Both men were briefed by David again, and once more summarily dispatched to tell Heckewelder and Edwards of the latest British imperative. David instructed them to relay Elliot's message exactly as it had been given, and to emphasize that there was no doubt that the entire Moravian flock, from all three of the settlements, would be included in the relocation to the Sandusky. David, the other missionaries, and the flock of converted Delaware had faced other crises before and God had always been gracious to them. Though they did not want to leave their precious valley, they also chose not to become martyrs. For now, the British held the upper hand, and David and the others had no choice but obey, and with silent resignation, the Moravian activities in the Ohio territory slowly came to a halt.

September 11, 1781

The seven days since Captain Elliot had issued his ultimatum passed very quickly. The earlier part of the week started slowly and routinely enough, but by mid-week, the other members of the distant flocks were beginning to arrive in Gnadenhutten. By dusk on September 10th, the Heckewelders and William Edwards had arrived with the last of their respective villages. Housing was a major problem, as the entire population of Gnadenhutten had swollen from nearly 160 to now almost 460. Some families were separated, as each of the families in the host village attempted to take in at least one of the families from one of the other missions, but because many of the older families were large, this was not always possible. Men, women, and children slept on the floor of the tiny schoolhouse, and the Gemeinen Saal also yielded to the influx of refugees, as pallets and blankets were spread over every tiny sheltered space throughout the village.

John and Sarah shared the cabin of a converted Delaware couple and William, due to the insistence of Susan and David, shared their personal quarters, as he and John had done almost two weeks earlier. Rondmanund, and his family, along with another determined, but as-yet unbaptized Delaware family simply camped near the cabin of his brother, Joseph, preferring to allow other Christians to have his place indoors. The weather was extremely kind to the Moravians and their converts during this most troubling time, and Indians like Rondmanund and his family experienced no real hardships.

In the hour just before dawn, Elliot and his men were already busy. The Captain had dispatched two of his soldiers, along with two of their allied Indians to each of the Salem and the New Schoenbrunn missions. Both parties were given simple orders by their commander: Hunt down and kill anyone caught attempting to stay behind, and raze the villages! Both of these detachments would then join up with the main column as it proceeded on a pre-determined route to Upper Sandusky.

Just before the sun began to appear in the low eastern sky, Elliot and the remainder of his troops began to assemble very quietly in the narrow street. By sunrise, the three British soldiers were stiffly at attention, Elliot astride his horse, while the other two afoot, and all facing the door to the church, while the accompanying Wyandot warriors were assembled in a rather loose, but orderly grouping to their rear.

When the three missionaries emerged into the growing sunshine of the day, they were amazed that Elliot had been able to assemble so many of his men without their having been heard. As they stood very near the door to the chapel, and holding bags of their personal possessions, some of the flock began to leave the building behind them. Around the village, family after family began to dutifully line the small street between the school and the church. From his elevated vantage point, Captain Elliot scanned the village in all directions, and it was clear to him that there were no more of the converted Indians scurrying to the central part of the village. There were no voices heard, as hundreds of the flock quietly and obediently completed their movement toward where Captain Elliot and the others awaited.

David was just about to speak to the Captain, when Elliot, turned in his saddle and barked to Pomoacan, who was situated just to his rear. The increased volume in the officer's voice was as much for the members of the flock as for the Wyandot chief. "Chief Pomoacan, I hereby order you to take charge of the Moravians and their Delaware brothers. Strip them of their clothing, their personal possessions, and their food. Gather each of them here, in this spot and prepare to get underway to the Sandusky. Commence immediately, Chief Pomoacan!" Before Elliot's words had quit ringing in their ears, the members of the flock began to buzz with protests and look and lean toward where David and his assistants and their wives stood, numb with a stark realization of what they had just heard. David, to be heard above the din of the excited converts, yelled to Elliot, "In the name of God, Captain, I pray you not be serious about what you have just said!" Elliot, turning slowly to his right to face David, then answered, "Yes, Zeisberger, it will happen precisely as I have just said. Corporal — I order you to shoot anyone who does not comply with my order to Chief Pomoacan." "Yes, sir!" was the reply from the corporal to Elliot's right rear, and he lifted his musket slightly to a ready stance.

"None of these children of God will give you and your men any trouble, Captain, please....." but the rest of David's plea was drowned out by the deafening roar of the soldier's musket, and a hush fell over everyone as Rondmanund staggered forward two steps and then collapsed with a mortal wound to his heart, and a large knife in his hand, just two paces from where Elliot sat aboard his mount. Rondmanund had not yet been baptized, and therefore did not feel wholly compelled to submit his family to the atrocious orders of the British. While he had been willing to join the others in a simple relocation to Sandusky in order to eventually be converted to Christianity, he was not pleased with the prospects which had suddenly developed. As the blue-white smoke from the shot dissipated, the seriousness of the day immediately seized the peaceful converts and there would be no more resistance from any of them. The strong smell of gunpowder hung in the early morning air as members of Rondmanund's family quietly wept around his fallen body, and the corporal quickly reloaded his weapon. Susan rushed to be with Rondmanund's wife and embraced her as the young Indian woman sobbed mournfully into her shoulder.

Tears filled the eyes of most of the flock. Tears of sadness, for the respected man just slain, but also tears of anger. The Wyandot braves had already begun their task of collecting the clothing and possessions from among those gathered at Gnadenhutten. Women and children were allowed to keep only the clothing and footwear that each wore, but the men were made to strip down to their underclothing. Those who wore no underclothing were permitted to wear only a cloth or hide about their midsection. None of the men were permitted to keep their boots. Food and bags of personal possessions were now beginning to pile high in the center of the village, and the Wyandots hurriedly arranged their booty on the several horses they had brought with them and on two mules which had been commandeered from the village corral. Those who had already been relieved of their goods were placed at the front of a developing two by two column, and were being urged onward by their Wyandot guards.

David, John, and William sat right down in front of the chapel and each stripped down to his undershorts and nightshirts, with Susan and Sarah Heckewelder acting as shields to the rest of the congregation. A Wyandot brave began collecting their personal effects to add to the growing supply in the near distance. William was especially happy that he had chosen to wear his undershorts on this day, as it was not his usual custom. After removing his clothing, David clutched his bible and deftly shoved it between his thighs to keep the Wyandot from snatching it, but he was too late. Elliot had been keenly watching the three missionaries, and he commanded the Wyandot to seize the bible also. With growing agitation, William leaped up and yelled at the soldier, while at the same time jumping between the brave and David, "Blast it all, Captain, what possible harm could this bible do you and your henchmen? You've already taken away our dignity and our food. We have no weapons. Have you no decency at all?" Elliot did not answer, but merely spurred his horse forward toward the head of the column. However, the lone remaining British soldier moved in their direction and pushed the Wyandot away from the still seated Reverend, then said nothing but turned away to join the others further ahead.

David's eyes sent a smile at William through the moist glaze covering his eyes as the younger man extended his hand to the senior missionary to help him to his feet. "Brother David," said William, "please forgive me for my outburst, but enough is enough!" Now clutching the bible securely, David patted him on the back and said simply, "Let us join the rest of our people before any more are killed. And William, where did you ever learn language like that?" All three of the men and the two wives then went directly to the fallen Rondmanund, and assisted his kinfolk in burying him quite literally above ground, under only a thin blanket of soil. The shallow grave was made necessary by the fact that any digging had to be done with only sticks and stones, and at the hurried prodding of the Wyandot guards. All those present bowed their heads as David led them in a speedy version of the Lord's prayer, which ended as John was urged along at the point of a Wyandot spear. The five whites fell into the column at a point near the middle and they began their tortuous journey.

The column was so long that David and the others with him could not see all the way to the front, although occasionally they caught a glimpse of Elliot as he rode back and forth, urging the Wyandot to keep the column moving and intact. To the rear, the end of the column was not visible from David's position either, and after the missionaries had walked no more than about a mile, there were the sounds of several gunshots from the vicinity of the village. When the men turned to look, as did others in the column, they saw huge dark coils of smoke circling skyward. It was apparent to those in the column that their beautiful dream village of Gnadenhutten was now being burned to the ground on orders of Elliot. What they could not know, but could only imagine, was that the remaining village livestock had been wantonly slaughtered in the streets and left to rot. Only two of the wooden structures serving as houses had inadvertently escaped being leveled by fire and crops that had been tended with love and painstaking care had been trampled and generally left to rot. Gnadenhutten virtually ceased to exist beyond this horrible day.

In blind obedience, due to their peaceful and God-fearing nature, the members of the flock trod sorrowfully onward in the course set by the devil wearing the red military tunic. There was little talk among the people comprising the column, except for the banter of small children, who failed to fully appreciate the seriousness of the situation. At least in the beginning.   All of the adults were extremely quiet except for muted whispers which were exchanged when their Wyandot escorts were not near enough to overhear. And this was not often, as the Wyandots had separated and half had taken up positions on one side of the column and half on the other. A fairly uniform pace between guards was maintained, so that talking and lagging behind was discouraged. Captain Elliot and Pomoacan rode at the head of the column, and from time to time, the officer randomly rode to the rear to check on the pace and close the ranks. One British soldier walked at the head of the column and one also brought up the rear. On those times when Elliot did ride to the rear, he would only go a little past the point where the missionaries and their wives were located, obviously to let everyone know that he simply enjoyed seeing these particular people suffer.

David and John, walking one behind the other, managed to hold a quiet, fragmented conversation along the trail, talking about how and why the shocking events had unfolded in the manner they did back in the village. "I just don't get it," said John, "Why on earth would Elliot suddenly turn over control of our entire flock to the Wyandot?" William, just in front of David, said, "I think it's because Elliot doesn't want any of our blood on his hands." "That might very well be, William, but I think that there's more here than meets the eye," offered David. He continued, "Neither the British nor the colonists have a lot of money just to pay off any of the tribes who help them. You saw and heard Elliot relinquish our control to Pomoacan, I doubt if de Peyster has any more to offer them beyond what they have taken from us." Susan then added a third perspective, "Is it possible that Elliot has overstepped his authority? Maybe de Peyster simply told him to have us get out of the valley, but matters have gotten so out of hand that now Elliot can just blame everything on the Wyandots."

There was a little truth in what each had just discussed. When Elliot had given his command to Pomoacan earlier in the village, he had been doing specifically what de Peyster had ordered him to do. The British commander at Detroit had nothing with which to pay the Wyandot mercenaries for their services, so they simply turned over the possessions of the Moravians and their flock to the Indians. Major de Peyster had also told Pomoacan that he and his men would receive nothing if the relocation was not carried out. And, in perfect candor, de Peyster's contempt for David Zeisberger was so great that it mattered little if the minister were killed while resisting Pomoacan and his braves. If this had occurred, de Peyster was prepared to face his superiors with the account of how blood-thirsty and unpredictable Wyandots wiped out an entire Moravian mission and the mostly Delaware inhabitants before British troops could intercede. Indian against Indian was something that the British command would easily accept.

This story would also be more acceptable to the French, other Indians, and any number of other ears in the Ohio Territory or other points north and west. It had been Elliot who had actually conceived the idea of turning the control of the converted-Delaware over to the Wyandot, and his suggestion to his superior was abetted by his ambition for his own command. He knew that the annihilation of innocent missionaries and their converts, especially such a large number, would work against any future promotion for him. The death of Rondmanund would be attributed to just another renegade Delaware brave attacking a lone British soldier — that is if anyone ever cared enough to ask. But the root of all the hatred and mistreatment of the Moravians and their flock by the British and the Wyandot had not yet been fully disclosed.

Luckily enough for the column members, the climate of late summer and early autumn in 1781 Ohio Territory would be extremely kind to them. To a person, they were sure that God had especially provided them with cool breezes during the day, and warm, humid nights. They would eventually be able to cover only about five miles a day, for the dense foliage was extremely hard to negotiate by everyone, but especially the women and children. Although all but five of the entire column were Delaware Indians, the members of the flock had long ago ceased to go barefoot, and had adopted the boots worn by their Moravian ministers. To travel, even a mile unshod would be difficult, but the entire long, grueling trip would be painful beyond imagination. By the end of the first day, there was only one or two who had no cuts or blisters, but *that* would only last one more day.

David and John had by now discussed their feelings about having subjected their wives to the indignities at hand. Though both were feeling pangs of conscience, David suffered the more, since Susan had been brought back from the east into this situation. At least Sarah was already in the Ohio Territory at the time she had met and married John. Both women were adamant about their men ceasing the talk about guilt feelings, but it failed to assuage the suffering husbands. Sarah, however, brought the conversation to an end rather deftly, when she finally said, "Oh John, where would our baby be without me here by your side?" John nearly caused a collision in the moving column at this point, by stopping dead in his tracks to exclaim, "What?" in a loud and surprised voice. The other missionaries and Susan then began beaming as proudly as the parents-to-be, while John was quietly filled in on the details by Sarah. The news of the baby eased somewhat the rest of the day's march.

Near dusk of the first day, the column was ordered to make camp for the night, alongside a small stream which flowed south. Or was it east? The fatigue and mental anxiety suffered by the members had already begun to take its toll. Most feebly sank to their hands and knees and drank from the cool water. Some collapsed in a heap at the edge of the stream and scooped water over their aching limbs. John and William were suffering from particularly nasty foot sores and each simply waded into the cooling therapeutic waters, and no one objected. Poor David was trying to figure a way to get both his feet and his mouth in the water at the same time, but finally settled in on first drinking, and then dousing his feet and forehead. A few of the children found small pools a bit upstream and took the opportunity to totally submerge themselves.

Susan had already appointed herself as midwife-in-waiting to Sarah and was attending to her comfort today, as she would do throughout the grueling march. Her assistance and concern for Sarah was a source of inspiration to all who were aware of the pregnancy, which was only in its second month. The British soldiers camped about 50 yards from the main column, and relaxed in relative comfort with bedrolls and dry rations, while their Wyandot allies rested on the other side of the column. Most of the column members moved very little after they stopped by the stream. They were simply too tired to move about.

Besides fatigue, hunger was the pressing problem at the moment. But not for the British and the Wyandot, who were camped and enjoying their usual rations. To the members of the flock, however, finding food along their trek to Sandusky would be a major problem every step of the way. A few of the mothers had managed to secret small apples or pieces of pemmican in their frocks beneath their aprons, which were reserved for the very young. But most were not as fortunate. Not only was hunger their enemy, but so was darkness. The hunt for food each day would have to occur quickly before it became too dark to find anything edible. It was a lesson that members of the column learned the hard way. Most were so tired and thirsty, that after stopping for the first day, most simply drank water and collapsed. When they realized that food could not be found after dark, it was too late.

The column was not guarded when they were stopped in the evenings, and the members could wander in virtually any and all direction for food — when and if it could be found. Basically the meals would be wild berries, crab apples, roots, mushrooms, and an occasional crawfish or sunfish from small streams. At a stream, the members would line up side by side at the edge of a small pool and walk slowly forward, methodically sweeping the water for whatever could be eaten. When one of the flock would find a small berry bush or patch, they would cry out to the others and soon dozens of hungry people would descend upon the vine and feast ravenously until the plant soon looked as if it had been attacked by locusts. In the days to come, the members of the column would also become much less selective about which roots they chose to eat. Bark, from certain trees also became a staple along the trail, as did select edible greens which were familiar to the converted Delaware women.

Camping and sleeping along the trail was not a major problem for the members of the column, thanks primarily to the cooperative weather. Family members huddled closely together and shared body heat. Where there existed an occasional single member of the flock, there were always families willing to share their warmth. David and John and their wives, along with William, actually managed to quickly get the sleeping sequence down to a science — or at least an art. On the first night, David and Susan slept in the middle, with John and Sarah on one side and William on the other. They agreed to alternate on each successive night, so that the outer person would only suffer for one night. On nights when it became very cool, or when someone had fish or crawfish to be cooked, the members simply built small fires. The first night's fires were begun from scratch, with tender, dried leaves, and twigs being ignited by sparking two large pieces of flint together. It was a slow, tedious process, but not at all unfamiliar to any member of the flock. On nights after that, they simply "borrowed" a burning ember from either the British or the Wyandot fires. Neither of the column's "hosts" objected to lending a hand in this manner to the flock.

Actually, the Wyandot were more humane to the members of the column than were the British soldiers. Some of the children would stand in the shadows of the soldiers while they ate their rations, but not one scrap was ever offered to the starved audience. On the other hand, the Wyandot, while not totally gracious, still offered most of their leftovers or outright gifts of pemmican to many of the children who watched them eat. The adult members of the column cleverly divided the children into seven groups, who took turns "staring down" the Wyandot braves while they ate. When scraps were given to the children, the group politely divided and shared what morsels were given them. Each day, a new group of children would appear near the Wyandot camp, and in this way, along with other food obtained, the children suffered the least hunger.

Besides Mary's new baby, little David, there were six other infants among the members of the column, but the babies always had benefit of their mothers' milks. To insure that the seven breast-feeding mothers would have an adequate supply, nearly everyone offered these women extra bits of food of all varieties. The concepts of love, brotherhood, and sharing would be magnanimously obvious among the members of the column the entire route to the Sandusky. Sarah and Susan watched quietly as one Delaware mother after another tended to the needs of their infant, and each made mental notes on the loving care they observed. It would escape the notice of the British and the Wyandot, but at no time during the trip would column members fight or argue over food or any other commodity, and *never* would they ask their guards for help. There was much suffering among the members, to be sure, but none overly complained.

Each night on the route, before anyone bedded down, David would lead the assembled flock in a small prayer service and read short passages from his bible by the flickering light of the tiny campfire. After the service, David would make his bed, with the sweet word of the Lord doubling as his pillow. David offered the use of the bible to Susan, but she preferred to snuggle into the hollow of his arm. When John first saw David place the bible under his head, he said, "David, is that the manner in which you get your inspiration for your wonderful prayers? Do they simply leap out of the book and into your brain overnight?" David never answered, but instead broke into a very robust laugh, and all five of the small party laughed almost uncontrollably over John's remarks. It was one of the few times that any of them would laugh again for a long, long time.

After about a week on what the flock now characterized as a "march," a scouting party of colonial militia from Fort Pitt happened upon the head of the column suddenly and were just as quickly put to rout by the British soldiers, who opened fire. Some of the Wyandot warriors gave chase for several miles, but the militiamen were able to escape with no casualties. The chance encounter had occurred in an almost face to face fashion, as the colonists had been coming south, from the general direction of Lake Erie, and were totally unexpected. When the initial shots were first exchanged, members of the column instinctively dived to the ground or took cover behind trees and in small hollows, and no one was injured. In fact, the forced members of the column had not been seen by the colonists at all.

The early afternoon colonial foray became a blessing in disguise for the column, however, because Captain Elliot and Pomoacan were forced to wait a short while for the pursuing Wyandot to return. After waiting about an hour and a half, the order to encamp for the rest of the evening was given, and the column enjoyed their only shortened day of the entire march. In addition, the encounter had occurred in an area blessed with apple trees, and everyone dined happily that evening. The long stop also meant more time for the members to bathe, gather food, and tend to near-serious foot wounds. For a change, the three missionaries and the two wives slept on an extra thick bed of leaves and fresh pine boughs which John gathered at an unbelievably leisurely pace. At the regular prayer service that evening, David quietly added an offering of thanks for the militia visitors.

Each day of the march would begin with Captain Elliot riding to the point where the rearmost members had bedded down for the night. Once there, he would order them to their feet and then ride off to the front of the column, shouting loudly along the way, "On your feet!" at the members. When he reached the front of the column, the members would begin to trudge forward. Elliot's boisterous urging was not required at all, because the members slept fitfully, if at all, and most were easily awakened by just the sound of the horse galloping over the dried leaves of the Ohio wilderness. The routine never varied, all the way to Lake Erie.

During the march to Upper Sandusky, the weather had been exceptional — probably the only thing during the whole episode that went well for the beleaguered members of the column. However, about midway to their destination one morning, the members were awakened by a very light rainfall. The temperature was several degrees cooler to be sure, but if it had to rain at all, the rain that fell was the gentlest and the warmest that the marchers could expect. By the time that Elliot reached the rear of the column on this day, everyone was already awake and prepared to move out. The rain continued all day and all night at the same steady pace.

Along the route, the marchers again made the best from a dreadfully oppressive situation. The women and children who wore boots, took them off and used the occasion to give their feet a change of pace in the soft mud, and those who had marched the distance barefoot were delighted to feel the soft, cool mud envelop and soothe their aching feet. The further back in the column, after nearly 500 people tramping and sloshing ahead, the mud became especially deep and refreshing. Had Elliot made the effort to look at the members' faces while they marched on this day, he would have seen smiles on many. The upbeat, optimistic, and utilitarian attitude of each of the members continued to be a source of burgeoning pride to the three missionaries.

Marching in a steady rainfall was one thing, but preparing to bed down in such weather was quite another. Seeking shelter from the rain would be a major problem. When the column was stopped that evening, members went about their usual hurried task of gathering food. On the flanks, the members could see the British and the Wyandot under their water-resistant lean-tos, warmed by their fires. Finding dry material for a campfire was extremely difficult and dry sleeping simply impossible for the flock. The best spots were those under large trees, but there were not enough such trees in the area. A few members were able to find low-hanging dense pine groves nearby, which gave comfortable shelter, but most were forced to sleep virtually unprotected in the slow but steady rain. Just before dawn of the next day, the rain eased to a halt, but added to the lack of food, foot problems, and fatigue, the rain only worsened the effects of the forced march. Ironically, at the end of the next day, the column camped along-side a small stream cut through a deep, rocky arroyo, having long, cave-like recesses cut into the bank which could have provided a great deal of shelter from the previous day's rain.

Prior to the one day of rain, John, along with perhaps 25 other members of the column had begun to develop a hoarseness and cough from the prolonged exposure. After experiencing almost 24 hours of the cool, steady rain, John's conditioned worsened and his temperature shot mad-deningly upwards. Sarah was beside herself with worry over her husband's condition, and Susan was worried that Sarah was getting too worked up. One of the women of the flock gathered an herb that was used to fight similar illnesses, but needed a vessel to prepare a hot tea from the herb.

John forbid anyone to ask the British for a tin in which to heat the anticipated treatment, and his suffering continued unabated. Nearly deliri-ous from fever and the effects of the cold, John plugged along, but was so weak that David and William practically carried him along the trail. David, fearing that John might even die, suggested that he might speak to Elliot about John's condition, and even though he continued to deteriorate, John steadfastly and emphatically said, "No!" Susan's pleas to her husband were similarly, though more delicately rejected.

Just when it looked as though things could get no worse, God appar-ently provided for the hapless missionaries and their flock once more. At the end of the day's march, David and the others made John as comfort-able as possible. Sarah was washing John's fevered brow with a cool, damp cloth, and the other three were gathering bits of food, when a young member of the flock ran up to them. "Reverend, there are some traders who have just arrived," he excitedly said, pointing in the direction of the front of the column. "Perhaps they may have something to help Brother John." Before David could react to the news, William, who had also learned of the visitors, appeared and volunteered, "David, I'll go and see if they can assist us. I'll be back right away." By now, John shook violently with chills and Sarah could only cradle the sick missionary in her arms in an effort to warm him. "Hold on, dear John," she whispered, and closed her eyes as she said a short, silent prayer.

The traders were three Englishmen, who were working the northern reaches of the Ohio Territory, and when they first encountered the group en route to the Sandusky, the first persons they came upon were the Wyandot and their chief. The members of the column were between the Wyandot and the British military contingency. Pomoacan, after checking them out, pointed the traders in the direction of where Elliot and his men could be found, and they started in that direction. When they encountered the members of the column, they were aghast at the sight of the wretched condition of so many of the members. "My Lord!" exclaimed the spokesman for the traders, "What is going on here?" Before any of the flock could answer, William arrived, and the traders' attention was drawn to this emaciated and bedraggled white man who approached. "We are Moravian missionaries and these are members of our flock, who are being relocated to Upper Sandusky, by a unit from the British army," said William, who continued, "If you have any compassion in you at all, please help me with my brother, John, who is dying yonder."

The traders looked in the direction that William pointed, and their leader then said, "Of course, we will help you if the British commander has no objections. We will check with him first, however. Are you under arrest, or are you prisoners?" Clearly the man was puzzled at the poor condition of so many people, and at the circumstances of their chance meeting in the Ohio wilderness. William mumbled that, of course, he understood, but never answered the man's question, and then headed back to where the others were tending to John, while the traders made their way to Captain Elliot to ask permission to help.

With obvious contempt for their charitable nature, Elliot waved the traders away from him and his men, saying sarcastically, "If you wish to help those who would commit treason against the crown, by all means, see to their needs." "Captain, we do not want to interfere with your mission. If you do not want us to communicate with your prisoners, we shall continue on our way," said the trader. "They are not our prisoners!" Elliot resoundingly bellowed. "Do whatever you damn well please!"

Rebuked and puzzled by the Captain's demeanor, the traders withdrew in the general direction of the column members, but first huddled within themselves as to whether or not they should even get involved. Because they, too, were Christians, they mercifully chose to see if they could do anything to help, and when they reached the other whites, they were astounded to learn that the only need requested was a vessel in which to boil water. Quickly the traders produced a small tin cup which was filled with water and boiled in order that John could drink the herbal tea. "God bless you," said David to the men, after John had been ministered to, and he introduced himself and invited them to sit at their tiny fire. "Thank you for allowing us to join you here, Reverend Zeisberger," said the trader, who, at the moment, felt embarrassed to be English, so uncivilized was Elliot's treatment of the Moravians and their flock. Before saying anything else, the trader produced a blanket from one of their mules and offered it to Sarah, who tenderly covered John's still shaking body.

The trader then opened the drawstring on a small leather pouch he carried and withdrew an even smaller leather pouch and handed it to David. "Here, Reverend, just in case the sick chap requires a little more than the herbal tea. It's quineen," as he gave the English pronunciation of the medicine. As David reached for the medicine, he clasped both of the man's hands within his own and said, "You have been sent to us through God's tender mercy. May He guide you and watch over you wherever you shall go." The traders also shared a pot of English tea with David and William and the two women before hunkering down for the night nearby. While David moved to the area nearest the largest campfire of the other members in order to hold his nightly prayer, Susan and William stayed behind to look after John with Sarah, and to hold some conversation with the three traders.

Eventually all of the traders spoke, and it was immediately clear to the Moravians that the men were well-intentioned, possessing none of the malice that had thus been exhibited by other British like de Peyster and Elliot. Richard Jones, Gilbert Pennyweight, and Percival Thorne were their names, and they had each chosen to come to America to make their fortune, and war or no war, they were going to continue their efforts. The trio were apolitical and would continue to function as traders regardless of the outcome of the war. Originally operating out of Massachusetts, Richard, the older of the three, met the others in Montreal, and they had come south to the Ohio Territory from off Lake Erie. When Susan found that Richard was originally from Massachusetts, she was quick to point out that she, also was from that area. It warmed them each to know they had encountered someone from familiar territory, even if it was miles and miles distant.

The trio traded whatever wares and commodities Indians, settlers, and other Europeans might need for furs or what-have-you, and then returned to the larger cities back east to resell their goods, bank their proceeds, and restock their mules. The missionaries had seen and heard of other traders who were not nearly as humane and charitable as the men who now shared their campfire. Stories abounded at Fort Pitt and other outposts of deceptive and unethical traders who would stoop as low as required to get the better of a customer, but not this trio, and not on this occasion. God seemed to continually watch over the Moravians.

In the morning, as Elliot rode his horse toward the rear of the column, David and Susan awoke to find that the three traders still slept nearby. "It is time for us to be on our way," said David, "I'm afraid that the Captain will not allow us the luxury of breakfast." He hesitatingly pulled the blanket from John, who appeared noticeably improved, and handed both it and the tin cup to Richard, saying "I really cannot thank you all enough, for your kindness." Holding up his open palm, as if to halt any more thanks, Richard said to David and to the others who were also by now awake, "Please keep them with our good wishes, Reverend. We may per chance need your assistance or prayers in the future." Gilbert and Percival then joined their leader in shaking hands with each of the Moravians before they began to prepare to continue on their journey to Detroit.

With the assistance of his wife, John wrapped the blanket about his shoulders and managed a weak smile and slight wave to the traders as the column began its daily push northward. To prevent the Wyandot from spotting and confiscating the tin cup, David gave it to Susan, who concealed it, albeit awkwardly, beneath her apron. The blanket would be eventually passed around among all of those in the column who were fevered or otherwise in need.

The English traders were not the only ones who encountered the column as it slowly made its way toward Lake Erie's south shore. A lone French trapper, and another pair of English traders, as well as two groups of Shawnee would meet and mercifully share ever so precious bits of food with the near-starving Moravians and their flock, and there were no objections from either the British or the Wyandot whenever this occurred. The acquiescence of Elliot and Pomoacan to these acts of kindness and charity toward the members of the column was the extent of their humanitarian character, however.

In truth, if any of the Moravians or their Delaware followers had starved or died along the way, they would have died as ignominiously a death as had the poor Rondmanund, back in the village. To Elliot, his mission was only to reach Upper Sandusky with "some" number of people from the Moravian missions in the Muskingum valley. His goal was to return to Detroit to a "Well done, Captain!" from Major de Peyster. Pomoacan's mission was to do whatever the British asked or ordered him and his warriors to do as long as they were given supplies and whiskey. The Wyandot chief had no other discernible goals.

As the column wound ever northward, a particularly high piece of ground provided the first glimpse of Lake Erie. The column was buzzing with excitement as, eventually, the entire column could share the excitement of the view. To each of the members, it meant that the relocation would be completed and that a new village and a new life could soon be started. From the point of their first sight of the lake, members of the column had begun to look about and size up the various locales as potential new homes. The attitude of the entire group became more optimistic, and the three missionaries began to make plans over the upcoming responsibilities involved with a new settlement. No one knew for sure what lay ahead, except for the knowledge that the long, punishing march would soon be over.

By the end of the day, on October 1st, the column had reached the shore of Lake Erie near the confluence of the Sandusky River. All but a handful of the members of the column, upon reaching the lake, jumped in and swam about in the waning temperatures of the steel gray waters. The chilly dip represented a cleansing of all of the dirt and grime, and misery and illness that the members had endured over the past three weeks. They camped for the night in small groups on sandy beaches, though northern breezes cooled the night air. Food, or more precisely, edible substances, were much less abundant at the lake's edge than back in the rolling countryside, but the joy of conquering such a harrowing trip, and its accompanying fatigue quickly overcame the pressing urge to feed. The members had gotten so accustomed to going to sleep hungry each night, that the lack of food went scarcely noticed.

The members' guards also chose to camp near the lake, and the soldiers flanked the group on the west or left side, while the Wyandot made themselves at home to the east. That night, at prayer, David gave an especially long and specific prayer which mentioned the heroic and unselfish act of each of the members and particularly Richard Jones and the other two British traders. After prayer, William led the members in song as several hymns were sung, but quietly; so as not to agitate the camps to either side. The members went to sleep that night without dreading the prospects of what awaited them in the morning.

Incredibly, when the members awoke the next morning, the sun was already high in the sky. Major Elliot had not ridden his mount up and down the column, screaming at the members to arise. In fact, the British soldiers were nowhere in sight. At dawn, they had quietly assembled and had begun the last leg of their own journey to their fortress at Detroit, across the waters of Lake Erie. David and the others were especially confounded by Elliot's evacuation. They had expected to discuss the next stage of their relocation, and how and with what tools they were expected to start life anew. Were they now simply to fend for themselves along the lake's edge, with only their bare hands as implements? Looking east, the members saw that the Wyandot were still in place. But why? There were many questions that could not now be answered.

The three missionaries then walked the short distance to where Pomoacan had set up his camp, near the edge of the dense brush which abutted the beach area. The Wyandot chief was sitting, facing out into the lake and puffing on a non-ceremonial pipe. "Chief Pomoacan," began David, "can you tell us what is to become of us now that we have reached this place?" The Wyandot chief did not change his gaze, and after inhaling a long puff of smoke from his pipe, answered, "Major de Peyster said that you are to remain here, and that we are to prevent your leaving." "We do not intend to leave Chief, at least not until the war is over, but are you saying that we are all prisoners?" asked David. "Major de Peyster said that you are to remain here and we are to prevent you from leaving," the chief repeated without a hint of emotion and without moving anything but his lips, still clenched about the pipe stem.

"Well, may we have some of our tools, so that we may construct some shelters for our women and children? Winter will soon arrive and we need to get these people protected," said John, as the other two looked on in dismay, Pomoacan merely grunted, and then waved the men in the direction of the Wyandot horses, where the possessions of the flock were kept. The three took the gesture to mean that it was okay to use the tools, and they began walking in that direction. About twenty paces from the horses, a Wyandot warrior abruptly challenged them, but a signal from Pomoacan told the warrior to allow them to reach the supplies. The trio was in the process of donning some of the clothing there when another Wyandot approached them and said, "No clothing. Only tools." The Moravians looked back in desperation to where Pomoacan sat, but he simply did not look in their direction, and they understood that they had once again been thwarted. In utter despair, the men took off the clothing and walked away from the animals carrying only an ax, a hatchet, a large hammer, and a saw. No Wyandot stopped them as they made their way back to the rest of the flock.

For almost two weeks, the members of the flock worked quickly and efficiently to ensure their survival, building only bare minimum protection against the elements in an area just into the underbrush and thin forest. While the men were busy constructing rudimentary shelters, the women and children scoured the area for substances that would pass for food. Edible roots, berries, and the other staples they had grown used to on the trail were once more gathered and supplemented the fish that were caught in the lake, river, and nearby ponds. Susan became especially liberal with her rations, preferring to always give a bit here and there to Sarah, urging her that "Your baby needs this!" Two groups of passing Shawnee also gave the members small scraps of pemmican, and one English trader also assisted with a scrap or two from his supplies, but that was the extent of outside help to the Moravians and their flock.

During this time, David managed to persuade Pomoacan to allow five of the healthiest adult members of the flock to return to Gnadenhutten to attempt to harvest grain from the ruined crop. If successful, there were many ways that the grain could be used in the coming months. Pomoacan also generously provide the five volunteers with a horse, with which they intended to pull a makeshift sled loaded with grain back to Sandusky. The five departed on October 8th, but it would be a long time before they returned, and work along the lake continued at a fevered pace. At the same time, Pomoacan and the Wyandot offered virtually no assistance to the members of the flock, but neither did they hinder the Delaware converts as they went about their work. The practice of sending the children of the flock to "stare down" the Wyandot in seven waves continued, and with the same successful, though somewhat progressively meager results. The Wyandot were not completely heartless; especially not to other Indian brothers.

On October 12th, David was overseeing the construction of an outdoor meeting place which would serve as a temporary chapel and school for the flock, when William interrupted him with the news that a British soldier was awaiting him at the lake. The soldier had arrived from Detroit accompanied by canoe — two canoes to be exact, and two Wyandot braves. The canoes stood beached in the sand as David and William approached the soldier, who was by now speaking with Pomoacan and the other two braves at lake side. When they got to within about fifty feet of the soldier, they were joined by John, who had been attending to a sick child nearby. All three approached the soldier warily, a corporal that David recognized from having been to Detroit previously.

"Reverend Zeisberger, I have orders from Major de Peyster, that you are to be arrested and brought to Detroit to face, along with John Heckewelder and William Edwards, charges of espionage against the crown. I presume that these men with you are the ones named in the warrant," he said, as he glanced at the unscrolled parchment in his hands. "That is correct," answered David, who suddenly now had a more complete realization of the totality of de Peyster's plan for the Moravians. With slumping shoulders exposing their dejected mood, the three missionaries looked sadly at each other and then bravely gathered themselves for what would forever seem to be the next leg of their odyssey.

The men were given only a few minutes to prepare for the trip, and their first priority was saying goodbye to Susan and Sarah. The husbands gave their tearful wives warm, prolonged embraces as William stood quietly by, eyes dejectedly cast toward the ground. John told Sarah to take special care of herself for the good of their baby, and Susan quickly interjected that she would certainly see to it. Then in a touching display of empathy, both women placed their arms around William, the bachelor and kissed him tearfully on each cheek. Then all five formed in a hugging circle and were led in the Lord's Prayer by David.

Joseph was placed in charge until, or if, the men ever returned from Detroit. With tears in his eyes, Joseph hugged each of the men and promised that the entire flock would pray for them, and a young boy arrived with David's bible. "Must we continue to travel like heathens, corporal?" asked William. And the young soldier quickly remembered that there had been additional orders to that effect. On de Peyster's okay, Pomoacan permitted the Moravians to retrieve some outer clothing and boots from among the confiscated supplies, and in less than an hour, the three were being paddled toward Detroit in the Wyandot canoes. On the shore, Susan and Sarah, arms around each other, waved uncertain good-byes to their husbands.

Essentially lame, from walking barefoot more than 100 miles through harsh, briar-laden and jagged rock-strewn terrain, the three, as well as the two wives and all the members of the column were gaunt, pale and skeletal zombies — listless from lack of food. A large number of the members would eventually have their lives drastically cut short due to ill effects suffered as a result of the arduous trek forced upon them in this most horrifying manner.

By now, each of the three missionaries weighed less than 120 pounds, and most of the others fared equally as poor, but miraculously, the unbaptized Rondmanund was the only one to have died as a result of the relocation. David, John, and William would face de Peyster and his charges bravely. To the consternation of de Peyster, Elliot, and the other British, the communal faith and survival instincts of the entire flock would be a unifying theme that would strengthen forever the bonds between the members of the Ohio Moravian missions.

October 13, 1781

Upon arriving at the English garrison at Detroit, David, John, and William were placed in the stockade, alongside a British soldier who was awaiting trial on charges of insubordination, two drunken Shawnee, and a French trader or trapper who was obviously insane, and for whom no one knew of or cared to inquire about his crimes. The most promising thing about the imprisonment of the missionaries was that while there, they had cots which were up, off the ground, and they were also given a daily ration of hard tack, a cold, watery unidentifiable salty soup, and a large tin of hot, black coffee each morning. It represented the first real meal that each had eaten in more than a month, and after saying grace, they partook happily of the prison meal. None of the others shared the missionaries' appetite for the prison food, however.

Both David and John were preoccupied with the wives that each had been forced to leave behind. Their talk the first night centered almost exclusively about what hardships the women had been made to endure since their respective marriages. The guilt that each of the husbands felt was sincere and near psychologically crippling. William, trying his best to make the best of the bad situation, spoke at length on how each of the men had been rescued from becoming a classic curmudgeon only through the good will of the women they married. William now felt comfortable in talking to the two about their wives, because by now, the women had come to look upon him as a sort of overgrown son. During and since the long march to Lake Erie, both couples had more or less adopted William.

But as light as William tried to portray their responsibilities, the subject remained a considerable weight for both David and John.

The next evening, Captain Elliot came to the stockade and informed the trio that their trials would be commenced as one, and that it would begin promptly at 8:00 in the morning tomorrow. In anticipation of their doubts of being given a fair trial, Elliot told the group that they had been appointed a barrister by Major de Peyster, an Englishman by the name of Silas Whitfield, and he literally snickered as he said the man's name. "He will represent you at trial and will probably call on you yet this evening," smiled Elliot.

With mock concern, Elliot then asked, "Is there anything that you can foresee as a need before your trial gets underway?" Since arriving at the stockade, the three Moravians had discussed the English accusations and were firmly convinced that they had no chance of proving their innocence against what were essentially trumped up charges. With this expectation, there appeared to be little that could be done to convince anyone of anything; especially the dubious Major de Peyster, who was to sit the trial as Magistrate, with Elliot as prosecutor in chief. In answer to Elliot's last question, the three simply waved him to be gone, and he happily obliged.

In less than a minute, an elderly, white haired man appeared at the bars of their cell and feebly announced that he was Silas Whitfield, their appointed representative, and that he wanted to confer with them. To a man, each of the missionaries instantly believed that this old man was in league with de Peyster and the others; owing mostly to the fact that he had been appointed by them, and then for suspiciously arriving only seconds after Elliot had gone. And if there were not suspicions enough, the fact that he was extremely elderly, and needed to produce a large ear horn to assist him in hearing their replies simply eroded any tiny shred of confidence that they might have had in their attorney. The old man looked as though he would not even live past the present interview at the stockade, much less the physical rigors and mental exactitude needed for a trial of this seriousness.

The longer the old man stood there outside their cell, however, the more confidence he inspired, physical appearance not withstanding. Silas Whitfield, an Englishman through and through, was educated at Oxford, and in his younger days had been an extraordinary barrister in the mother country. Though now of advanced age, he was as much feared because of his brain, as he was also needed because of it, and the King had "selected" Whitfield to assist with the extended task of legalizing treaties, checking contracts on boundaries, notes in general, and what have you in the new world. The inconvenience of the war had, for the moment, trapped the old man in the western outpost of Detroit.

Whitfield already knew their names and enough about their history in the Muskingum valley that three things were imminently clear. One, that he had done his research on them carefully. Two, the old man had a remarkable memory, for he, at no time, referred to notes for names, dates, or anything. And three, that de Peyster had long been planning this charade of a trial. Whitfield told them that he had been notified by de Peyster of his appointment as their defense on July 4th, and that since that time he had been gathering what he could to assist. The old man was visibly upset because he had not been notified of the arrival of the missionaries the day before. "Could it be that we are actually going to get a fair trial, Mr. Whitfield?" asked John incredulously. After having had the question repeated into his ear piece, the old man answered.

"Major de Peyster is a man who is quick to accuse, and is often found to be wanting in terms of facts. He earnestly believes that each of you has somehow conspired to assist the Americans in this damnable war against the throne of England. Excuse me for my filthy mouth, Reverend Zeisberger. The conditions to which I have been made to adapt have made me a bit less than civil, I'm afraid. Major de Peyster has assembled an array of witnesses against you, but I have talked to them, and I do not believe that they are as convincing as what he believes. As for me, I care not whether you are guilty of treasonous actions against anyone. I shall defend you zealously, whether you plead guilt or innocence.

My only concern is that none of you has violated your own ethical canons and done anything against your church or your God. I am a Christian, and I am aware of another place and time in which the man on trial, also tried for treason, was eventually crucified. He died at the mercy of his accusers, but I am not about to let that happen to you. You most certainly will receive a fair trial, because I have been appointed to see to it. If you have no questions of me now, I must complete my strategy before the morning. Good day! Chin up, lads!" And with that, the old man ambled slowly away from them.

The soldier now confined with them laughed heartily, and said, "I hope for your sake that the old fart is still alive by the morrow, gents. No offense, Reverend." After a few hours of discussing what slight strategy that they could, themselves, engage in, the three men shared a hushed prayer in the corner of the cell and then attempted to get some sleep.

Sometime before dawn, William whispered, "John, do you think that they will hang us if we are found guilty?" The stirring of the younger two men was indicative that neither had yet completely fallen asleep. From the direction of David's bunk came a whispered response to John's question. "I believe that is the usual penalty for espionage in the midst of a war. But are you really afraid to die? Either of you?" and David sat up slowly on his cot. "No, of course not, David," whispered John, "because I am at peace with my God." "And I," said William, who by now had moved to the center of the small cell. Both David and John met him there and they all embraced tightly. With unseen smiles in the darkness, the men returned to their hard beds, reaffirmed of their belief that God's love and tender mercy would be their sole and only necessary support. David and John also had the images of their wives soon enter their consciousness and their hearts grew heavy once more — not for themselves, but for the suffering they believed they had introduced to the women.

The three had barely closed their eyes when the jailer awakened them with a gentle tapping on the bars of the cell. "Time to arise, gents. We have hot biscuits and ham and eggs for your meal this morning before your trial," he said. But when the meal cart was wheeled into the narrow space outside the bars, it contained only the usual hot coffee and hard tack that could barely be pierced by human teeth unless it was first dunked in the thick, syrupy coffee. The jailer howled at the humor in his sick joke, but no one complained. John and William then acted as if the meager breakfast was actually the sumptuous meal previously advertised, and the jailer watched them with a great deal of interest, as they pantomimed a great feast of the food before them, complete with finger bowls and napkins. The act was enough to get the attention of every person in the cell — including the French idiot, who simply sat slack-jawed and stared at the two. When William began to clean his imaginary silverware with the tail of an imaginary tablecloth, the brief performance brought a large smile to David's face. When everyone began to laugh, the jailer became annoyed and walked sullenly away.

At exactly 8:00, two young British soldiers appeared outside the cell housing the men and ordered them out. Obligingly, the three missionaries gathered themselves and took places in the narrow hallway adjacent to the lone cell, with one soldier in front, and one to the rear. David walked first, still clutching his bible and he was followed by John, and finally William. There was no conversation; not a word, and as the jailer re-locked the door, the other prisoners sat silently watching. The three prisoners were marched through the stockade office, which also doubled as a sleeping area for the guard, through an exterior door, and across a dusty courtyard which stood between the military offices and the stockade.

Once across the courtyard, William glanced back over his shoulder to see a gallows at the far end of the area. He did not have time to count, but there were at least two nooses — more probably three — dangling idly from the large crossing beam. Once across the courtyard, the men walked a short distance on a covered wooden walkway and then stopped outside a closed door. The door was the entrance to the assembly room, probably the largest room in the garrison, and it had been converted to a courtroom. The lead soldier opened the door and entered, and the men followed him inside.

To the right, along the far wall, was a long table, behind which sat Major de Peyster in the center, and flanked by two junior officers. It was later learned that the junior officers, with de Peyster having the decisive vote, would decide the fate of the accused. Beside each junior officer sat another officer, one an aide to de Peyster, while the other attempted to record the proceedings with quill and ink upon a stack of fresh parchment before him. Immediately to their right, and at the end of the long table stood the union jack. A flag identifying the garrison's regiment stood to their left.

The bright red military tunics and the brightly colored flags were a sharp contrast to the plain black and wrinkled clothing worn by the three men who were escorted to the table to the far left. Old man Whitfield sat at the near end of that table. At another table a few feet to the right, sat Captain Elliot, who smugly eyed the prisoners as they took their seats. Behind the men and their counsel sat several men and an Indian or two that none could instantly recognize. The trio had no way of knowing that everyone there had been called for the sole purpose of testifying against the Moravians. There were no spectators, which might have also legitimately been called impartial witnesses as to what was about to occur.

In a loud, and somber tone, Major de Peyster rose and began to read the charges against the missionaries, "In the matter of the accused, Moravian missionaries David Zeisberger, John Heckewelder, and William Edwards, who are on this 15th day of October, in the year of our Lord, 1781, hereby accused of conspiring with the colonial rebels against all the good people, and His Majesty, King George, of England, in violation of the Treasons Act of 1581 and charged specifically with espionage during war. How say you to the charges before this court?" Attorney Whitfield then leaned toward the men seated with him and after whispering instructions to them, together they all stood and answered in unison, "Innocent." Then all again took their seats.

Major de Peyster then continued, "And who shall represent the accused?" This time, Old Whitfield rose, although much slower than the men seated at the table with him, and said, "Silas Whitfield, Esquire, for the defense, your honor," and he went into a coughing spell which caused his complexion to turn from ashen white to near beet red. His powdered wig also became comically tilted on his head as a result of his violent coughing, causing those to the rear to snicker aloud. Even Elliot was forced to stifle a laugh at his worthy opponent's expense. de Peyster quickly regained order, "Captain Matthew Elliot prosecuting for the crown. Captain Elliot are you prepared to go forward?" "I am, your honor," said Elliot as he rose. "You may present your evidence, Captain," said de Peyster as he took his seat.

"Your honor, and other esteemed members of the court," started Elliot, "Since the colonial rebels declared themselves a sovereign and independent nation on July 4th, 1776, there has existed a state of war between the rebels and the crown. Much of the area just to the south of where we now convene this tribunal is known as the Ohio Territory. Since May of 1772, Reverend David Zeisberger and his assistants have operated a Moravian religious mission in the area known as the Muskingum River Valley, and they have done a rather splendid job of bringing Christianity to a good number of Delaware Indians.

However, in their capacity as missionaries for that region, they have, on several occasions, caused the death of several British soldiers and the sudden and unnecessary interruption of the business of His Majesty, by passing strategic information to the colonial militia at Fort Pitt, and also by giving aid and comfort to the same rebels. With the witnesses we have today assembled, we shall show that Reverend Zeisberger and his two assistants, John Heckewelder and William Edwards are therefore guilty of the crime of espionage, if not treason, and for that reason, should be put to death." As he made notes, himself, de Peyster then said without looking up, "You may call your first witness."

Elliot spun on his heel and peering intently at the back of the room, said, "The crown calls Owen Stanley." A shuffling noise at the rear of the room was soon followed by the footsteps of Owen Stanley as he walked to the area immediately to the right of Elliot's small table. Major de Peyster then swore the witness in and allowed questioning to begin as Elliot walked to the side of the room nearest the defendants. "Mr. Owen, what is your occupation, sir?" inquired the Captain. "It's Stanley — Owen Stanley," he corrected, "and I am a trader by trade, sir. I trade commodities for furs and such in the undeveloped areas."

"Are you an English citizen, Mr. Stanley?" asked Elliot. "That I am, Captain," said Stanley, who added, "God save the King." "Are you familiar with the area of the Ohio Territory known as the Muskingum region?" asked Elliot with a pleased tone at Stanley's previous response. "I am, sir. Most of my trading over the past ten years has been in the Ohio Territory," he answered. "What have you done for your country and your King during the past five years?" he was asked by Elliot. "I have worked as an agent of the King while buying supplies at Fort Pitt, and while engaging in my trade in the Ohio Territory," answered Stanley again.

"And in your position of agent of the King, do you contend that you have received payment from the crown for your services?" pressed Elliot. "Yes, sir, I have," replied Stanley. And then Elliot pointed to the table with the three defendants and asked, "And what have you learned of these men who are today seated at the table as accused? Zeisberger, Heckewelder, and Edwards?" "The word at Fort Pitt is that the Reverend there, and his men, too, are the eyes and ears of the rebels in the Muskingum region. According to what I know, those gents pass along information about British troops in the area by means of some of their Indian converts, what visits Fort Pitt regularly," answered Stanley. "Can you give this court an exact date on which you have personal knowledge of any or all of these men giving specific information to the rebel forces at Fort Pitt?" asked Elliot as he zeroed in on the trader.

Scratching his head, as if he hoped to trigger his memory process, Stanley began, "In the spring of '79, April or May, it was, while I was dealing with some of the rebel militia at Fort Pitt, I heard the commander there, say that the Reverend had convinced some of the Indians in the Musk-

115

ingum region to leave the British and return to their own people." "Did you hear how many or which Indians had been persuaded by Reverend Zeisberger, Stanley?" asked Captain Elliot. "No, sir, I did not, but everyone knows that at that time, the Wyandots, the Mingos, the Shawnee, and the Delaware were all in the employee of the British," answered the trader.

"At this time, Mr. Stanley," added Elliot, "did you hear of any loss of British troops that could be attributed to the actions of Reverend Zeisberger or his people?" "The rebel commander looks right in me eye and says, "Stanley.....we defeated a British unit this week and it would not have been possible without the work of Zeisberger," answered Stanley again. "I have nothing further. You may question this witness, Mr. Whitfield," said Elliot as he sat down and appeared to gloat again.

With a great deal of difficulty, old Whitfield rose from his chair and tottered in the direction of where he had heard Stanley's voice earlier. Whitfield's eyesight was nearly as poor as his hearing. "Please speak up, Mr. Stanley, as I am hard of hearing," said Whitfield, as he readied his ear trumpet. "You say, Mr. Stanley that you are a trader, and that you trade in the Ohio Territory. Is that correct?" "Yes, sir," boomed Mr. Stanley in response. "Tell the court please Mr. Stanley, what sorts of commodities — I believe those were your words — that you trade for furs and such," prodded Whitfield, who had by now straightened his wig. "Oh, several commodities, like tobacco, food and rum," said Stanley. "And how many times have you personally traded with anyone in the missionaries of Reverend Zeisberger or his colleagues?" queried Whitfield. "Why, I never did trade directly with anyone in the Moravian missions, sir," was the reply from the trader. "Never?" "No, sir. Never." "And why not, Mr. Stanley?" "Well, sir, everyone knows that Reverend Zeisberger doesn't allow any drinking or tobacco use in his villages," answered Stanley. Whitfield pressed on, "Well, if Reverend Zeisberger doesn't permit alcohol or tobacco in his villages, with whom *do you* trade your commodities in the Ohio Territory, Mr. Stanley?"

"I trade with the Wyandots, the Mingos, Shawnee, and the Delaware, sir," answered Stanley. "Didn't you just tell the court that you did *not* trade with Reverend Zeisberger's villages, the Delaware?" Whitfield asked with the trumpet pointed in Stanley's direction. "No, sir," Stanley corrected, "I mean I trade with the Delaware what work with the redcoats; *not* the Delaware from the Moravian villages." The old attorney slowly turned to walk in the direction of his table, then stopped and turned once more to face Stanley. "Tell me Mr. Stanley, in the spring of '79, were there ever any exact figures discussed as to the number of Indians allegedly persuaded by the Moravians to leave the service of the crown? And were there ever any exact figures of the number of fallen redcoats, as you call them, which were attributed to the alleged collaboration of the Moravian missionaries with the colonists?" asked Whitfield as he steadied himself at the edge of Elliot's table.

"No, sir," answered Stanley, "no exact figures were mentioned." "Could the figures have been several hundred?" prompted Whitfield. "Why, yes sir!" beamed Stanley in response. "Could the figures also have been only one or two?" he shot back at Stanley. As Stanley looked sheepishly at the floor, he answered, "Yes, sir." Whitfield again pointed his trumpet at Stanley and asked, "Was that a yes, sir?" "Yes, sir!" boomed Stanley again. Old Whitfield again made his way slowly back to his seat at the table with David and the others, and as he reached the table, he steadied himself and asked while looking in the direction of his chair, "By the way, Mr. Stanley, have you ever been in the Ohio Territory region known as the Tuscarawas River valley?" "No, sir," answered Stanley. "I thought not," Whitfield muttered quietly to himself, and then said, "Nothing further!" With a great deal of effort, and some obvious pain, Whitfield lowered himself into the uncomfortable chair. There was no one laughing at him now, even though his ear trumpet clanged to the floor.

"The crown now calls Lieutenant Jonathan Kent," said Captain Elliot, as he rose from his chair to question the next witness. David and the others slowly looked over their shoulders to try to pick out Kent as he came forward, but Lieutenant Kent, unlike the others, had not been sitting in the rear of the room. He entered, instead, from the exterior door, after being summoned by one of the guards outside. He strode to the spot at the side of Elliot's table where he was sworn in by de Peyster in the same manner as had been Stanley. Upon looking for Kent in the back of the room, David had spotted the old Delaware chief, Captain Pipe. Since 1778, Captain Pipe had harbored a grudge against David and the Moravians for dividing the once powerful Delaware tribe. David knew that Captain Pipe would be more than happy to put an end to Moravian activities everywhere. Captain Pipe's presence did *not* bode well for the missionaries.

"Lieutenant Kent, will you please tell the court of any conversations or meetings that took place between you and any of the accused Moravian missionaries seated at that table," urged Elliot of the witness. "In the late summer of 1776, I took a patrol of several men and a group of Wyandot into the Muskingum region and called on Reverend Zeisberger on orders from my commander," said Kent, as he nodded toward Major de Peyster. "And please tell us, Lieutenant, what was the gist of that conversation with Zeisberger?" "I told him that we suspected a colonial offensive shortly from Fort Pitt, and that we believed he knew something about it. He denied it, of course," answered Kent. "Could you please tell us why you suspected any involvement by the Moravians," asked Elliot. "Because," answered the young officer, "the Moravians had been doing a great deal of their trading with the colonial rebels at Fort Pitt. And in addition, the Delaware were the only tribe in the area that we could not persuade to join us in the war effort. Not at first, at any rate."

"What was Reverend Zeisberger's attitude while you spoke with him on that occasion?" "He was very cocky, and he refused our offer of protection against the rebels," answered Lieutenant Kent. "In your official opinion, Lieutenant Kent, do you believe that Zeisberger and the other Moravians or their converted Delaware had knowingly conspired to assist the colonials in their insurrection against the crown? And if you do, would you please tell this court why?" asked Elliot pointedly. "Yes, sir, I do," answered Kent, who went on, "First of all, since Zeisberger and his associates entered the Ohio Territory, there has been a steady decline in the number of Indians that have sided with the British effort in the war. Second, every time that we have sent a detachment of troops into the Muskingum region, they have been ambushed by the insurgents, and have generally fared quite poorly. Third, our people in and around Fort Pitt tell us that the Moravians are the source of the information which is leading to the ambushes." "You may question Lieutenant Kent, Mr. Whitfield," said de Peyster as Elliot returned to his seat.

After conferring briefly with David and the others for a minute or two, the old man once more straightened the eyeglasses upon his nose and picked his ear trumpet off the table before him and slowly made his way toward the front of where Lieutenant Kent stood. "Are you a Christian, Lieutenant Kent?" asked the old man. "Why, yes, I am," answered the officer, as if troubled that anyone would doubt the fact. "Do you have any problem with the Moravian church claiming souls? Even Indian souls, Lieutenant?" asked Whitfield straight away. "No, sir, none at all," crisply replied the officer. "Why, of course you don't, Lieutenant. Hell — none of us in this room are against Christianity, are we? I beg your pardon, Reverend Zeisberger," Whitfield turned toward the missionaries as he apologized for his language again, and then refocused on Lt. Kent. "Would you say Lieutenant, that the character of your *only* conversation with Reverend Zeisberger was centered more on religion than on military strategy?" asked the old man. "My questions to him concerned things military, his answers were more on religion," shot back the younger man.

"How many times since '76, have British soldiers been set upon by rebels in ambushes in the Muskingum region of the Ohio Territory? If you know?" asked Whitfield. Not wishing to give away any military secrets, Lieutenant Kent correctly said, "I do not know that I can answer that exact question, sir." After a brief conference at the front of de Peyster's table, with Elliot, Kent, Whitfield, and de Peyster all adding something to the moment, they all returned to their places and Kent answered simply, "Every time!" "Very well, Lieutenant Kent," continued Whitfield, "You say that *our people at Fort Pitt* accuse the Moravians. Tell us, please, sir.....Who, exactly, **are** *our people at Fort Pitt?* If you know?" Whitfield mimicked the tone of his previous question and waited again for an answer as Kent squirmed over the sensitivity of his possible answer. "I don't know.....I'm not sure I can.....er, Am I allowed to answer that?" he finally asked of Captain Elliot, and again a conference at de Peyster's table ensued. Afterwards,

Kent answered, "In the name of military secrecy, I am not allowed to divulge the names of our people at Fort Pitt, sir."

"I see, Lieutenant Kent. You visited Reverend Zeisberger in the Muskingum to talk military strategy and he talked of winning souls. You tell us that every time British troops go into the Muskingum region that they are set upon by rebels, but military prudence forbids that you tell us how often this has occurred. You also say that the blame for these ambushes are bolstered by the claims of our people at Fort Pitt, but you cannot name one of them. Again, observing strict military prudence. Are you aware, Lieutenant, that Mr. Owen Stanley has already testified for the crown in this matter?" and Whitfield began gesturing toward Stanley, seated in the rear of the room, with his trumpet. Kent turned and scanned the room until his eyes met those of Stanley. "Yes sir, I am aware." "Might Mr. Stanley be what or whom you have characterized as *one of our people at Fort Pitt?*" asked the old attorney. "Yes, sir," answered Kent. "Nothing further, your honor," said Whitfield, as he once more shuffled off in the direction of his chair, and clutching his ill-fitting barrister robe lest it fall off. The smug tone of his last remark left no doubt as to how much he felt he had accomplished with his questioning of Kent.

For the rest of the morning, two more British officers gave rather questionable testimony about alleged Moravian collusion with the rebels within the Ohio Territory, but their contributions to the trial appeared to be the weakest of all who would eventually testify. For all his age, which David and the others would conservatively estimate at 85, Silas Whitfield had thus far proven to be an extraordinarily pugnacious and capable attorney. As the morning progressed, it became apparent to the defendants that not only would they get a fair trial, but that the old Englishman chosen to represent them was far more formidable than *anyone* had expected. After the last of the two officers had testified, de Peyster, clearly agitated, called a recess until 2:00 that afternoon. David, John, and William were again marched back to their cell, and just in time to partake of the room-temperature soup, which they happily devoured, along with another hot cup of thick, black coffee.

Having not slept well the previous night, each of the missionaries chose to lay down on their bunks until they were later summoned to the courtroom. David and John resumed the never-ending thoughts of their wives, while William tried simply closing his eyes, but their afternoon rest was disturbed shortly by Mr. Whitfield, who announced his presence in the stockade by dropping his clattering ear trumpet upon the hard wooden floor. "Tell me what you can of this Delaware chief, Captain Pipe, can you, lads? He appears to be the best witness for the crown," said the old man, who knew that the best witnesses were usually held until the last.

"One of my good Delaware friends was chief White Eyes," said David, "and Captain Pipe was probably his best friend. White Eyes was murdered by a group of colonial militiamen who thought, incorrectly I might add, that he was a British ally. This happened three years ago this month, and Captain Pipe has not spoken to me since then. I feel that he believes I, too, am responsible for the British losses in the Ohio Territory. I know that he blames me for White Eyes' death." "What can he truthfully say against you, Reverend?" asked the old man. "Only what I have told you, Mr. Whitfield," answered David. Neither of the other missionaries could offer a clue as to what Captain Pipe's testimony would hold for them. "Very well," said Whitfield, "I'll just have to wait and watch as this unfolds. Chin up, lads!" he repeated, as he slowly turned and left the cell area.

In a short time, the original two soldiers reappeared at the cell and once more escorted the three men to the courtroom over the previous path. All three looked up into the warm October sky as they crossed the courtyard, and their thoughts immediately took them back to their beautiful Tuscarawas River valley, though each was totally unaware of the other's mind. William pictured his arrival in the valley for the first time. John was reminded of a day of harvest in the fields, alongside the members of the flock. David wondered when, and if, they would ever see the beautiful Tuscarawas again. The sound of their own boots against the hard floor of the walkway and then the courtroom brought them back to the reality that they were all on trial for their lives.

To open the afternoon session, two more Indians were called to bear witness against the Moravians, and they were Indians that were not instantly recognizable to any of the three men on trial. According to Elliot's line of questioning, each of the men testified that David had tried to convince him to leave the British for the colonial rebels. Old Whitfield really shone in his examination of the pair of Indians, one a Wyandot and the other a Shawnee — neither proficient in the white man's language. After skillfully getting the Wyandot to refer to Major de Peyster as the Fort Pitt commander, Whitfield asked permission for the second witness to step out of the room while the first tried to identify David Zeisberger from among the three defendants seated at the table. Afterwards, the first would leave, while the second did the same. Since all three of the Moravians were dressed in black, and all were approximately the same size, it would be a fair test. Elliot protested, but de Peyster allowed the exercise and neither Indian could do any better than say that all three men looked alike. Elliot's face turned nearly the same brilliant shade as his fine jacket. His blood fairly boiled within his head.

"The crown now calls the Delaware chief, Captain Pipe," said Captain Elliot in a sing-song sort of voice that seemed to say, "Now I've got you." When Captain Pipe had made his way to the witness area, Major de Peyster swore him in, and then Elliot's questioning began in earnest. Unlike the previous two witnesses, *this* Indian not only spoke the English, but knew David Zeisberger well. "Captain Pipe," said Elliot with a smug grin, "would you please identify Reverend David Zeisberger for us today?" And the Delaware chief walked over to the front of the defense's table and pointed his long, weathered index finger directly at David's nose. When Captain Pipe returned to his witness area, Captain Elliot asked, "How long have you known Reverend Zeisberger?" "Oh, long time now. Long time. Maybe nine years," answered the Indian. "Have you ever been asked by Reverend Zeisberger to leave or quit the employ of the British army, Chief?" asked Elliot. "Oh, yes, many times. Many times," answered the chief.

"And did Reverend Zeisberger ever ask you to or suggest to you to begin working for the colonial rebels?" continued the British captain. "Oh, no. No, never me, but he asked many Wyandot, Shawnee, Mingo, and Delaware," answered Captain Pipe. Elliot's chest swelled noticeably over the old Indian's most recent answer, and he took a spot to the far right, near the door, where he could see the three Moravians in the distance while looking at the witness. "Captain Pipe," started Elliot anew, "do you have any knowledge of any messages or information that David Zeisberger or either of his assistants or any of his Delaware mission members passed along to the rebels at Fort Pitt?" Appearing a slight bit confused, the Indian hesitated before asking a question, "Oh, who? The Delaware?" "Yes, yes, Captain Pipe, the Delaware. Those Delaware who now live with Zeisberger and the others in the mission villages," said Elliot. Again, the chief appeared slightly confused, and he hesitated even longer before saying, "Oh, Delaware, yes. Christian Delaware, no." Elliot then returned quickly to his table and began rummaging through his notes, as it was obvious that he had failed to elicit the correct responses from the Delaware chief.

Silas Whitfield immediately leaned over and began a brief whispered conversation with David which ended when de Peyster angrily urged the proceeding to move along. From his table, Captain Elliot asked, "Are you friends with Zeisberger, Chief?" "Oh, no. Not friends. Not enemy. Not friends," the Indian answered truthfully. "How do you feel about the colonial rebels at Fort Pitt, Captain Pipe?" questioned Elliot. "Oh, whites at Fort Pitt are my enemy. They kill many Delaware. I kill many enemy, too," he said, as he proudly held up his scalplocks for all to see. It was apparent that there were several white men numbered among the chief's victims. "One last question, Chief," added Elliot, "Do you believe that Zeisberger has ever conspired against the British or assisted the rebels in any way?" "Oh, yes. For sure," answered Captain Pipe. And then with that glimmer of incriminating evidence dangling before him, Elliot asked, "Can you name one specific example or time that Zeisberger conspired against the British or assisted the rebels?" "Oh, yes," Captain Pipe answered, "Moravians convert many Delaware to religion. If Delaware not religious, they fight for British against rebels. More Delaware mean that British win war soon. Oh, yes." Elliot sat down, by now, completely flustered, and it was next Whitfield's turn.

The old attorney stood awkwardly and shuffled slowly to the front of his own table, before saying, "I'll get straight to the point, Chief. You said that Reverend Zeisberger here has asked you to leave the British several times — many times, I believe, were your exact words. Do you remember just one of those times? Any one time that occurred?" "Oh, yes," responded Captain Pipe, "in the village of Goschachgunk, just after White Eyes died." Whitfield then leaned toward the witness with his ear trumpet for a date. "That would be about three years ago?" asked Whitfield. The chief answered, "Oh, yes. Three years." "Do you remember the exact words that the Reverend spoke to you on that date, Chief? And your response?" continued the old attorney. "Oh, yes. Sure. He tell me quit British now. He ask me join mission, not fight anyone. I tell him, I fight enemy. I fight colonials. Colonials kill White Eyes," answered the Indian.

"So the Reverend never did say to you that you should join the rebels or fight the British, is that your testimony, Captain Pipe?" asked the old man. "Oh, yes. All true," acknowledged the chief. "You also said that the Reverend had asked many Wyandot, Shawnee, Mingo, and Delaware to begin working for the colonial rebels. Do you recall saying that, Chief?" asked the old defense attorney. "Oh, yes. Sure," was his answer. "How do you know this to be true, Chief — that all these other Indians had been asked?" questioned Whitfield. "Oh, everyone know truth," said Captain Pipe. "Please, Captain Pipe, if you can," Whitfield carefully worded his question, "Name me just one of these people who know this truth?" and he fixed his trumpet in the Indian's direction. "Captain Elliot know truth," said Captain Pipe innocently, causing Elliot's face to again redden. "And Major de Peyster?" added old Whitfield inquisitively. To any unbiased observer, it would have seemed that de Peyster slowly began to sink in his chair. "Oh, sure. Him too," came the not-unexpected answer. "I see," said the old barrister in a low voice, exhibiting no emotion. A shiver of excitement ran through each of the three Moravians with this revelation, but Whitfield was not done. Not yet.

"Captain Elliot asked you a short while ago if you had any knowledge of any messages or information that any of the Christian Delaware passed along to the rebels at Fort Pitt, and you said Delaware, yes — Christian Delaware, no. Do you recall that question and your answer?" asked the old man. "Oh, yes. Sure," was the new response. "Which Delaware do you know for certain that passed messages or information about the British to the rebels at Fort Pitt?" pressed Whitfield. "Oh, Delaware chiefs Wannantuha and Bird Nest. They plenty smart. They take money from British. They take money from rebels for British information. *Plenty smart*," Captain Pipe said the last two words with a great deal of emphasis. Although the names of the Delaware chiefs disclosed by Captain Pipe were not familiar to most of the people in the room, David, John, and William recognized them to be two of the men who took control of the Delaware tribe and splintered it upon the abdication of Gelelemend. In a low tone, Whitfield simply said, "Thank you, Chief," and again made the agonizingly slow effort to be reseated.

When it became obvious that Elliot had no further witnesses to call, it was now the defense's turn, and old Whitfield had originally planned to question all of the missionaries, if for no other reason than to have each of them simply face the court and say, "I did nothing." However, the weak case put forth by Elliot had made the testimony of the three missionaries totally unnecessary, and when Major de Peyster instructed the defense to call witnesses, the old man merely said, "No witnesses," and feigned getting up to make the statement, although he had *no* intention of standing.

Captain Elliot then rose and began to offer a summation of his fine case against the Moravians. "The crown believes that it has shown that Reverend David Zeisberger, John Heckewelder, and William Edwards, and any number of the Delaware tribe which they have converted to the Moravian religion, have practiced a deliberate subversive campaign against the armies of King George. They have systematically attempted to convince numerous of the King's valued Indian allies to leave their service to him and join the rebels in their insurrection. British army losses in the Ohio Territory, particularly in the Tuscarawas River valley and the Muskingum region have been significant, and all because of the presence of the Moravians. The court has heard testimony to that effect today from not only our own agents in the area, but also from our respected Wyandot, Shawnee, and Delaware friends. We believe that each of the Moravian missionaries who sit at that table," and he gestured at the defense table, "deserve the full measure of the law for their treasonous collaborations with the enemies of the crown. We ask for the sentence of death to be pronounced."

Now, old man Whitfield had to rise, and he did so with the same deliberate slow speed with which he had always taken his seat. One could almost feel his pain as he slowly struggled to his feet. "Captain Elliot would have you believe that each of the men seated at this table are actually militiamen, whose uniforms are no doubt tattooed to their bodies, under these simple garments they wear. But these are men of God's army. They carry bibles, not muskets. They save lives, not take lives. Yes, they have attempted to convince members of the tribes of the Ohio Territory to quit the British and join them, but this is only because they are missionaries. This is what missionaries do. If the colonials had any Indians as allies, they would also be asked to quit the colonials and join the Moravians in their mission villages." The three Moravians nodded in agreement to Whitfield's observations as he continued.

"Captain Elliot offered Owen Stanley as evidence of the collaboration of these men. Owen Stanley is a fine example, he who sells the devil's own products to our Indian friends. Owen Stanley, by his own admission is more of a liability to the British than any of this contrived evidence against these three fine men would have us believe today. Owen Stanley, who has never even been in the Tuscarawas River valley. Lieutenant Jonathan Kent told us how he talked military matters with Reverend Zeisberger, but got soul-saving religion in return. For this we wish to hang these men? No man of God anywhere is safe by these standards — including the Archbishop of Canterbury!

And finally. Finally...." Old man Whitfield looked as though he were about to pass out from the strain, as he dabbed perspiration from his brow. "Captain Pipe came here to tell us that Reverend Zeisberger was working for the colonial rebels and that everybody knew it, but who is everybody? Only the very men who have brought this action for the crown. God save the King!" said the old Englishman instinctively. "You have all heard, direct from the mouth of this splendid ally of the British that the very people who *do* continue to collaborate with the colonial rebels are those traitorous Delaware allies who have taken your supplies and also taken same from those at Fort Pitt. I know who should be on trial here today, gentlemen, I know who should be hanged, and so does everyone in this room. It is not these three good, kind, and gentle men of God." After a short pause for effect, he ended with, "Thank you." Whitfield practically crawled around the edge of the table to his seat, and allowed his body to simply fall into the seat. David hurriedly turned the chair so as to make the landing a successful one for the old gent.

Major de Peyster then announced that he and the other two judges would take the case under advisement and that their decision would be rendered as soon as all of the evidence had been reviewed. Mr. Whitfield asked that the three missionaries be released to his custody while the judges were deliberating, but Captain Elliot objected, and it was ordered that the three be returned to their cell. As the military judges all left, everyone arose, and Attorney Whitfield leaned toward the trio and said, "I'll be along in just a few minutes to talk with you." The young soldiers entered the room and once more marched the missionaries back to their present home in the stockade.

All three sat on David's bunk in the cell, and smiles embraced their faces, but they also knew that de Peyster had yet to declare them innocent. David said with a perfectly straight face, "I really do not fancy sitting here in this cell, but at least we have this wonderful food." And this brought a laugh from John and William. "Imagine," said John, "that Wannantuha and Bird Nest have been the ones passing the word to the people at Fort Pitt. All this time!" "Poor Captain Pipe," added William, "all this time his fellow chiefs have been dealing with his enemy." "Ever since White Eyes was shot, Captain Pipe has held some sort of grudge against the mission. It's almost as if he believed that we were responsible for pulling the trigger," mused David. "I still can't make out why he feels that way about us." The fact that Captain Pipe was once a very good friend and was now estranged from David and the other Delaware in the flock always bothered David and would forever continue to haunt him.

The sound of footsteps in the corridor told them that someone was coming, and when they looked up, they could see that it was their appointed defense, Silas Whitfield. Mr. Whitfield's face was extremely flushed and his face was bathed in perspiration. He was dabbing at his lips with his hanky as he came into view, as though he had just had another near fatal coughing spell. The old man said, "Well, lads, I think that we gave them the best possible show, but I do not want any of you to get too elevated thus far. Major de Peyster is not a benevolent man, and I believe that we heard enough today from that Delaware chief that he and Elliot certainly hold something against you. We are not yet out of the woods. Had de Peyster released you to my custody, I would have been fairly certain that he means to acquit you, but since that did not occur, I must be frank in telling you that I am still concerned for your lives. Any fool can see that this was a rigged case from the beginning. Still, I don't know....." and his voice trailed off as he appeared to see if anyone from the jailer's office was listening.

David reached out between the bars and took the old man's hand to shake. The old hand was cold and clammy, but gripped with the acknowledgment that its owner was still a person to be reckoned with. The confidence in the handshake made David say, "Mr. Whitfield, I cannot thank you enough. God will look kindly on you for what you have done for us." "Thank you, Reverend Zeisberger," replied the old man. "I believe in you and your work," and he shook the hands of John and William also. "I must go now, but I will stay abreast of things for you." And then his characteristic ending comments, "Chin up, lads!" The men smiled in amazement *and* admiration as he made his way out of the stockade again. That night, the three prayed with an absolute optimism, buoyed by the performance of their seemingly ancient representative in court, but still tempered somewhat by the devious nature of Major de Peyster. For the first time in many nights, however, the men would finally get *some* sleep.

The morning sunlight which filtered into the small cell brought with it new hope that the three missionaries would soon be free, and it was the first thing on each of their minds as they awoke. Without even bothering to check if the others were yet awake, William lay in his bunk and looked at the wooden ceiling and said, "I just know that the Major is going to release us today. There's no way that he can possibly justify keeping us here." John then rolled on his side, facing William and said, "I dreamed that we were released today by de Peyster. It would be an excellent end to what has been a terrible hardship on everyone." His thoughts obviously included the poor suffering souls back at Lake Erie, with their Wyandot chaperons. David, who was berthed in the bunk immediately below William, now sat up and allowed his legs to touch the floor slightly. He spoke to both his assistants, although he looked only in John's direction, "Knowing de Peyster as I do, I am not yet ready to believe that he is through with us. Especially after hearing what Mr. Whitfield told us last evening. I'm afraid that the Moravians will never be popular with too many whites in this country, but especially not the British." There was a certain truth to David's prophecy which would eventually be revealed to all three men, but not today.

October 16th came and went very slowly for the three men without benefit of a verdict from de Peyster's court. So did the days that followed, and soon the days began to grow into weeks, but still no news from de Peyster. In the interim, they had been visited several times by Mr. Whitfield, who had attempted to cheer them up, but could offer no real clues to when, or if, they would ever be released. On his visit of November 10th, Whitfield told the men that he would call on Major de Peyster in person to see if he could once more persuade the officer to release the men into his custody. The following day, old man Whitfield returned to the cell and his dejected appearance gave away the bad news that he bore for the men. Each of the Moravians had almost imperceptibly begun to slip further and further toward despair, although their religious foundation remained very strong. Now, with Whitfield's downcast looks, each man's faith was again put to the test.

"I'll give it to you straight, lads," said the old man, who by now looked physically as though he were at death's very door. "Major de Peyster and his two lackeys have decided that they need to hear from the two Delaware chiefs who were named in the trial. He's decided that he will keep each of you here until, and, most importantly, *if,* he is able to get a confirmation on Captain Pipe's testimony. I am told that a squad of British soldiers were dispatched by de Peyster the very day following your trial to find and bring in both of those other chiefs. How long that will be, one simply cannot say. Also, and I think it only fair to warn you, that what each of the Indians say when they speak to de Peyster will be extremely crucial. I have demanded that I be present when the two are examined by the court, although de Peyster can simply tell me to go hiking. But....." and the old man's voice trailed off slightly, "he hasn't done this yet and I intend to be there when he questions these men. Any questions from any of you?" he asked, as he pressed his ear trumpet against the bars of the cell. Visibly disappointed now, none of the three had any questions for their representative, and after telling them to keep their chins up, Whitfield again tottered off precariously down the passageway.

Ironically, and without anyone as far west as Detroit knowing, the entire matter of the suspected Moravian duplicity became a moot question on October 19th, 1781, when the British commander, General Cornwallis, surrendered his troops to General George Washington of the Continental Army, at Yorktown, Pennsylvania. Armed hostilities between the two sides would continue on for nearly two years, but the war was now officially over. In any case, old Whitfield would continue in his efforts to try to get the men released.

It would be several more days before the men saw or heard from Mr. Whitfield again, but the news would not be good in any case. The English soldier originally confined with them had already done his time and had been released. The two drunken Indians had been replaced by two others, then three new drunks, then a new pair or so until the two new braves who now shared the cramped cell. Only the blathering French fool remained from their first days in the wretched place, and by the looks of him, it would seem that he would be there long after they left — one way or another. The Moravians regularly held their prayer service each evening in the stockade, and surprisingly enough, had even managed to convert a couple of the now-sober Indians to Christianity, but the trio remained in custody.

On November 20th, the men received possibly their worst news in many, many days. The jailer who seemed to antagonize them the most appeared at their cell early that morning, even before breakfast, and said, "Bad news for you chaps, sure enough. Word has it that old Silas Whitfield was found dead in his bed last evening. 'Seems he'd been there for several days. Will you be dining in this evening?" he asked with a sarcasm which was totally uncalled for, because the hearts of the Moravians were crushed with pity for the old gentleman who had fought so brilliantly for them in court. So great was their grief for old Silas Whitfield, that none of them even considered the seriously negative consequences of what Whitfield's death might possibly mean to their own case. David called for an immediate prayer, and as the three formed a circle with their arms about each other's shoulders, everyone in the cell became respectfully quiet. Tears for the old man filled the eyes of each of the men and at last David ended the prayer with, "God rest his soul."

Later that same evening, Captain Matthew Elliot also came to the stockade and gave the same news to the men that they had earlier received from the jailer, except Elliot did it with an English dignity which was totally appropriate, and which, despite his antagonism of them, revealed his admiration for the legal wisdom of the departed worthy adversary. Elliot had not come to gloat, and neither had he come to further dampen the spirits of the missionaries. He was merely doing what had seemed like the appropriate and British thing to do. After giving the three his condolences, Elliot started down the hall, and then, as if only by an afterthought, said, "Oh, yes.....our men have returned the two Delaware chiefs who were singled out by Captain Pipe, and Major de Peyster will be interrogating them tomorrow." The pace of Elliot's steps had nearly carried the last few words out of the stockade with him, but when they each looked at one another in disbelief, they knew what they had heard, and their spirits immediately soared. There would be a particularly long and detailed prayer offered up in the stockade this night! For the first time in many nights, the men's last conscious thoughts and dreams were pleasant ones. John dreamed of seeing his first child in Sarah's arms. David had visions of Susan, gently patting his hand and calling him, "Darling," while William dreamed of a hot bath, followed by a sumptuous meal.

All through the next day, the men nervously paced their cell but heard nothing of the proceeding being conducted by the British Major. Even the hateful jailer had no bad news with which to taunt the three men. Another prayer service and another night in the squalor of the stockade. Each of the men had by now been infested by lice, and by crabs, which were rife among the dingy and unsanitary bedding and clothing of each of the inmates. A goodly portion of each evening was spent picking lice from each other's heads. The wait for word from de Peyster was maddening and affected the sleep of the men as well. In addition, since leaving Lake Erie's shore, none of the trio had shaved, and scraggly beards now adorned their faces.

By dawn on November 22nd, the only thing on each of the men's mind was the unknown consequences of that which had transpired in Major de Peyster's office. Each man awoke with the first rays of light into the darkened cell. John went to the window, and standing way up on his toes, could see that activity around the stockade had not yet begun. He never really knew why he looked out the window, but it was to see how free people simply went about their daily tasks. Having never been without his freedom before this occasion, John had never before given it that much thought. He went back to his bunk and climbed up, and said, "David, I have never told you how much I appreciate what you have meant to me. Your enthusiasm for winning Indian souls has been an inspiration for me that has taken control of wherever my life will lead. With no regrets, I tell you now that I would join you in our beautiful Tuscarawas River valley again, no matter the consequences." David rolled toward John and said, "John, your existence here, as well as William's, in this cell with me is proof of your thanks for me. I fear that I have placed each of you in harm's way, and I only pray that somehow, we shall each be given the opportunity to once more return to our valley and the wonderful people of our flock." "Amen," said William, who was also awake.

In a very short while, the obnoxious jailer pushed the cart containing the daily ration of hard bread and coffee for the prisoners down the narrow hall, and each man came to the bars of the cell to get their meal. However, before they could even begin, the same two soldiers who had been their escorts during the trial appeared in the hall and ordered the three missionaries to fall in between them. To David, John, and William, it seemed as though their trial was now continuing. Each man dressed fully, and David grabbed his bible as they fell in step with the two redcoats and began the same route to where their trial had earlier taken them. But on this day, upon leaving the stockade, the guards led them toward the other end of the courtyard, toward an area where David had been before. Quietly he whispered to the other men, "We are being taken to de Peyster's office."

At Major de Peyster's office, the men were led through the adjutant's office, belonging to Captain Elliot, and directly into the office of the commander. Only Major de Peyster was there, standing in front of his desk, with his arms crossed across his chest. The two guards left and closed the door behind them. "Sit down, Reverend Zeisberger," he said, as he gestured to the three wooden chairs before him, "Please, all of you, have a seat." The British officer leaned back against his desk and squarely looked into David's eyes before saying, "I'm afraid that we owe you an apology, sir. Each of you. We confirmed only yesterday, in questioning Wannantuha and Bird Nest, that they have, indeed, been the source of the information being supplied the colonial rebels in the Ohio Territory. I realize that what I have just told you is a hollow consolation for the rather shabby treatment to which you have been subjected, and I can only say that I am truly sorry for your inconvenience."

The three missionaries could hardly believe their ears, but they were much too weary and wreaked with anxiety to show any emotion or enthusiasm, including a smile, and the only hint of their relief was a glazing over of their eyes. David rose slowly from his chair and asked, "Then may we now go home, Major?" "Of course, Reverend Zeisberger, and I have already instructed my aides to assist you in your journey back to Upper Sandusky," said the Major, "and I have had them assemble a small ration of food and clothing for you. You may check them over and add to them as you wish. My quartermaster has been instructed to assist you in any way possible." "But what about our flock and our wives, Major?" asked John, who stood now along with William. "They have had their clothing and supplies taken from them and are likely starving at Lake Erie's edge as we now speak."

"I regret, very much, that your families and your people have had to endure any hardships during this inquiry," said de Peyster, "but we cannot go back in time and undo what has already been done. We shall do the best that is possible from this moment on. Do you not agree? I have instructed my men to have Chief Pomoacan return all of the supplies taken from your people. He will give you no further trouble." The English officer then offered his hand, and it was obligingly taken by each of the men, though it was a handshake which conveyed no genuine friendship or trust toward de Peyster. "The men who brought you here will take you to where your canoes are waiting," said the Major, as he took his seat behind his desk and appeared to begin to go back to his paperwork.

Before the now freed men left the garrison, David made it a point to inspect the small store of goods that had been provided courtesy of Major de Peyster. In addition to a dozen old army blankets, two dozen sets of longjohns, and about 50 pairs of socks, the British commander had ordered his quartermaster to lay up a supply of coffee, sugar, salt, flour, quinine, and candles. "Anything else, Reverend?" asked the quartermaster, a sergeant with many years of service. "Yes," answered David, who took note that all of the clothing was used, but clean. "We'll also take more of these," and he tossed another dozen blankets on his pile of supplies. The sergeant's eyebrows lifted, but he said nothing.

"We'll also have some of that delicious hard tack that we were served while in your stockade, and a supply of pemmican or bacon, or both if possible," added David. The remarks about the stockade bread had caused both John and William to laugh out loud. "We ain't got any bacon just now, Reverend, but here's five pounds of pemmican to go along with the hard tack that should suit you," said the old quartermaster. "Oh, yes," said David, "We are going to need several pounds of corn seed for our spring crop." "Will that be all, sir?" asked the sergeant. David then leaned forward and whispered in the quartermaster's ear, which made him smile, and he said, "Certainly. 'Be back in just a spot!" When he returned, he hoisted a large cloth sack of grain, probably about ten pounds, on the counter before him, and then he pressed a small packet into David, hand, which was quickly stowed in his pocket. "Thank you, very much," said David, and the three men left the supply depot with their goods.

The exhausting trial of David Zeisberger, John Heckewelder, and William Edwards had, at last, brought to an end the wrath and the opposition of the British military against the religious operations of the Moravians in the Ohio Territory. But the punishing forced march from Gnadenhutten to Sandusky, the cruel months of cold deprivation, and the harsh treatment of the members of the flock by the Wyandot guards had begun a festering blight upon the Moravians and their religious converts that would, perhaps, never heal. Most importantly, the spirits of all of the men had been terrifically strained, if not irreparably broken. Only their steely faith in God remained strong. The three missionaries would soon return to Erie's south shore, but to what? Their mission dreams lay in three pitiful ruins alongside the Tuscarawas. Crops that had been carefully nurtured now lay rotting in the unattended fields. Rondmanund, and several others, they would soon learn, had already lost their lives to the absurdity of the fears of those outside the Moravian family. And many, many more were yet to die. As their canoes sped gracefully and quietly south through the cold lake waters, the thoughts of the three missionaries were focused upon the myriad of uncertainties that now awaited them in the Ohio Territory.

November 22, 1781

As the first of the canoes reached the south shore of the lake, the three men peered eagerly along the beach to see what and who they could see. David specifically sought out the figure of Susan, while John was making the same sort of search for Sarah. On the beach, in the direction of the area that had been occupied by the flock, they could make out a few children playing, but the waning hours of the dusky sun forbid easy identification of any of the people who began to slowly walk toward the water and the arriving canoes. Behind him in the second canoe, John and William were also having difficulty in making out those on the beach.

At last, David recognized a familiar face, as old friend Isaac stepped up to the now beached canoe and said, "Oh Father David, welcome home. Your flock has missed you." The Delaware wrapped his long, thin arms around the wispy man of God and each began to sob quietly into the other's shoulder. John and Sarah had already been reunited, a short distance away. David glanced in their direction long enough to see John examining the bulge that would soon become their first child. To the west, a few feet further away, William was greeted in similar fashion by those from his own previous village. As soon as Susan came running up to David at the canoe, the picture was complete. She threw her frail arms around his neck and kissed him passionately through his whiskers. It was a happy time for all.

David grasped Susan by the shoulders, and stepped back slightly, and said, "Let me have a look at you, my love. You are so thin. Has the food situation gotten no better since we left for Detroit?" asked the missionary. Before Susan could answer, Isaac bowed his head, in obvious reverence, and said, "We have lost some of the flock, my brother, and I fear that many more are very close to death's door. We have so little to eat in this place." Susan nodded her assent to Isaac's statement as tears of joy and sadness mixed in her eyes.

David partially turned toward Isaac, and gesturing toward the supplies that were stacked in the canoe, said, "We have brought some provisions which will see us through for a while. Get someone to help you carry these things up to the shelters." The approaching darkness had, by now, almost hidden the entire beach area from view, but a few small fires to the east, where Pomoacan and the Wyandot still camped, began to stand out in the darkness. David glanced their way, and noticed that the British soldiers who had escorted them were already walking in that direction. He and the others, however, began to walk in the direction of the shelters erected by the members of the flock. William, joining John and Sarah, had already left the beach on their own way back.

Upon reaching the shelter which had been used by he and Susan before the arrest and subsequent trip to Detroit, David could see that his loving flock had made some improvements in the place. A thick layer of leaves was spread over a generous covering of pine boughs, in an effort to make sleeping a bit more comfortable for the missionary, who was by now 60 years old, but looked and felt nearer to 80. On the rear wall, hung the same tin cup that had been given the members of the column by Richard, the friendly English trader. David searched his memory quickly for the trader's full name, but was too exhausted to be successful. He smiled at the little extra touches that he had been accorded by his flock, and then he turned and said to Isaac, "Assemble the flock in the meeting place for prayer service tonight and we shall fill each other in on what has occurred during our absence. We shall meet in one hour." Susan encircled his waist with her arm as they walked into the shelter.

Isaac left to begin his notifications just as William and John reached their shelters and they, too, were pleased at the condition of their quarters. David shared with them the news of the scheduled meeting and prayer service, and then all three men happily prepared to bathe for the first time in several months. David then produced a small packet of lye, which had been what he had quietly requested of the quartermaster in Detroit, for aiding them in ridding their bodies of the parasites that had been a constant source of irritation. They all smiled at the sight of the lye, which David had been careful to keep from the eyes of Susan and Sarah.

Before dipping themselves completely in the chilly waters of the lake, the three men paid a quick visit to Pomoacan and the supplies which had been long taken from them. The soldiers had already conveyed Major de Peyster's orders, and Pomoacan gave them no trouble. Each of the men would, for now, take only what was of immediate need, and that was a large kettle for boiling water, and a change of clothing for each of them. The three missionaries placed their fresh clothing in their shelter after filling the huge kettle with water from the lake. William carried a burning branch, which would be used to start their own fire. The thoughtful flock had already laid in a supply of seasoned firewood for them, and in no time at all, there was a dandy campfire and the water was slowly heated.

After the icy bath, the men rubbed each other down harshly with handfuls of fine sand from the beach as a prerequisite to using the lye, and then raced hurriedly to escape the brisk November winds which blew in off the lake. Susan had already been warned to wait for them with Sarah, in her and John's shelter. At David's shelter, they happily added their old, soiled, and heavily infested clothing to the fire, as David mixed the lye in the now heated water. With the tin cup, they each took turns pouring the hot mixture over each other's head and backs, as they simultaneously rubbed the lye mixture into their skins with their hands. The hot mixture burned sharply as it found its way into the sores upon the three men's bodies. They shivered and winced in between hot cupfuls of the mixture, but knowing that they would soon be free of the pests that had infested them was relief well worth the discomfort. Not one area of their body would escape the caustic action of the water and lye, save for their eyeballs, and for this they were each grateful.

Dressing hurriedly to escape the bitter cold, the three men looked each other over with simple approving smiles. Now the only thing about them which remained to be altered was the beards which they each sported, but the hair on their face could wait one more day. David reached down and picked up his bible, and the missionaries walked in the direction of the meeting place to do what they had always looked forward to with much relish. They were about to minister to the needs of their flock. Soon they were joined by the two women and all of them walked contentedly, arm in arm.

When they reached the meeting place, they found that the construction, which had only begun the day they were arrested, was now complete, and the converted Delaware had done a remarkable job of making it as close to what David, himself would have wanted. There were now crude benches in the center of the area — enough for everyone in the flock. A huge fire burned to the front of the gathered assembly, and immediately to the left of a beautifully constructed altar that had been made. David beamed with pride as he walked to his place at the altar. His vision into the audience was somewhat limited by the unsteady light of the fire, but what faces that he could see were beaming as broadly as his own. To the rear of the altar stood a large cross, which had been placed into the ground. It was a splendid effort at recreating the place of worship that had been destroyed by Pomoacan's men on orders from Captain Elliot.

To each side of the altar was a smaller bench, and John and Sarah took their seats there, while William sat next to Susan on the one to the right as

David laid the good book upon the altar, still smiling broadly. "My wonderful, wonderful brothers and sisters, we have missed you dearly. We prayed for you daily while we were gone, and God has been merciful to us all." As he spoke, however, David and the other two men could sense the sadness that enveloped many of the flock. Audible sobs could be heard in areas to the rear and to the sides. Each of the men peered intently into the night air, trying, without much success, to locate the sources of the anguish.

Continuing with the news of their arrest and trial, David left out very few details. The members of the flock were keenly interested in the news concerning Wannantuha and Bird Nest, because each of the Delaware chiefs had close relatives within the flock. Even Captain Pipe had relatives among the converted Delaware now living in the Upper Sandusky region, and after the meeting, all three missionaries, for several days to come, would be almost constantly deluged with requests for information about this chief or that. David also spoke of the kindly and ingenious ways of the late Silas Whitfield, and of how much he had meant to their ultimate freedom — and to the very freedom, however painful, that the flock enjoyed at this exact moment. He also told the shivering audience that Major de Peyster had agreed to have Pomoacan and his many warriors return all the personal goods and supplies that had been confiscated in Gnadenhutten so many weeks prior. This drew a loud, enthusiastic response from the flock, who had done without for so long.

"What has been done in regards to our food supply for the flock?" David inquired of some of the senior converts, who traditionally took the closest seats to the altar. Levi stood and said, "Brother David, you will be proud to learn that we have gathered every berry and fruit that is fit to eat from everywhere within a one-day walk of this spot. We have also gathered and have managed to store some of the roots and mushrooms upon which we survived when we were first brought to this place, but I fear that the meager stores that we now possess will not feed the flock for long come winter, and winter approaches soon. Some of the men have taken up the old ways, but only of a necessity, Brother David, of hunting live game with the tools of our ancestors. It has been the only way that we have survived thus far. Please forgive us for our transgressions."

All three of the missionaries were deeply touched by the honest and plaintive confession of the man who stood in the glow of the fire before them. David raised both hands with palms out and open as if to let them all know that their regression back to the use of bows and arrows and other means of survival was by no means a blight on any of their souls. And he told them as much. He also told them of how, since the forced march from their village that he had resorted to using his bible as a pillow, and after a few low, audible gasps, everyone relaxed and laughed about their reverend's utilitarian and inventive nature. David also told the flock that Major de Peyster had given orders for Pomoacan and his warriors to return the goods and supplies taken from them earlier. Then David asked of the five members of the flock who had left, with Pomoacan's blessing, to gather some grain from the neglected crops at Gnadenhutten.

Samuel, one of those men, rose from off to the right and walked forward to a point where he could be seen in the glow of the fire. Levi, noticing that the fire was ebbing, began to stoke the flames with more wood, before taking his seat again. "Brother David," began Samuel in an apologetic tone, "the party that left here to retrieve grain from our village at Gnadenhutten arrived there in very good time, but we were set upon by a party of armed militiamen from Fort Pitt." "Were there any casualties, Samuel?" asked David, before the man could finish his story. "No sir, none of us were harmed, but we did not succeed in our mission," said the young man. He continued, "As soon as we approached our village, the militiamen sprang from the brush alongside the village and took us prisoner. Because we were not dressed in the manner of civilized people, the rebels would not believe that we were Christians. We were taken back to Fort Pitt as hostile prisoners and were told that we would be hanged for aiding the British. At Fort Pitt, the militia commander questioned and examined us for several days before he was satisfied that we were of the Moravian mission, then he released us. But they kept our horse, so there was no way that we could gather and return with any grain. Brother David, we are all so ashamed....." and he hung his head and could not continue.

William was seated closest to Samuel, and he rushed to offer solace to the young man. He put his arm around Samuel's shoulder, and spoke reassuringly to him, and gradually he spoke again. With William still beside him in support, Samuel continued, "Brother David, I must warn you that despite what you and the others have just endured at the hands of the British in Detroit, things at Fort Pitt bode no better for any of us. While at Fort Pitt, we were cursed and spat upon by most of the people. They did not see us as men or as Christians. To them, we were simply murderers. There is a great deal of hate in the Ohio Territory for all Indians, and I am afraid that you and your assistants are as much outcast as any Indian. No one seems to have love in their hearts, Brother David. No one!"

"Samuel, you and the others are to be commended for your efforts to retrieve the grain at our former village. You did everything the right way, but you are wrong," answered David. "Though we may be the only ones, there is still love in our hearts. My heart, yours, and in the hearts of every member of the Moravian mission," he said. "Amen," said John loudly, and a chorus of "Amens" echoed in the night air. Samuel then returned to his seat, as did William, and David continued, "We have all been set upon by first one side and then the other, but we are still together, and we still have love in our hearts. Has any one of you, man, woman, or child lost that love?" He looked in all directions for anyone bold enough to answer that question in the affirmative. David stared at them for a long time without saying anything, then asked again — "Well, have you?" His voice was now almost a shout, and it was very unlike David Zeisberger, who was not thought to be a fire and brimstone sort. The tone of his voice, however, was invigoratingly loud, and the assembly answered him with a slow but resounding, "NO!"

"I thought not," said David with a quiet smile upon his face, which brought similar smiles from the crowd before him, because they had first thought him to be angry. Susan however, knew otherwise, and had covered her lower face with her hands so that the rest of the congregation could not see that she was stifling a large grin. It amused her greatly that her husband had suddenly taken to this unfamiliar brand of preaching from the pulpit. David went on, "Probably one of the most unpopular men on the face of this earth was our savior, Jesus. He had a small number of those who believed in Him, but even more who doubted. And He had an entire nation and army who hated Him enough to slay Him, or so they reckoned. And all of this time, He never lost the love in His heart — even for those who nailed Him to the wood. Our Lord suffered the ultimate sacrifice and never lost that love, and we shall do the same. We are being tested — no doubt about that, but we shall all persevere. Our Christian beliefs are too powerful to succumb to the wills of those in Detroit, Fort Pitt, or any other place. We are God's children, and we shall go on spreading His word and His love, and that love will never stop. Let us pray."

"O Lord, we are here tonight — in this place — not to try to escape from our problems, though we would like to! O God, how we desire only to be left alone. We would but withdraw into a distant ivory tower, far enough distant and behind high walls; to close our eyes, our ears, and our minds, and forget the turmoil and war, evil and injustices that are about us. We desire not to know of hunger, pain, suffering and death, and pray they never exist. If we could but go about our own pursuits unfettered and unmolested. But God we cannot!

Even now, we are all too aware of the unreasonable demands, threats, and violence, but they are cries of frustrated, unhappy, and impatient people — and we must not lose the love in our hearts for them. O Lord, You know the ill-conceived words that have been hurled upon us, the bitterness and jealousy that has poisoned life as we know it. Cruel minds abound with evil and explosive thoughts. Protect us O Lord that we are safe in this place from those who would seek to do us further harm, and let us go forth and spread Your love and guide us that our thoughts and actions might be the same as Thine, in the name of peace and love. Amen."

For a long time following the prayer service that night, David and the two other missionaries were surrounded by many of the flock who wished to convey personal hellos, thanks, or to inquire about news of a relative among the many Delaware still serving the British at Detroit and other places in the territory. Susan and Sarah willingly gave up their places at their husbands' sides during this time. Among the first of the women who greeted the three returned Moravians was Mary, the young woman who had named her baby after David. The tears in her eyes betrayed the message that she was about to deliver, and David hugged her close as she sobbed. Baby David had died only a day or two after the trio had been taken off to Detroit, and there was no doubt in anyone's mind that the harsh treatment at the hands of the British and the Wyandot had been responsible in great measure.

The three men who had been gone for so long also learned that several other members of the flock had perished as well, and their hearts were extremely heavy for the loss of such close and devoted friends. A small cemetery had been set up in the clearing immediately to the rear of the assembly area, and in the morning, David, John, and William would visit the gravesites and say a special prayer for each of the departed friends. It was now clear to the men why they had heard such sorrowful weeping among the flock during the prayer service. When the last member of the flock had wandered home to their own crude shelters, the three missionaries scattered the ashes and dying embers of the once roaring campfire and began the short walk with the two wives to their own shelters.

As David and Susan prepared for sleep that night, they talked of the individual miseries and tragedies that had befallen the members of their flock and they vowed to do their best to give as much comfort, love, and aid as possible. John and Sarah had much the similar conversation in their shelter. After adding a few new sticks of firewood to the small blaze which he had used to heat his chilled bones, William looked up to find Ruth, one of the senior women in the flock nervously standing just in the edge of the night. "Yes, Ruth, what is it, sister?" asked William, who failed to notice that the woman carried the blanket which had been given John by the English traders while he lay sick and fevered on the march. "Here, Reverend," she said, "we would all want you or one of the others to have the blanket on your first night back. It is our gift to you, and all that we can give." William began to fumble for words to express his thanks as well as the thanks of the others, and to insist that she keep and use the heavy cloth, but she had turned and zipped back to her own family before he could stop her. "These are the most wonderful people in the world," said William aloud to himself, though no one could have disagreed.

In the morning, about an hour after dawn, a young male member of the flock awakened David and Susan from their sleep with his shouts from the area of the beach, "Father David, come quick, the Wyandot have gone!" Arising quickly, and donning their outer garments against the brisk morning breeze, they hurriedly made their way in the direction of where Pomoacan and his men had previously camped. Sure enough, they had left quietly at dawn. A moment of terror then gripped David, and soon John and William, who had by now joined he and Sarah. The men slowly turned to look in the direction of where their confiscated possessions had been kept by Pomoacan. From their vantage point, they could not see all that they hoped and they started slowly toward the supplies, then more quickly, until all five of the missionaries found themselves running.

Upon reaching the supplies, it became sickeningly evident that Pomoacan and his men had plundered the goods and possessions belonging to the hapless members of the flock. Not every thing was missing, to be sure, but most of the really important items such as tools were gone, along with blankets and housewares that would be vital if the flock was to survive the coming winter months. In fact, thought David and the others, their very survival depended in great measure on the goods that were missing from among the supplies that lay scattered upon the ground. John forlornly sank to his knees and raised his eyes to heaven and managed a quiet, "How much more, O Lord?" before he was consoled by first Sarah, and then David, Susan, and William. The trials and tribulations that were by now being foisted upon the innocent members of the flock in never ending succession were beginning to wear on the patience of even these trusting messengers of God. In a short time, Levi and some of the others began to arrive at the scene, and before noon, the entire flock had learned of their latest misfortune.

Most of the mens' clothing had been spared by the Wyandot, and there were a fair amount of small, but useful utensils strewn about here and there. Luckily, the Wyandot had overlooked one straight razor among the supplies, and each of the three men would put it to good use later in the day. William quickly organized a group of the women of the flock to collect all of the items — intact or not and take them to the storage shelter where most of the flock's store of berries and fruits were cached.

William also prayed silently to himself that the Wyandot had not raided those supplies, but his fears were groundless, for the shelter was close enough to some of the members' own shelters as to prevent such an occurrence. At the shelter, the women sorted and stacked items neatly in piles like clothing, bolts of cloth, and even scraps of things thought to be potentially useful. The shelter would become a community store, where any member could simply take what he or she felt necessary. The Moravians had taught their flock so well about sharing and having love and compassion for their fellow man that greed or selfishness was simply not a concern. It never had been, nor would it ever be, among these selfless people.

The three missionaries then brought forth the small amount of supplies that de Peyster had given them upon their departure from Detroit, and they, too, were added to the stores in the shelter. Because none of the converted Delaware had yet acquired the white man's penchant for hot coffee, the three missionaries kept the small supply of coffee with which they had returned. They also kept and shared the original, solitary tin cup for the purpose of brewing their coffee, but were more than willing to share it with whomever needed it at any given time. Since the three had been gone, many of the flock had worked feverishly to fend off some of the ravages of living in the wild, and they had crafted clay pots and plates which had been permanized by baking in an earthen oven, set in a bank of clay. Nothing fancy, to be sure, but certainly useful. Susan and Sarah had both become quite talented at fashioning the ceramic vessels. Those pieces also were added to the stores, until it would be possible for everyone to once more possess their own goods and belongings — if, indeed that would ever come to pass.

In the few days that followed, David sought and received a volunteer from among the flock who would attempt to reach the nearest Moravian settlement, at Friedensstadt, which was about 40 miles north of Fort Pitt. The young man, Noah, was to relate the misfortune of the Moravians and their members to the missionary at Friedensstadt, who was to then either send help and supplies or arrange to have the main Moravian settlement in Bethlehem provide assistance. It would be one of the rare times in his long career as a missionary that David Zeisberger would ever ask the church for assistance, but it was now imperative, and he had no misgivings about his requests. Noah was needlessly instructed to stay clear of both British and colonial patrols, and the recent experience with the Wyandot had also left the young Delaware wary of any other Indian. Early on the morning of December 2, 1782, Noah set off on his mission to Friedensstadt, with the good wishes of the entire flock. It was the last that anyone would ever see or hear of Noah again, as he never reached Friedensstadt, and his fate was never learned. The dangers of the Ohio Territory were simply not confined to the utmost reaches — disasters were a reoccurring peril for those who dared to stay.

The approaching winter was almost upon the ill-fated members of the flock, and they worked feverishly to put up their best defense. Each of the individual shelters had been enlarged and shored up with additional timbers to where they could withstand the most fearsome of Erie's legendary storms. Coarse mats had been woven from among the many varieties of saw grass abundant near the water's edge, and these made fine bedding for frigid nights. The members of the flock were remarkably industrious and artful in their zeal to head off the ravages of winter, and many of their natural Indian skills were put to good use. The hunters among the flock were still able to make fine bows and arrows and the younger members were taught the ways of their parents and grandparents as they learned to hunt the many kinds of game nearby. Deer, rabbits, squirrel, and pheasant were regularly taken, and fishing was very good in some of the bays where the Sandusky River met and mingled with the big lake. There was a great need for grain, however, as bread had not been a part of their diet for a long time, save for the stale hard tack which the three missionaries had actually come to look forward to while confined in the Detroit stockade.

It was decided that at some time in the near future, when provisions were adequate in both number and protective qualities, that a large group of the flock would eventually return to the more than 300 acres of neglected fields in the Tuscarawas valley. They would attempt to salvage what dry grain could be found, and also to bring back any implements or supplies which had neither been burned or otherwise destroyed by Pomoacan's warriors. The small quantity of seed which the three had been given by de Peyster's quartermaster would not suffice for a crop to sustain more than 400 people. More seed might be obtained from the fields in the Tuscarawas valley.

It was estimated that more than a hundred volunteers would be needed for the long and perilous journey so that many baskets of grain could be salvaged and returned to the area of the Upper Sandusky. Rather than have such a large number of the men of the flock go, it was decided that entire families would make the trip. Besides, none of the families wished to be separated for what was sure to be an extended period of time. For morale purposes alone, it made sense that women and children should be allowed to accompany their husbands and fathers. Life on the trail could not be any more perilous than facing a devastating winter along Lake Erie's edges. Or so they thought.

In preparation for their trip back to Gnadenhutten, men, women, and children all spent their time weaving baskets which would be needed for the grain they hoped to retrieve. Again, Susan and Sarah worked extremely hard at crafting the woven baskets to assist in the retrieval of grain. The overall plan was flawless and remarkably sensible — each person constructed a basket which would fit inside another, which would fit inside another, and so on until four baskets could be easily carried inside one that was larger. In this way, smaller members of the flock could carry the empty baskets south, while the burden of the full baskets would be shared by the physically able on the return trip. It would also allow heavier or bulkier provisions to be carried on the outbound trip by the larger members of the families.

During Christmas, it was so cold that David went from shelter to shelter to give all of the members his blessings, rather than have the entire flock attempt to assemble in the icy outdoor area. Susan stayed behind — it was that cold. After a heavy snowfall, and just as the plummeting temperatures set in, the entire landscape, for as far as the eye could see, was transformed into a beautiful but crippling, white-clad environment. Nightly prayer service was canceled indefinitely and David or one of the assistants would make "shelter calls" as needed to reinforce the members' spirituality.

David and Susan spent most of their inside time playing checkers on a custom made checker-board mat woven as a Christmas gift by one of his close friends from among the flock. The game was complete with wooden checkers, which had been delicately sliced from dark and light branches, and functioned as well as any game either of them had seen. Occasionally, either John or William would take part by challenging the winner in a kind of small tournament, but for the most part, the three missionary men spent the majority of their time planning for the spring planting season and the months ahead. William easily became the most proficient checker player in camp, and seemed to win all of the tournaments. He found, after only a short time, that opponents were beginning to be hard to come by.

As the days wore on, stronger and more frequent winds blew in from the north, across a now frozen lake which simply made the gusts even more destructive, and made the existing temperature appear unbelievably lower than it was in actuality. As luck would have it, the winter that was to descend upon the members of the flock as they fought to survive would be the coldest imaginable. The Moravians and their converts could not have faced a more debilitating winter unless they had chosen to camp at either of the global poles.

For a period of 22 days, the temperature at the camp near the lake stayed well below freezing, and was magnified far to the negative side on the strength of the prevailing north winds. Drinking water was only available by boiling chunks of ice in the, by now, well-traveled tin cup. More than one person in camp made the mistake of grasping the cup too firmly, only to have large patches of their skin pulled off after they became firmly frozen to the metal surface, including poor John. It was a very painful injury that would heal so very slowly in the Arctic-like climate.

Near the first week of February, the weather began to break slightly, though it still was miserably cold outside, to be certain. The freezing temperatures had abated somewhat, but not yet enough to the point that any extended activity could be carried out. Food stores were shrinking drastically and even the hunters were unable to consistently bring meat to the table. As any hunter knows, game will also take refuge in very cold, biting weather, and there were simply too few signs of wildlife outdoors. David had been regularly monitoring the levels of the food stores and when it became so evident that the supply would soon be exhausted, the long anticipated trip to Gnadenhutten became a necessary reality.

Word was passed among the members that the trip would soon be getting underway, and the people were preparing as rapidly and as best they could. Snowshoes were made for each of the hundred or so persons who would take part in the return to Gnadenhutten, so that any difficulty in walking in deep, or icy snow would be minimized. Many of the thin woven, more flexible mats had been carefully altered and pieced together to form a crude but efficient kind of outerwear for protection against the weather and wind. A fair share of the flock's food stores had to be, by necessity, taken by the departing families, even though what they took with them and what was left for the others would not suffice either of their intended purposes.

The decision to return to their former villages had become, ultimately, a life or death situation, that had been forced upon them through the selfish and mistaken actions of others. If they stayed in the area of the Upper Sandusky, a fair number of them would slowly perish, for there was no food to be gleaned from nature, and that which had been stored now ebbed dangerously low. If they made the trip to Gnadenhutten, there *was* at least some chance that enough grain could be culled from the ruined crops to save the entire flock. The decision to go was simple, and when the temperature rose above the frost mark on February 6th, word went round that the trip would commence at dawn on the following morning.

At dawn, despite the fact that a fresh three inch snow had fallen overnight, the departing families quickly and excitedly assembled in the ice-crusted and snow-covered assembly area. All of the members of the flock were there except for one or two very ill members, who remained in their shelters. Amid much hugging, tears, and a quick but heartfelt sendoff prayer from Reverend Zeisberger, the departing families headed south toward the interior of the Ohio Territory. The only positive aspect about the departure of so many of these dedicated converts was that they would have Erie's icy winds to their backs for the outbound portion of the trip. The *only* thing positive.

February 7, 1782

Upon leaving the frozen shores of Lake Erie, the returning party of just over a hundred and twenty headed south, up a slight rise. Although no "leader" had been chosen or even thought necessary, Isaac, would eventually assume the mantle of leadership. In the beginning, Isaac had been near the front of the new "column," and as each new day began, Isaac would again lead his people south. Isaac also selected each evening's camp site. It was not so much that Isaac had taken command, but that the other members of the column did not seek a position of leadership. There was no animosity or doubt over Isaac's role, anywhere in the group.

Since becoming a Christian, almost ten years earlier, Isaac had become a popular figure among the converts. Nearly everyone admired him for his boldness in debating with David over the length of a man's hair prior to being accepted into the mission. Because he had used the biblical Samson's hair as grounds for keeping his own long hair intact, he had also earned the occasional nickname of "Samson," from among some of the flock. He accepted the ribbing in very good nature, too, for he indeed was the most Samsonesque of all the flock. Before the forced march and the extreme shortage of food, Isaac's physique was proportionate to his height, which was well over six feet tall. Before becoming drawn, and somewhat emaciated, he had a very muscular body. He also had the longest hair of any converted Delaware.

Isaac was now 38 years old, and was accompanied by his wife, Leta, and two small sons, Jacob and George. An experienced and expert woodsman, Isaac was deft at reading trails and he also had a keen sense of direction. In assuming the lead spot in the column south, Isaac also was careful to set a pace that was not only comfortable to the others behind him, but was also expedient enough to be able to be of value to those still at the lake. He was a very practical person, and ideally suited to lead the expedition back to Gnadenhutten.

The woven-mat snowsuits served the column members well, and there was minimum discomfort from the weather as the group made its way south again. Because the mats were not as flexible as hides or cloth, there was some initial problems with rubbing and chafing. After several days of wear, however, the mats began to feel quite natural. The snow shoes were invaluable. Without them, travel would have been utterly impossible, as waist deep drifts were encountered and traversed without incident. The supplies that were taken by the column members were monitored closely by each individual family, and appeared to be slim, though adequate. They were also closely watched by Isaac, who would be the first to share his rations with anyone.

Each evening's campsites began at dusk, which came much earlier at this time of year, and each new day began just after dawn. Isaac also led a simple prayer service each night around his own campfire. The service began with only his family, but included virtually the whole column in just three days. Except for the one main meal in the evening, all other food was consumed in small amounts while on the move. A very short rest stop was permitted near the middle of the day. If nature called a member of the column, he or she had the sole responsibility of re-catching the column. Usually that person's family lagged behind to provide security or assistance for the pausing member. The position of members and their families in the column was thus constantly changing.

Other than one near-blizzard just two days into the trip, and another two inch snowfall at about the midway point, the weather was cold, but generally cooperative all the way back. During the day, temperatures climbed to the mid or upper 30s, and at night, it was always at or near the frost. Large campfires and close sleeping arrangements kept the members warm, and all remarked that they were much more comfortable on *this* trip. The free march south was much more exhilarating to the returnees' morale.

On February 17th, a group of eight pro-British Delaware warriors, westbound, encountered the column at about its midpoint, and late in the afternoon. Although the Delaware could easily tell that the members were Indians also, they were startled by the strange winter dress of the members. These Delaware were returning from a successful raid on colonial units nearer to Fort Pitt. After learning that the group were Zeisberger's converts, the Delaware began laughing hysterically at the make-shift protective clothing being worn. The two groups also began a friendly reunion which lasted into the night, as the column and the warriors set up a joint camp for the day at that exact site. Once the warriors had learned of the circumstances of their converted relatives — and there were many — they ceased laughing and became very angry, vowing revenge on Pomoacan and his men, who were not well liked by the Delaware anyway.

Although Isaac and the other Christians asked them not to exact revenge upon Pomoacan, the tragic predicament of the Moravian converts would not soon be forgotten by these warriors. After giving much of their provisions to the pitiful column, the scouting party bid them a safe journey, and the two groups parted. Though the members of the column would never learn of it, later that same year, Pomoacan would die from a slashed throat, inflicted by avenging members of this same scouting party.

The return to Gnadenhutten would be made even more swift than the previous trip in the opposite direction for three reasons. First, the latter trip was *not* made under duress. There were no Wyandot guards on this occasion. Second, there was a pronounced, but unspoken sense of urgency to this mission, unlike the dread of each step of the first trip. Third, most of the way from Lake Erie to Gnadenhutten would be over terrain which featured a gradual downhill slope. The second half of the present trip would encounter problems of a much different nature.

On February 25th, the column at last reached their former homes at Gnadenhutten, along the Tuscarawas River. An eerie quiet now enveloped the village where many of the younger members of the column had been born. From a vantage point just across the river, in the same spot that Elliot and Pomoacan and their men had camped, the column assembled in a rather large huddle and looked at the village with a profound sadness, almost hesitant to go any closer. Isaac motioned the group forward, however, and they crossed the shallow, but icy river with some difficulty.

Only two of the original structures remained standing, and they were virtually uninhabitable, but would provide a great deal of protection for members who would spend the night there. Most of the members just looked about and shook their heads with bewilderment. They could not fathom why anyone would want to be so cruel to other human beings. While the others were preparing the two skeletal structures for camping, Isaac chose to walk out into the fields and see if there were anything which could be salvaged and returned to the others.

In the field, he shook a light covering of sparse snow from several prone plants and peeled back dry yellow husks to reveal row after row of hard, bright yellow corn. He smiled to himself, knowing that he had, thus far been successful, and things suddenly looked brighter. Soon he was joined by Leta, who also checked a plant or two. Isaac placed an arm around his wife and said, "You know, Leta, Reverend Zeisberger is right — God is surely smiling on us. All this destruction and here in this field we find seeds for a new beginning. Life is amazing." Leta and Isaac then walked hand in hand back toward the others, eager to share their good news.

In the area which had been the main street, there lay several rotting carcasses, now frozen, and partially snow covered, but another grim reminder of the utter waste and destruction that had been visited upon the peaceful converts. Just about the only thing which had not been destroyed at Gnadenhutten was the cemetery, which looked peaceful and serene under a patchwork blanket of light snow. The tracks of a single rabbit laced its way diagonally across the plot, but otherwise it was undisturbed. Before night, many in the group would visit the cemetery to pay respects to those left behind in the cold earth. Isaac led the relatives in a simple, though touching prayer service.

One hundred miles due east of Gnadenhutten, at precisely the same time that the column members were catching their first glimpse of their former village, a group of angry colonial militiamen were busily preparing for action. A Delaware raiding party — the same warriors who had encountered the column in route to Gnadenhutten — had recently entered the area and attacked two groups of settlers who lived just beyond Fort Pitt. The people in and around Fort Pitt were frightened, angry and in a retaliatory mood.

The county lieutenant for the Washington County, Pennsylvania militia, James Marshal, was busy attempting to muster his troops to mount an attack on the hostile Indians of the Ohio Territory. Particularly those found in the Muskingum region. Marshal had gone door to door, and word of mouth had already spread of the damage that had been done, and of the lives that had been taken by the marauders.

The militiamen would be led by Colonel David Williamson, a colonial regular from Fort Pitt. Colonel Williamson was a short, stocky man of 50 years. A merchant by trade, he had offered his services early on in the war, and had seen considerable combat in the Ohio Territory — both in the outlying areas and also around Fort Pitt. His experience at fighting Indians was, however, limited. In fact, his only contact with Indians had been to see an occasional prisoner at the fort. His value to the Washington County men lay in the fact that he had experience in leading large numbers of men. By the time that Lieutenant Marshal had done his job, Williamson's command would consist of 55 men, most with no real military experience. Their mission objectives were simple: capture or kill any hostile Indians that they encountered.

Upon preparing for their departure, Colonel Williamson selected five of his best woodsmen to be his advance scouts. This group would start ahead of the main body, and would maintain a buffer distance of approximately five miles. In the event that a large body of hostile Indians were discovered by the advance scouts, the rest of the main body would have a better chance of survival. The scouts were all expert marksmen and were fearless, for their positions to the front would be extremely dangerous.

At a briefing, before anyone began the mission, either scouts or main company, Colonel Williamson reminded each of the men of the existence of Zeisberger's three missions in the Muskingum region. He stressed that the Delaware Indians which had become converts, were not hostile and were *not* to be engaged. Williamson had been briefed by veteran Indian fighters, and he knew that the Wyandot, Shawnee, and Mingo represented the gravest threats to colonials. He was also told that, for the most part, the members of the Delaware tribe were not a problem, because most had been Christianized by the Moravians. Those at Fort Pitt were unaware, however, of the situation involving Zeisberger and his converts and their protracted persecution by the British and their Indian allies.

Meanwhile, back at Gnadenhutten, the members were looking through the rubble that had been their village to retrieve whatever they could for use in their new settlement to the far north. A small cache of candles were found, two unused livestock harnesses, and some small hand tools. All would eventually be useful. A large cooper's mallet was found, and it was simply leaned up against the wall outside one of the two remaining structures until it would be needed. Several of the families that had made the trip back to Gnadenhutten were from the other settlements at New Schoenbrunn and Salem, and they wanted to try to reclaim some of their possessions that had been hurriedly left behind also. They met with Isaac to discuss the matter and he agreed that it would be safe for them to return for a small salvage operation. Besides, they reasoned, there were also crops left behind at the other two sites, and they took their grain baskets along for an additional harvest.

Salem was just a short distance away, to the south, but New Schoenbrunn was much further to the north, and each of the two parties set out early so as to complete their mission in a timely manner. Upon their arrival at the respective villages, they sadly learned that Pomoacan's men had also razed both the villages. They scrounged around in the hovel and ashes and managed to locate small, insignificant items, but concentrated instead, on filling the grain baskets. The weather during this time, turned from very nice to extremely forbidding, and then to a very warm spell, which caused a large scale thaw. For two days, members at each of the three sites were forced to halt their work and simply take shelter. When they emerged with the thaw, they worked with unbridled enthusiasm.

On March 5th, as the members at New Schoenbrunn gathered the last of the grain in the field, they were unaware that they were being watched from the brush by Colonel Williamson's scouting party. Quietly the scouts had worked their way close enough to the former mission to see that all of the people there were Indians. The leader of the scouts, Robert Everett, cautioned his men to do nothing because they were outnumbered. Everett and the others believed those at New Schoenbrunn to be hostile Delaware — perhaps even the same group which had raided near Fort Pitt. The strange straw coverings they wore on their bodies also lent credence to this theory. Everett sent one of his men back to alert Colonel Williamson's men of the "hostiles" that had been found. In the meanwhile, the other scouts would continue on to the south.

As the four militia scouts were about half way between Gnadenhutten and New Schoenbrunn, they came upon an isolated 16 year old boy, Joseph, a son of one of the families at Gnadenhutten, who was attempting to catch a meal for the members of his party. Joseph's mistake was that he had stripped down to the waist, as he fished a quiet pool in the Tuscarawas River. He had also found a large turkey feather on the ground, which he stuck in his thick black hair. Believing him to be a hostile, a militia marksman dropped the youth from a distance of 75 yards with a single musket ball. When the scouts went to check on their casualty, they discovered that he had only been wounded in the shoulder. Begging for mercy, Joseph was hacked to death with several tomahawk blows and then scalped.

When the messenger scout reached Williamson's men, he told them that he believed a large raiding party of hostile Delaware were presently located at New Schoenbrunn, and for some unknown reason, Colonel Williamson then diverted his 50 or so men south toward Gnadenhutten, bypassing New Schoenbrunn altogether. It is possible that both the scouts and the main body had planned originally to meet first at Gnadenhutten, and then to move in other directions, but by doing so, the members at New Schoenbrunn were completely unaware of the presence of the militia in the area.

Having completed their grain gathering mission, those families at New Schoenbrunn, which numbered about twenty, began the short trek south to Gnadenhutten. When they reached the spot on the river where Joseph had been fishing, they found his body and were horrified at what had occurred. It was obvious to them that Joseph had been slaughtered and scalped by whites, and probably militiamen. They hurried on toward the others at Gnadenhutten, only to come upon signs of a large movement of troops from the east, which, of course, had been Williamson's men. Frightened of the consequences of dealing with the militiamen, especially after the ghastly discovery of Joseph's body, the members quickly decided to flee the area and return immediately to David's group with the grain that had already been gathered. It was definitely the right thing to do.

At Gnadenhutten, the four scouts now unobtrusively spied upon the activity of the members there from a vantage point across the river. When they saw Colonel Williamson and his men approach the main village from the east, with weapons raised, the scouts closed in from the west and sealed the village, unarmed and harmless as they were, in the middle. As the men approached the converts, they were shouting for the people there to raise their hands. Dumbfounded at what was occurring, the men and women in the field, simply put down their baskets and did as they were instructed.

Isaac, with hands raised high, walked in the direction of Colonel Williamson, who by now was easily identifiable because of the way that he was barking orders. "Hold it right there, you murdering heathen," a militiaman yelled at Isaac. Isaac stopped and turned in the direction of the man who had just yelled at him, and said, "We are peaceful Christians at work for the Lord. Why are you here?" With that, Isaac was smashed across the brow with the butt of the colonial musket and he spun to the ground with blood gushing from his wound. Leta ran instinctively to his aid and very nearly received a similar blow, but another man grabbed the gun and prevented the blow. As she tended to her husband, she said tearfully, "We are all members of Reverend Zeisberger's Moravian mission, we mean no harm to you or anyone, can you not see that? Look — we have our children here and we are all starving. We are simply gathering grain!" She directed her plea to no one in particular, as she looked from man to man.

A few of the men were advising Williamson that these were the same Delaware who had raided their homes in Pennsylvania, and they were convincing. Coupled with his own inexperience with Indians, Williamson was quickly persuaded that *these* were clearly hostiles, never mind that they spoke near perfect English, wore mostly the clothes of the white man, had close cropped hair, were using Christian phrases, and in a village which was known to be used by Moravian converts. A few of the men even began to doubt that these people were hostile, but by now Williamson and the others had been caught up in the fever of the moment.

Questioned by Williamson, Isaac, who was by now on one knee, with the assistance of Leta, again repeated that they were Christian converts of the Moravians. "Are there any other of your members about?" asked Williamson, already aware of the group at New Schoenbrunn. Isaac, fearing for the others' safety, then said, "No, sir — just us." "You miserable liar," said the man to Williamson's right, as he placed his musket against Isaac's head, prepared to fire, "we seen a bunch more of your kind up-river at the other place. See how they lie, Colonel?" Realizing that he had been caught in a lie, Isaac now truthfully disclosed that another group of their people were also down river at Salem.

"Take 16 men and fetch the others here from down-river," Williamson ordered Lieutenant Marshal, knowing that Salem was only a short distance away. "I reckon that the other group up-river will soon enough come back here, and if they don't, we can get them on our way back." he continued. "Yes, sir," said Marshal, as he began to pick his 16 men. "Sergeant," the Colonel ordered, "start separating these prisoners. I want all the women and children put in that one cabin, and all the men in the other. I have to figure out what we're going to do with them." "I know what we gotta do with 'em, and by God, I'm ready!" came an anonymous volunteer solution from the rear. "Now hold on, here. Nobody's going to do anything until I give the order. Is that clear?" the militia commander asked as he scanned his men for dissenters.

Marshal and his men reached Salem in a very short time and handled the members there with a much different manner. The militiamen simply marched right up to the main group and Lieutenant Marshal said, "We have your other group just up-river, and if you know what's good for you, you'll come along too." Peacefully and obediently, the members at Salem obeyed, and they carried their full baskets of grain back to Gnadenhutten. In each of their minds they knew that something had gone wrong, but they did not say anything. Yet. Better to let Isaac do the talking for the group, they were all thinking.

By the time Marshal and his men arrived back at Gnadenhutten with the prisoners from Salem, it was nearly dark. Those members with Marshal were separated, as had the others been, and placed in the appropriate cabin. None of the prisoners had given any of their captors any problems whatsoever. There were no attempts to escape and the prisoners made no noise, they merely talked quietly among themselves, and later they began to pray and sing hymns. From the cabin which housed the women and children, occasionally a young child could be heard crying, but that was not unusual. The militiamen camped in the area between the two structures and posted guards — needlessly — to prevent the prisoners from escaping.

In the morning, Williamson dispatched Marshal and his same 16 men to New Schoenbrunn to bring back the members that were there, unaware that they had already fled back toward Lake Erie. When Marshal returned, he reported to Williamson that the up-river village was clean. He also told that they had found a young Indian's body that had been hacked to death, shot, and scalped. Marshal said that he believed it to be the work of a band of hostiles, and the four men who had, in fact, done the deed said nothing. Anti-Indian fever among Williamson's troops was exceptionally high, and every little occurrence simply continued to fan the flames. Colonel Williamson said, "I'll decide later tonight," as he yawned and stretched, "what we have to do. Do you have any suggestions?"

Marshal then told the Colonel that several of his men were expressing reservations about keeping these particular Indians as prisoners. "The men — at least some of them — believe that we have captured a bunch of Moravian Christians. There's talk among some of them that we ought to just turn them loose and go on back to the fort." Colonel Williamson then swallowed hard and said, "What would you think the men would say if I put it to a vote?" "I think most of them would say, 'Kill 'em!' Look Colonel, almost every man here has lost either a relative, a friend, or neighbor to some damn Indian, and they want some revenge. I only wish you could've seen what they did to that poor lad up the river — you wouldn't be asking anybody's opinion, sir. It was ugly. Real ugly!" said the Lieutenant. "Call the men to muster, Lieutenant. I'll put it to them tonight," said the commander.

Just after dark, around a roaring campfire, the men assembled in their usual, predetermined muster positions. Williamson addressed his men, "Look men — we have us almost a hundred Indians here, and I know that some of you are feeling a little squeamish about it — thinking we got us mostly Moravian converts, but I'm not so sure. There's a badly butchered and scalped boy laying a little up river from here, and I think these people did it. I, personally think they ought to pay for this and for a whole lot of other attacks on innocent people. But I respect your opinion, and I'm going to give you a chance to be heard on it. How many of you think we ought to take them back to the fort?" asked Williamson.

About ten men raised their hands immediately, amid catcalls from some of the others, and slowly more hands went up. ".....thirteen, fourteen, fifteen, sixteen," counted Williamson out loud. "How many of you don't want them to go anywhere?" he asked, and most of them began jumping and whooping with delight in an almost uncontrollable frenzy.

"All right — all right, settle down!" he said as he tried to regain a little order, a large smirking grin on his face. "In the morning, you sixteen soldiers will go on back to the fort, ahead of the rest of us. We'll hang around here for a while, and be along directly," he said, again with a smile, and again the men cheered and stomped their approval. "Better turn in now and get some sleep, and put some more wood on that fire there, it looks like it might get cold as hell tonight. Dismissed!" he said simply.

During the night, the temperature did drop sharply, causing a great deal of discomfort for the soldiers. The sixteen that had voted to spare the Indians were sleeping very poorly, anyway. The other 39 went to sleep easily, as if they planned to do something very ordinary in the morning. In the cabins where the prisoners had been gathered, the people inside were not sleeping, either. Leta, with her ear to the cracks in the cabin closest to the muster, had overheard the Colonel's vote and subsequent decision, and she did not like what she had heard. With a sense of foreboding disaster, most of the adults — women *and* men — were spending the night singing hymns and praying. They scarcely noticed that the weather had once again turned extremely cold.

At dawn, the sixteen dissenting soldiers were up and about and ready to go. Marshal arose also, and said, "You men wait here a minute, I'll see if the colonel wants to say anything to you." He then gently shook the colonel, and said, "Colonel, some of the men are going back to the fort now. Anything you want to tell them before they go?" Williamson looked up and squinted, and said sarcastically and emphatically, "Hell, no!" then turned over and tried to go back to sleep. Marshal then gave them a sign and they left for the fort, never looking back and never discussing the incident all the way home.

Overnight, the cold, moist air laid down a killing frost, and a thin translucent covering was on everything. When anyone breathed or spoke, great clouds of white condensate gathered and practically hung from their faces. There was a sharp cracking sound when anyone walked or moved along the ground. Still, it would be a fine day to do what had to be done by the remaining soldiers.

When all the soldiers were up and stirring, Williamson said, "All right men, let's get this thing going." Marshal asked if there were any particular plan, and before Williamson could answer, a soldier standing nearby said, "Look, colonel, here's a great big cooper's mallet that we can use!" "Great idea," said the colonel, "take them out of those sheds one at a time and do it over there," he gestured toward the cemetery. The soldier quickly grabbed the mallet and practically ran to the cabin housing the men. Pausing outside, he could hear them singing Christian hymns. He opened the door, and the carnage began.

One by one, the innocent and constantly abused converted Delaware were led to the area of the cemetery and clubbed over the head viciously while they bent in prayer. Two soldiers would then grab the body and carry it a short distance to the edge of the nearby woods, where it was simply cast away. With each successive killing, the excitement grew within each of the men allowed to swing the giant hammer. Each of the soldiers took a turn swinging the death blows except the Colonel and the Lieutenant.

The smell of death was in the air and it took a long time to kill each of the men and then toss his body aside. Each victim simply walked from the cabin and knelt where ordered, and was summarily crushed from this life. It was a simple slaughter and the victims could not have been more compliant had they been sheep. In fact, some of the onlookers began to bleat derisively like sheep as each successive victim was slain. The sound of the hard maple mallet striking the victim's head echoed harshly through the still Ohio countryside, and a puff of steam would erupt from each exploding skull as it shattered. The warm blood that gushed from the wounds had, in places begun to freeze, and gave a strange rosy appearance to the frosty earth.

In the structure which had been housing the women and children, Leta and several other women pressed against the walls for a partial view through the slim cracks in the wall, for the cabin had no windows. They were aghast at what their eyes revealed. Leta hurriedly grabbed her youngest son, Jacob, and held him tight against her body, as if to deny the murderers a chance at him. Then she quickly rushed him to the far corner of the cabin and began digging frantically at the mud which had been used to seal the cracks in the boards which formed the wall. In uncontrollable fear, and with her adrenaline racing out of control through her own body, she kicked and kicked at the bottom two boards, thrashing loudly about and kicking so hard that her feet began to bleed.

She began to kick even harder when the door to the cabin was opened by the soldiers who now began taking the first of the women and children victims. Others within the tiny darkened space began weeping quietly when they began to realize the fate of their own loved ones. So great was the urgency of Leta's action and the fear for her children that her own bladder began to give slightly, in an internal physical response to fear that was simply ignored. Another mother saw what Leta was doing and soon joined her in attacking the same two bottom boards in the corner. They backed against the wall and alternated in kicking and kicking and kicking. Both of the women were covered with blood from their own wounds, but it only made them kick harder and harder. Eventually, they heard a small cracking sound and hesitated to make sure of what they thought they had heard. Sure enough, a small vertical crack appeared in the weathered bottom board, and they now kicked with even greater determination. When a piece of the board broke loose, it opened a hole about 4 inches by 10 inches, and they stooped and pulled at the board above it. Frantically, because the number of people in the room had begun to noticeably dwindle, they alternately kicked, punched, and pulled at the next board until their hands were also bloody. Finally, with one almost superhuman effort, Leta knelt and pulled the next board with all her might, and it snapped free, causing her to fall backwards, with the piece in her hands. Now the women had a hole about 8 inches by 10 inches and Leta grabbed Jacob, and kissed him hurriedly and with such force that it hurt the child. Then she literally crammed and shoved him out the hole, which was barely bigger than the child's head. Her only instruction was for him to run and hide, and Jacob did exactly as he was told.

Leta next looked over her shoulder for her son, George, and as she reached for him, the door opened in front of her and the soldier simply reached inside and grabbed for another body. The man grabbed George by the arm and began to pull him outside, but Leta grabbed her son by the other, and each tugged violently in opposite directions. Leta hung on to her son with such force that she felt her own body also being pulled toward the open door, and her grip sliding away because of the wounds which she had caused to herself in trying to free Jacob. She desperately tried for a better grip, but lost ground with each attempt. As the boy was being pulled away from her own bloody grip, she shrieked a long and mournful, blood curdling, "nnnnnNNNNNOOOOOooooo!" which echoed over the entire valley, and finally ebbed. Then George was gone. When the same soldier returned for the next victim, Leta, with tears streaming down her face and with blood from one end of her to the other, simply stepped forward with numbed resignation and was the next to be jerked out of the door. She went to her death convinced that, at least, she had saved Jacob. Other women tried to also force their children through the small opening, but the children were too big, and try as they might, no one else was able to escape through the tempting but impassable opening. A 12 year old girl was the last to be taken for execution, and she bravely went to her death without a whimper.

Many of the hammer swingers were covered with droplets of blood, which had anointed them with each head smashed. The other men were also covered by blood as they carried body after body to the edge of the woods. When they were done, 97 bodies lay gruesomely heaped and the soldiers were smiling and sweating profusely. Killing 97 people in that manner was hard work, even if 35 of them were children. With a huge heave, the deadly mallet was tossed into the woods in the direction of the steaming bodies by the man who had had the last "honor" of wielding the murderous weapon.

It was decide that they would all wash in the river before getting underway for Fort Pitt, but before they did, many of the men wanted to take home souvenir scalps. In a grisly instant, more than 25 men went to the steaming and bleeding pile of dead and dying Christians and methodically took the scalp of the nearest or most accessible body. It didn't matter that most of the accessible bodies were those of women and children, which had been dumped on top of the pile. After bathing and joking about the execution, and constantly reinforcing their evil deeds by saying how much fun it was, the men set out happily for home. It was not yet noon.

Young Jacob had fled to the other side of the river as soon as he had escaped, and for the longest time, he simply hid in the brush and did not move. By late afternoon, he raised his head and peeked in the direction of the village, but saw no movement. Slowly and with a great deal of trepidation, the young Indian made his way back across the river and slowly entered the camp, pausing every two or three feet to be certain the soldiers were gone. He did not yet know for sure what had happened that day, and he was not certain that he wanted to, either. A screaming Blue Jay dived closed by, and its sound and movements almost stopped his heart, then he continued slowly.

When he reached the center of the village, he still had no clue as to the whereabouts or condition of the others. Jacob continued roaming the village, slowly at first, then in a mild panic, for he desperately did not want to be alone. Eventually his attention was called to the steaming pile of bodies, because from his vantage point, it appeared to be a smoldering fire. As he neared the pile, he began to see that it was bodies, and he was so revulsed that he retched and threw up. The smell and the sight of all the bodies was simply too powerful for a ten year old to take. Still, he walked closer, and was about ten feet away when he heard a low moan coming from the right side of the pile of bodies, near the top. His first instinct was fear, and he started to run, but then his Christian upbringing enveloped him and he knew that he had to help.

From somewhere in the pile of dying flesh, the low moan continued, and as Jacob pulled and prodded toward the sound, he had no way of knowing that the desecrated carcass immediately in front of him was that of his own mother. The body of Isaac, his father lay almost at the bottom of the same heap of what had once been human beings. Leta had been scalped, and was so horribly disfigured that she was beyond recognition. One more low moan arose and Jacob saw its source, a small boy about his size, but hacked and gashed beyond recognition. "Help me Jacob," said the injured boy, and he extended his hand for Jacob to grasp. Jacob gave a mighty pull and the boy came free from the pile of corpses. "It's me, Thomas," said the boy. "Don't you recognize me?" The survivor was a boy his own age, and one of his regular playmates, but he, too, was unrecognizable. "Let's get out of here, quick," said Thomas, and they quickly began to walk from the scene.

Instinctively, they began to walk in the direction of their village on the shores of Lake Erie, and although they were a long, long way from there, they were not worried. As they crossed the river one last time, they stopped and looked back at the scene of the carnage. Each had lost every living member of his family, and it was an experience that few could ever survive. The horror of what each had seen, endured, and shared would be a haunting for the rest of their lives. They turned, sadly, and hurried up the slight hill before them. The sun was already sinking into the western sky, and the temperature was again beginning to plummet. The coming night promised to be cold and scary, but nothing compared to this day's killing frost.

Late March, 1782

The two small survivors to the massacre had finally reached the others at the lake and had told their stories, and the entire camp grieved openly for those who had perished. There had already been a terrible fear by those at the lake that some dreadful thing had happened to the people at Gnadenhutten, because the twenty who had collected their grain at New Schoenbrunn and had come upon the mutilated body of young Joseph had returned only a few days earlier and told their tale. The fears of the entire village were finally confirmed when Jacob and Thomas arrived.

Now David stood and stared out across the cold gray waters with a feeling of numbness which caused him much pain. John and William, after tending to the two boys, and administering spiritually to so many of the flock, quietly took a spot next to their leader and each placed an arm around him. Susan, sensing David's immediate needs, chose to remain a respectable distance away from her husband, allowing the other two missionaries to share the quiet moment. Sarah joined her and the two watched silently. The three men had already endured a life of grief together.

In response to their show of concern for him, David encircled each of them with his arms. "My two friends," said David with a heavy heart, "we have endured so much, but there is still so much to do. What do you think we should do now? Is it possible that we have foolishly let ourselves believe that we know what is right for these gentle people, even though we have led them to the brink of extinction? I thought that we were always doing the right thing — God's work. Have I — have we been in error?"

"There was a poignant tone to his questioning voice which caused both the other men to feel even more grief now.

Avoiding each other's eyes, to escape further pain, John spoke first and said, "David, you and I have known each other for such a long time. Our families were martyred and persecuted long before this country was formed. It is true that as a race, we have not suffered nearly as much as our flock, but we are now a part of each of them, and when they bleed, we all bleed with them. Men have always been inhuman to other men and it continues to be so in this new world. Would it be any different if we were still in Saxony? No — only the faces are different. The hate, the misery, and the injury goes on and on. We have given so many of these children of God a reason to live. We have not taken that reason from them, others have done it, and it would have occurred were we with them or not. Do not doubt all the good that you, and the rest of us have done. You know it is the Lord's will."

William shivered slightly in the chilly wind and said, "David, you may not have known it but I had a life of relative comfort in Maryland. However, something was missing. I felt incomplete. Oh, I always knew the Lord, to be sure, but until I joined you two here, I really did not know what I was doing or where I was going in life. We have done so much of God's work here among the Delaware, but we are a long way from being done. We have not brought any of this misery to the hearts of our flock, it exists in the hearts of those about us. Here among the flock is the *only* place that I feel complete and utter contentment, and I have just spoken to so many of them who feel the same. They do not blame us, and neither shall any of us accept the blame. I know that we all share the need to be among these kind and gentle souls who mean no harm to anyone, and I know that we all need to be together."

It was spiritually gratifying to David to hear each man's testimonial as they stood beside the lake, and each of the missionaries silently vowed to continue to be a tower of strength to themselves and the whole of their beloved, though severely diminished flock. David turned and looked over his shoulder in the direction of the shelters, and said, "God has brought us to this place, thus He must intend for us to stay. Come, my brothers — we have a lot of work to do," and they walked toward first the wives and then the others.

That evening, after the prayer service for the victims, the missionaries announced plans to lead a group of volunteers back to Gnadenhutten to give the deceased a proper burial. All three of the men knew that it would be a very difficult task for everyone involved, and they tried to soften the experience as best they could. In addition to David, John, and William, the burial party would include only volunteers — preferably non-blood relatives to any of the victims. Women were not encouraged to join the group, although there were several, in addition to Susan and Sarah, who insistently volunteered.

Tactfully, and with great sensitivity, David and John convinced the women to not only remain behind and assist with the needs of the flock, but to also convince the other women to do the same. There was plenty of difficult work enough for everyone, and the men of the flock simply elected to handle the most gruesome of the tasks by themselves. Altogether, there were only five men who had no blood relations lost at Gnadenhutten, although all of the members were close friends. Five other men, although directly related to the victims, were selected because of their strong spirituality and physical constitution which could withstand the powerful emotional drain which lay ahead. The ten volunteers were also cautioned by David that he could not guarantee anyone's safety, especially if additional encounters with the colonial militia were to occur. Not one man changed his mind.

The group of thirteen men left the following morning, despite the lingering dangers which lay ahead in the Ohio Territory. The group also took as many of the congregation's baskets as they could carry, in one final effort to retrieve the precious grain that had been left behind. The trip back was without incident, although the weather was extremely cold at night, and food was still a major problem. Along the trail, as they made their way south, the group foraged for what food they could, in almost identical manner to their previous forced march in the opposite direction. The expeditionary group had elected to take only a bare minimum of supplies — preferring to leave the vital supplies for the women and children of the flock.

Upon reaching Gnadenhutten, the group was astounded at the devastation which had overtaken their former homes. They stood, stunned in silence, and gazing at the ruins which had occurred behind them as they had been forced onward, away from the village. It did not take them long to locate the bodies, as several large vultures and crows were circling overhead, while others were already at work on the corpses. Instinctively, each of the thirteen men rushed forward and began shooing the birds away, but they were unable to protect the massive heap of decaying flesh before them.

Weeping openly, with the stench of death overpowering their nostrils, the group first began to bury the bodies individually in solitary graves, but after only three such burials, they changed their minds and decided on a single mass burial. It was also decide that a religious service would be delayed until each of the victims had been interred. So great was the grief of volunteers that it was impossible to be done otherwise. To facilitate such a burial, Edward located a short piece of ground, a small bluff, which was about five feet higher than the surrounding terrain. It required that each corpse be carried almost 200 yards from where the massacre had occurred. There the bodies were laid, one by one, side by side, with heads toward the high ground. When the ghastly heap had at last disappeared, the men then positioned themselves above the bluff and began shoveling earth down upon the dead. In a very short time, sweat replaced tears, as the men worked to near dehydration — stopping only when absolutely exhausted to sip a few mouthfuls of water.

From the ruins of the village behind them, the men used pieces of siding from the cabins to fashion crosses, which were placed above each victim. The entire burial took the men until long after darkness, and though it was unspoken, none had wanted to camp anywhere near the scene of the massacre. But the late hour made this impossible, and it was decided that they would encamp near the Tuscarawas river, as far from the scene as possible. With a roaring campfire lighting the makeshift cemetery, the group assembled for a final service for the 96 stilled bodies.

"Oh Lord," began David, as the others wept quietly with heads bowed, "we commit to You these souls so needlessly wasted. Welcome each one of them into Your heavenly home and know that they were among the best that mankind has ever offered to You. Thank You Lord, for making their suffering as short and as painless as it was, and let not their passing be in vain. Use the goodness and mercy within Your heart and theirs to purge the hatred and evil from those responsible for this act. Keep these 96 helpless children of God close and they shall continue to serve You forever more. Amen." David had kept the prayer short and directly to the point, knowing the strain upon each of the volunteers, and they also were relieved to put this part of their life behind them. Although fatigue, hunger, and cold took their toll upon them, the images of the slain were so fresh in their minds, that it was a difficult night for sleeping, and most got no rest at all. The evening prayer at the small campfire was much longer than that offered up for the deceased.

The bright early sunlight awakened the men early and within an hour, they had nearly filled their baskets with the precious grain which remained in the fields. As they made their way north again, they searched in vain for young Joseph's body, but were unable to find it. Possibly it had fallen prey to a larger beast, and had been dragged off into the brush. Weary, but satisfied at what had been accomplished on this, the final trip south, the group began the cold and lonely trip back to Erie's shore. It would be an unusually uneventful trip, given the nature of the recent treks back and forth for the persecuted Moravians and their Delaware brethren, but welcomed for its finality. They were free and, at last, going home.

There had been so many tragedies rained down upon the Moravians and their converts in the Ohio Territory that, by now, they had come to expect it as a normal part of their lives. However, the end of the Revolutionary War would give the tiny commune a measured respite from the rigors and the tragic losses so recently endured. With steadfast determination, the missionaries and the flock slowly and painfully rebuilt the physical and the spiritual infra-structures that had been so badly damaged. The trip in 1780, when he and Susan had been married, was David's last trip back to the Moravian enclave in Bethlehem, as time and all of the punishing experiences that he had endured had simply taken their toll upon his body and, more importantly, his spirit. Neither was he overly anxious to appear again before the Council of Elders and explain in great detail the circumstances that had culminated with the massacre of so many of his flock.

A rather dry, perfunctory report, devoid of nearly all subjectivity was submitted to the Church, and later this was followed up by a visit to the flock from a Church designate. The grief felt by all within the Church was appropriately relayed to Reverend Zeisberger and his associates and David was also assured that his culpability had never been an issue. To David and the others who had been so closely connected to the tragedy, the massacre was still fresh enough in their minds and spirits that they felt it could never be forgotten. There continued to be tremendous pangs of frustration among the missionaries over the fact that there seemed no person, agency, or authority with whom they could lodge a fitting protest over the atrocity.

For whatever reasons, the Moravian authorities at Bethlehem never ever took an official position on the massacre of the poor Delaware. It may have been to avoid an "I told you so" type rebuff from the colonial government, who really did caution the church about the dangers of operating missions in hostile Indian territory and also an extremely volatile war zone. And the Moravian Church was not the only entity warned, either. Similar warnings were made to other churches, commercial land companies, traders, and even to individuals setting out for destinations beyond or within the Ohio Territory from Fort Pitt and other points east. They did not warn anyone, however, that the greatest threat might come from within their own forces.

It may also have been because the Moravian officials believed that David Zeisberger, in fact, really had been engaged in some sort of espionage activity during his time in the Ohio Territory — which was in direct violation of Church policy. The earlier arrest and subsequent confinement of Reverend Zeisberger by British forces in New York did lend credence to what seemed to be at least some degree of culpability on his part. He also had not been officially *disciplined* by the Church for the first incident — a fact not lost upon the colonial authorities. Perhaps in many minds at the time, Reverend Zeisberger *was* acting in some capacity for one side or the other, although history would later reject or at least mitigate this theory.

And finally, perhaps the Church authorities did nothing because there was an immense feeling of guilt among the elders for not having exercised more control over the activities of David Zeisberger in the Ohio Territory. If they felt that anyone should be blamed, it could only have been themselves, for not being more wary of one of their own. One who already had been suspected of political activity from the time of his first arrest by the British. How could the Church possibly award David Zeisberger his own mission assignment, knowing full well of his proclivity for political involvement, and then later complain to the colonials about an incident involving his political activity?

Then too, even if the Church authorities chose to truly believe the innocence of Zeisberger in all that had ever befallen him and his fellow mission members, what chance would they have had that the colonials would even listen to their charges of a colonial faction committing such an atrocity?

First and foremost to be considered in this regard was the prevailing attitude about Indians in general. The colonials had always been plagued by hostile Indians. Hostilities between whites and Indians literally dated to the arrival of the first whites in this new land. The arriving whites alienated their native hosts by being greedy, destructive, dishonest, and just plain mean. When large numbers of whites began to fight over the land, first one side and then the other convinced the Indians to join their side. The British had merely been the latest to enlist the aid of the Indians, but apart from that, many innocent whites had long been obliged to deal with the hostile Indians. It created a pervasive negative attitude about not only hostile Indians, but *all* Indians. Many whites were simply unmoved by revelations of death and destruction suffered by any Indians, so great had been their aggravation with the Indian. To far too many whites, things like the Ohio Territory massacre would have been perceived as something that Indians simply had coming to them. It would literally fall on deaf ears were anyone to complain openly about brutal treatment of Indians. Even Christian Indians.

At the time, there was no Department of the Interior, and no Bureau of Indian Affairs, although in 1775, one of the first acts of the Continental Congress was to name a Committee on Indian Affairs. Though not a cabinet-level office, the new Committee did name three departments of Indian Affairs and urge the likes of Benjamin Franklin and Patrick Henry to take proactive roles in the administration of these departments. However, given the prevailing mood concerning hostile Indians, and the non-existence of official directives or policy, it is unlikely that anyone would or could do anything about the massacre or any other real or alleged mistreatment of Indians. In fact, it is more likely that hearing such a report, most members of the new government would have paid it little or no attention.

The evidence of colonial apathy to the Indian plight is both plentiful and powerful. Shortly after the creation of the Committee on Indian Affairs, the new government's policy on dealings with Indians in general, and the Delaware tribe in particular was set forth in the Treaty of 1778, America's First Indian Treaty. This treaty was significant for several reasons. First, it was the *very* first Indian treaty enacted by the fledgling United States government. Its status as first was no accident. It was a showcase move on the part of the new Continental Congress, who sought to gain the aid of the Indians in their fight for independence from England.

Secondly, the treaty was signed by only *three* Indian individuals — Chief White Eyes, Captain Pipe (the very same Captain Pipe who had ostensibly testified against the Moravian missionaries in Detroit), and John Kill Buck — all of them members of the Delaware Nation! In addition, the treaty was officially entitled "Treaty with the Delawares 1778," and the *only* tribe mentioned in the entire treaty was the Delaware.

Thirdly, the Delaware Nation was selected for the first treaty because of their respected status among Indians and their history of being honest and honorable in dealing with other warring factions. In fact, other tribes of the era so respected the Delaware that they were often referred to as the "Grandfather tribe" among Indians. As co-signers to the first treaty, the Delaware were selected and recognized for their place of honor and respect among Indians.

The first contact between members of the Delaware tribe (originally called Lenape) and Europeans began with the arrival of Italian explorer Giovanni da Verrazano, under contract to France, in 1524. In the narrow straits to New York harbor, which now bear his name, Verrazano and his crew entered the waters of the new world and began almost immediately to alienate the Indians. At first, and during much of Verrazano's visit, there was a good deal of mutual trust and respect with the Indians, which ended when he and his men attempted to kidnap some of the natives and return them to Europe as slaves.

For almost a century afterwards, the Delaware, as well as other smaller tribes in the area, became targets of raids of other Europeans who also sought to enslave them. Subsequent incursions into Delaware lands included those by the English, Dutch, and French. Though trade was the primary objective, specifically with furs as the most prized commodity, slavery was the continuing source of violent confrontations between the Indians and the whites. This sort of contact with the foreign invaders naturally began to turn the Delaware unfriendly toward the whites.

From the early part of the 1600s until the mid- and late 1700s, the Delaware tribe was methodically thinned in numbers due to periodic direct conflicts with the scheming Europeans, a series of smallpox epidemics (also courtesy of the whites), and confrontations and raging wars with other tribes. The conflict among the various tribes in the region was based almost wholly on disputes over land, hunting rights, and trade agreements instigated by first the Dutch, then the English, Swedish, French, and Germans. The Delaware saw their numbers, power, influence, and lands systematically dwindle from vast holdings of the eastern seaboard and upper New York to the northern middle-Atlantic regions until they were finally relegated to just two small areas. About two-thirds of the tribe ended up along the upper Ohio River, near the present Ohio-Pennsylvania-West Virginia border while the rest continued to remain in the original Delaware homeland in the area of the upper Susquehannock River.

That the Delaware were accorded the honor of signing the first treaty of the United States was in no small measure because of an earlier treaty with William Penn, which some historians point to as the *only* treaty between whites and Indians never to have been broken. The successful treaty with the Quakers also introduced them to a kindler, gentler type of European, and the influence of Christianity as well. While the other Europeans had also talked of Christianity, their actions belied their faith. But there was no such hypocrisy among the Quakers. Aside from the Quakers, only the Moravians had remained unwaveringly honorable in their relations with the Delaware, primarily because of mutual trust, and the gentle and peaceful manner in which each lived. To almost everyone in the western Pennsylvania region and Fort Pitt, the Delaware were recognized as a peaceful, non-aggressive people. To everyone but a handful of Indian-hating colonial militia, that is.

Scarcely a month after the signing of this nation's *very first* Indian treaty, it was broken by those who had initiated it. The aggressive and vengeful colonials who wantonly attacked and murdered Chief White Eyes, one of the three Delaware signers of the treaty, would go on to perpetuate even more death and destruction against the hapless Indians. Obviously, the colonial party which killed White Eyes and broke the treaty were not operating with the consent or knowledge of the colonial government, but they *were* official representatives of the United States. The incident would also mark a continuing pattern of deception and betrayal that would characterize virtually every ensuing treaty ever signed with the Indians.

On September 17, 1783, Great Britain finally signed a treaty with their former colonies which formally recognized their independence at the Treaty of Paris, and the new country proudly called itself the United States of America. But the brothers and sisters of the flock had long ago learned this spirit of unity, through the sharing and the teachings of their Moravian brothers, David, John, and William. The official end of the war now had little significance for most of the members.

Through the passing of the U.S. Ordinance of 1787, provisions for the governing of several areas, including the Northwest Territories became law, and things bode well for the flock, since the Ohio Territory was deemed a part of the Northwest Territories. Established government policies would soon protect all the citizens of the region, including, at last, the Moravian converts.

For several years — in fact, for longer than they had ever stayed in any one village in the Ohio interior — the Moravians and their flock reestablished their roots along Erie's shore and the flock prospered and grew. John and Sarah's child, a daughter, was born that April, following the massacre. She was named Susan, in honor of David's saintly wife. In the next few years, they would produce two more daughters. And the flock grew in quite another unexpected manner.

The former Delaware Chief Gelelemend, who had fled during the night and into the southern Ohio countryside in March of 1781, suddenly appeared with his family along the shores of Lake Erie in 1788, and was warmly welcomed by his old friend, David Zeisberger.

As David sat preparing his sermon for the evening service on a warm Spring afternoon in May, he saw a familiar youngster from the flock approaching with a non-Christian Indian, who limped slightly. Rising to greet the guest, he squinted in disbelief when, at about ten paces, it became obvious as to just who the Indian was. David dropped his materials and stood with his arms outstretched to the guest as a tear began to trickle from the corner of his eyes. With that, the Indian picked up his pace and hurried into David's waiting embrace. It was Gelelemend.

Both men sobbed quietly while they hugged, and the boy who had brought the man to the Reverend slipped away swiftly — somewhat embarrassed by the poignant reunion that he had just witnessed. After several seconds, the two men separated but David kept his hands gently on the man's upper arms and said, "Gelelemend, I have thought of you often, and you have always been in my prayers. I am.....I mean we are all glad to see you." A broad smile now graced his wrinkled face. David sniffed a beginning tear literally back into its duct, and he wiped his eyes with the back of his hand as Gelelemend began to speak. "David, my old friend, I have traveled many paths since I last saw you, but your warm greeting tells me that I have never been far from your heart. All of the cruel journeys that my family and I have endured since we last met have been lost in the glow of your wonderful and lasting friendship. I feel very good to be back among my people. Tell me sir, does your mission have room for an old, unsaved man and his family?"

"Oh, Gelelemend," replied David with an ever-burgeoning smile, "I'm sure that we can always make room for you and your family. So much has happened since we last met, that I don't know where to begin....." His voice trailed off, as he looked out toward the lake and began to choose his words. "We lost so many of our people to an attack by the colonials from Fort Pitt....." and before he could finish, Gelelemend told him of how he had already heard whispers of the incident during some time that he had spent at the fort. He also told David that he had been concerned that David might have been among those killed until a trader visiting the fort had put those fears to rest. After almost an hour of catching each other up on the other's business, David and Gelelemend walked to the spot in the mission where Gelelemend's family had already stopped to reunite with distant relatives and friends. A special prayer was said for Gelelemend and his family that night and at least a week of celebrations followed, leaving no doubt that *these* lost sheep were, at last, home.

The legacy of David, his assistants, and his mission members not withstanding, Gelelemend was an amazing story in himself. After fleeing the insurrectious members of his own tribe, Gelelemend had headed almost due south with his immediate family. Reaching and crossing the Ohio River, the family somehow made its way up river, until reaching the area of western Pennsylvania in which he had been born and raised. It is most ironic that he was given protection from his Delaware enemies by unnamed persons at Fort Pitt — perhaps by some of the very persons responsible for the 1782 massacre at Gnadenhutten. Upon arriving at Lake Erie, and after several weeks of convincing a skeptical Reverend Zeisberger that he was sincere in desiring, and worthy of being accepted, Gelelemend was all set to become a Christian. However, he was set upon by several of his old Delaware nemeses at a treaty signing, and beaten within an inch of his life. In 1789, after he had recovered fully, David finally baptized him and he took the Christian name of William Henry.

When the Ohio Indian wars began, shortly after William Henry joined the congregation, David, John, and William once more felt the same haunting anxieties for the welfare of their members of the flock. The Ohio Indian Wars began because of the massive influx of settlers from the east, as more and more families sought land, that was virtually free for the taking. However, most of that "free" land belonged to various Indian tribes, who resisted bitterly the advance of civilization of the new country. When the hostilities escalated to armed, violent conflict, even though the Moravians were basically far from harm's way, they felt that something had to be done.

David, John, and William once more met in the Zeisberger home to discuss the fate of the congregation. In a great surprise to everyone, John suddenly announced, "David and William, I have been with you both a long time and have delighted in sharing what God has given us, but I must now think of my family. As you are well aware, Sarah's family, the Ohneburgs, have moved close to Fort Vincennes, and my children have never seen their grandparents. Sarah and I would be pleased if you would both give your blessings on our joining them." Tears began to flow freely around the room, as first John, and then the others began to initially contemplate the separation of John, Sarah, and the girls.

David and William reached across the table, in unison to take John's outstretched hands. Susan moved close to John from behind and placed her arms about him in a gentle bear hug. "Oh, John," she cried softly, I will miss you and Sarah and those lovely girls!" "No question about it, John," said David, as he wiped his eyes and nose, "you have been with me so long, now. Of course you have my blessings, but I want you to know how deeply I will miss you and your family." David's long association with John had taken a slightly paternal twist, as it had with William, owing to their differences in ages. Now it was as if the eldest son had just announced that he were leaving home.

William, much closer to John in years, truly looked at David with fatherly respect, but his relationship with John was more akin to that of brothers — extremely close brothers, and he would not get over this separation soon. "John, my brother," he began, before rising from the table to embrace John, "I barely knew my own brother, but you have more than filled the void. You may go west to join Sarah's family, but you must always remember that you are in my heart." The moment became overwhelming for Susan, who excused herself to be alone outside the room.

When dry eyes had at last returned to the table, John informed them that he and his family would be leaving the mission within the week to join Sarah's family. David then asked John to stay on through the meeting, for his input and advice would certainly be needed and respected. The three of them discussed the possibility of moving the flock, owing to the circumstances of the Ohio Indian War, and eventually it was decided that the flock would, perhaps, be better off in a place farther away from the conflict. Several possibilities were discussed, including west, near where John intended to move; to the north, and into Canada, and to the south, in the area to which Gelelemend had originally fled. After much discussion, it was decided that Canada would be the best area for them. The Moravian Church, after being written by David, also confirmed this choice in return correspondence with David and William. The Church also passed along its best regards to John and his family.

And in June of that same year, the remaining two missionaries and their flock once more relocated, this time under voluntary circumstances, and without casualties. Setting off north across the great lake, the flock re-established itself on the Thames River in Canada, just south of the present day city of London, Ontario, and they called their mission Fairfield.

At the Battle of Fallen Timbers, deep in the interior of the Ohio territory, on August 3, 1795, General Anthony Wayne and his American troops defeated a massive Indian alliance and in a short time, a peace was finally reached when the Indians and whites signed the Treaty of Greenville, in which the tribes ceded to the whites land that now comprises most of the present area of Ohio, as well as parts of Indiana, Illinois, and Michigan. There would never again be armed conflict between whites and Indians in the Ohio territory, and more and more white settlers poured into the area.

David and Susan, in correspondence with John and Sarah, learned that in 1792, John had become Assistant Peace Commissioner for the United States Government in Vincennes, and was later doing the same assignment in Detroit. Both David and Susan laughed when they learned of John's Detroit assignment, for they never believed that any of the three original missionaries would *ever* want to return to Detroit, under any circumstances. They were, however, extremely happy for John and Sarah and their daughters.

David, Susan, and William ministered lovingly to the flock in Canada, and they had many productive years in which their mission grew in size, albeit much more slowly than in the halcyon years in the Muskingum valley. However, with no war raging about them, they were now truly left to do the peaceful work that God had surely intended for them. Still, each of them, but especially David, could not get the memory of the beautiful missions along the Tuscarawas River out of their minds or their hearts.

In August of 1798, at the age of 77, and with the blessing of the Moravian Church in Bethlehem, David Zeisberger and his wife, Susan, returned to the Ohio Territory and the beautiful and beloved Muskingum valley, along with 33 of the original surviving converts. His good and loyal friend, William Edwards, passed up the opportunity to lead his own mission and chose to accompany David and Susan back to the original mission of their dreams.

As they had done so many times in the past, the nomadic flock of David Zeisberger once more established a new mission, along the Tuscarawas River, and they called it Goshen. The mission at Goshen was located a scant few hundred yards from Zeisberger's first establishment of Schoenbrunn. Among those who joined the old missionary in the return to the Muskingum region were Jacob and Thomas, who brought with them their own families and children. The two survivors of the Gnadenhutten massacre would remain closest friends for years to come, both dedicated to David Zeisberger and the Moravian faith.

In December of 1802, as members of the flock were preparing for the Christmas season, Jacob and Thomas, working together in the fields, discovered the body of an old man laying at the edge of the woods, just north of the mission. He had been stabbed in the chest, and though the wound looked fresh, the man appeared to be dead. When they picked him up to take him to the cemetery for a proper burial, he emitted a low, but audibly distinct gasp. While Thomas tended to the man as best he could, Jacob ran toward David's residence to get help.

"Reverend Zeisberger," cried Jacob frantically, "come quickly! Thomas and I have found the body of an old man yonder and he is still barely alive, but hurt badly. It looks like he has been shot through the heart!" David and William both reacted swiftly, grabbing whatever cloth was readily available, as well as a small supply of sulfa, and hurried in the direction in which Jacob ran, and where Thomas waited with the man. A small gathering of onlookers had also started to move in the same direction.

Upon reaching the man, it was immediately obvious to both David and William that the injury was gravely serious, and that death was a distinct possibility. The man was already on his back, and semi-conscious while David cut away the shirt which covered a nasty looking hole in the upper region of his left chest. Dark red blood oozed hurriedly out of the man until David applied direct pressure to the wound with a balled-up cloth, which began to turn crimson as the man lost more and more of his precious blood. Pausing the pressure only long enough to sprinkle the infection-fighting sulfa into the wound, David quickly bound the makeshift bandage tightly to the man's chest with strips of another cloth. During the entire time, David kept speaking words of encouragement to the man, while William softly led the gathered group in a low and most somber version of the Lord's Prayer. Many of the young men and women present watched with hands clasped in a prayerful stance and heads bowed.

During the ministrations to him, the old man opened his eyes only once, but was unable to focus clearly on any of his would-be rescuers, although Thomas knelt at his head, in his line of sight. Upon seeing the man appear to gaze at him, Thomas said, "Don't worry my friend. You are among friends. We are Christians of the Moravian faith." In response, the man weakly replied, "Bless Jesus. Thank you." Then the man closed his eyes once more. For nearly an hour, until the wound stopped oozing and began to clot, the man lay in the same place, except someone had fetched a blanket to cover him.

The fact that his pockets had been turned inside out and were completely empty at the time he was found gave every indication that he might have been the victim of a violent robbery. His manner of dress indicated that he was not a hunter or trapper, and was more than likely a traveling merchant, although nothing connected to him was found in the surrounding woodlands. There were no weapons, horse, wagon, or anything else found in the area. Attempts to trace his path to the area by means of following his trail of blood were fruitless — the blood disappeared after a few yards back into the underbrush toward the east. The lack of clues to the man's identity was as baffling as his mysterious appearance at the edge of the mission.

As the man started to become fevered, David had Jacob and Thomas carry him gently to the nearest cabin, which happened to belong to Thomas and his family. They placed him on the bed and Thomas began a long vigilance over the helpless figure. Thomas would wash a cloth with cold water and dab it at the man's hot forehead. After rinsing the cloth, he would dip it in the water again and squeeze droplets onto the parched lips of the old man. In the interim, Thomas would read appropriate passages from the bible, in hopes that God's word would have a more positive healing effect. David stopped by several times throughout the evening to check on the old man and he and Thomas pondered the question of who he was and why had he been stabbed. When David was prepared to return home for the evening, he and Thomas knelt beside the man and prayed for his recovery. It did not pass on David that Thomas's eyes were thick with tears and that the young man had a great deal of empathy and concern for the older white man lying before them. David gave Thomas a warm pat on the shoulder before they both arose and before he left for the night.

Sometime during the night, perhaps an hour or two before sunrise, Thomas — still seated beside the man — but now asleep in an upright position, was awakened by the sensation of the man squeezing his arm feebly. Opening his eyes to the man, Thomas saw his eyes glazed open again for an instant, and the bearded old man stiffened, and said simply, "I'm sorry." And then he was gone. Thomas sadly pulled the blanket up over the old man's head and buried his own head in his hands and cried quietly to himself, not wanting to awaken his wife and child. This incident had been the most traumatic for him since the slaughter of his people, which had very nearly claimed his own life. This death would stick with him for as long as the others.

After sunrise, David arrived to check on the patient again, and was given the news by a weary-appearing Thomas. Looking into Thomas's bloodshot eyes, and knowing the gentle, caring nature of the man, David said, "God knows that you did all within your power to help this poor, unfortunate creature, Thomas. God will also be merciful to this man's soul." The kind words from his minister helped allay the situation somewhat for the young man. When Jacob arrived shortly, the two younger men carried the old man up to "God's Acre," where another man was already beginning to prepare a final resting place for the old man. Seeing the Reverend approach with the other men carrying the body, the worker called out to David, "Is this spot okay over here, Reverend?" The spot in question was across the cemetery from all the other graves.

"Please Reverend," said Thomas, "let him rest up here, by the others. It's so lonely way over there." Jacob shivered in the breeze and nodded his second to the motion. David smiled at the continuing benevolence within Thomas and also signaled his approval to the gravedigger, who moved his operation to the spot next to the last grave in the cemetery. While the grave was being dug, the trio laid the man gently upon the ground and waited for the hole to be finished. They mused together that they did not even know a single thing about the man about to be buried in the cold Ohio soil, and David said, "I do not enjoy burying him anonymously, although I'm certain that God will accept his soul just the same."

With Thomas at his head, and Jacob at his feet, the two men began to lift the dead man in preparation for placing him on the ropes by which he would be lowered into the grave. As Jacob began to lift first, he lifted with slightly more force than Thomas, causing the man's left boot to come off. "Wait a minute," said Jacob, "I've got to put his boot back on." As he knelt on the ground to replace the boot, he looked into the boot and found a piece of aged, folded parchment. "Hey, look at this," he exclaimed, and then handed the parchment to the Reverend, who opened it and read aloud:

"This is to identify Colonel David Williamson, of the Continental Army of the United   States. Colonel Williamson is hereby authorized to conduct business on behalf of the United States in the Northwest Territory as a senior member of the Commission on Indian Affairs. Please show him all due courtesy and respect. Signed, Brigadier General Lach'n McIntosh, Commanding Officer of the Western Department. Fort Pitt. August 13, 1798."

Each of the men then looked at each other in near complete shock. Could this possibly be the man who had been wholly responsible for the terrible act which killed almost 100 of the mission members, and who was responsible for very nearly taking the life of both Thomas and Jacob, as well? This man who lay on the ground at their feet? Was it really him? The irony of the moment was overpowering, and all three men wept. It was Thomas who spoke first, saying, "I was not seeking justice and I did not want to see even this man die." Looking toward the heavens, he continued, but now in prayer. "Please Lord, accept this poor man into Your kingdom. Forgive him for his mistakes and let his loved ones not suffer over his passing. Cleanse my heart, dear Lord, and let the pain of the moment suffice for a lifetime."

The men in the cemetery that morning quietly buried their former antagonist in a simple grave among their own loved ones and friends. It was never learned how or why the man died, or even what manner of business had delivered him to the very men he had once so savagely victimized. It is clear that the same men gave him all the attention and respect in death, that they would have given one of their very own. It also appeared as though the man knew of and appreciated their tender mercies as he drew his last breath.

None of the participants in the ceremony of burial that morning ever revealed that they believed the man they had buried in "God's Acre" had been their mortal enemy. Nor was it ever learned why the man had been in the area, or what had befallen him. A simple wooden cross, bearing the name "Williamson" marked his final resting place. Within a very short time, the death of the stranger was forgotten by all in the village except those who laid him in the ground.

Several years later, in 1814, a David Williamson, age 74, was *allegedly* buried in a pauper's grave in Washington, Pennsylvania. Whether *that* man was Col. David Williamson, however, is pure speculation. And though the identity of the man buried at Goshen would never be certain, Reverend Zeisberger, Thomas, and Jacob earnestly believed that it *was* Col. David Williamson.

On March 1, 1803, Reverend Zeisberger and the members of his flock celebrated with quiet and happy relief when the Ohio Territory formally became Ohio, the 17th state of the young nation. And in the waning years of his life, David was content to be among the people to whom he had long ministered. He died quietly in his sleep on December 12, 1808, at the age of 87, with his devoted Susan at his side. William Edwards died at age 77, and was laid to rest a few feet from David Zeisberger. In Goshen's cemetery, the simple inscription on the headstone next to that of David Zeisberger and his wife indicates that it is that of William Henry (Gelelemend), grandson of Netawatwes.

Despite all his harrowing efforts and wishes, the dreams that David and the others had sought for so many years in the Ohio Territory — that of a simple Delaware/Christian society, filled with love and hope — were never fully realized. The weather, on the day of his death, though extremely cold, was nothing compared to the killing frost which descended over this beautiful and tragic valley during that spring of 1782.

Epilogue

Although this work is based on actual events, including the horrific massacre of 1782, as a writer bent on adding character and dialogue to historical events and persons, I necessarily had to "bend" certain facts to make sense of what time has caused to be recorded with great gaping holes. Recalling events of more than 200 years requires a great effort and more. In this instance, it is called *artistic license*. Much of what we know of David Zeisberger and the Moravian experience of the Ohio Territory has been learned from the diaries which were kept by the man, himself. Except for a very short unexplained period of time in 1776, when no diary record was kept, the diaries were the primary source of information. I mean no harm to any person, living or dead, by anything contained in these pages, although where possible, I have used the actual names of the persons involved.

I must also confess that, like everyone else on earth, I am not free of my biases. In 1990, I confirmed through family genealogical research that my great grandmother, Cynthia Dixon, wife of Nathaniel May, was a full-blooded Cherokee Indian. With great pride, and having never used or attempted to use this to my financial, legal, or social advantage, I have, since then, considered myself to be a Cherokee. According to law, as a one-eighth descendant, I may legally do this. I wrote this book with an obvious bias for the Indians involved. And although I am not a Moravian, I am, however, a Christian. Upon learning of my own Indian heritage, I have become fascinated with the history of Indians, and I have been deeply saddened to learn of the many instances in which Native Americans have been defrauded, betrayed, and martyred.

Since the arrival of the first white men upon this nations's shore, the Indians have suffered. They have been lied to, cheated, stolen from, and murdered by the whites. Lands that from time immemorial had belonged to the Indians, was first taken away by well-meaning explorers, settlers, and adventurers who simply felt that Indians, because they were uneducated in the European manner, and owned no written record of their history and existence, were "savages." The Europeans were thus easily able to out-trade, outsmart, and simply trick or swindle the Indian. It became even easier when the Europeans realized that the Indians had an extremely low tolerance for alcohol. A drunken Indian was much easier to outsmart.

As an example, consider the legends that the island of Manhattan was "purchased" for only $24, or that the area of the United States comprising parts of Virginia, West Virginia, North and South Carolina, Tennessee, Georgia, Alabama, and Mississippi was originally "purchased" for a sum in excess of $3 million dollars. These deals are not proof of good real estate acumen by either of the parties, but looks suspiciously like someone got some Indians drunk and stole a whole lot of valuable property from them. If the current consumer fraud laws were in place then, those "deals" would have been negated in a heartbeat.

The concept that Indians were "savages," and hence, uncivilized, led to well-meaning Europeans desiring to educate and Christianize the Indians, when in fact, the Indians already possessed religion and education of their own, which served them very well. In truth, the people who sought to change them were driven to do so because the Indians were simply *too different*. The holocaust, apartheid, and the recent ethnic cleansing in eastern Europe are more recent examples of what happens when someone begins to think someone else is *too different*, whether the root difference in question is education, race, or religion, or something as banal as length of hair.

The Moravians, and particularly David Zeisberger, were quite a bit different than other missionaries, however. They did not think the Indians were too different, they felt that the Indians simply had not had the benefit of being introduced to the European brand of religion. The same religion that had been wholly spiritually satisfying to them. They did not try to change any Indians, including the Delaware. The Moravians first just lived among the Indians, and did not take advantage of them in the process. This was done to learn and appreciate the Indian spirit and character, and more importantly — to let the Indians know that the Moravians could be trusted. When a Delaware wanted to become a Christian, he or she had to prove that they were willing to forgo tobacco use, dancing, gambling, and drinking. Fighting was also prohibited, but with the other elements removed, fighting was not much of an issue, anyway. If the Indian could not meet the Moravian standards, he or she simply was not accepted. The rejected, or more precisely, the *nonaccepted* Indian could still live in and around the missions, and might even one day be accepted yet. These people were also **not** mistreated by the Moravians.

And neither were any of the other Indians of the Ohio Territory. No matter the tribe, the Moravians and the Delaware maintained a relaxed and peaceful neutrality with them. Only the British, on one side, and the Americans, on the other, were problematic. Both of these war opponents wanted the Moravians and their Delaware members to assist them. Because of their strategic situation in the middle of extremely valuable territory, they were a prized ally sought by each side. The British already had most of the Indians in the northern and western territories as their allies, but the Moravian-converted Delaware were not among them. The American colonists had frequently been subjected to brutal British-inspired Indian raids, and for this reason, did not trust *any* of them, including the Delaware.

The Gnadenhutten massacre of 1782 is, in my mind, and in the minds of many others also, the most shocking and atrocious act of inhuman treatment of Indians in recorded history. But in the years to follow, Native Americans would suffer countless atrocities at the hands of the white man.

The Trail of Tears of 1839, in which literally thousands of Indians were force marched from their homes in eastern lands to reservation lands in Oklahoma is a blight on the federal government of which all Indians are well aware — especially the Cherokee.

The Sand Creek, Colorado massacre of 1864, in which more than 150 Cheyenne and Arapaho — mostly old men, women, and children — were murdered by troops commanded by an overzealous, publicity-seeking colonel-turned-politico is another example of a senseless act directed toward Indians.

Generally, the Battle at Wounded Knee Creek, South Dakota in 1890 is thought of as the most devastating single event for American Indians, as several hundred warriors were killed. The battle is popularly known as the Wounded Knee Massacre, but at Wounded Knee, *both sides* were engaged in armed combat.

On December 24, 1997, shortly before this work was completed, the following article appeared in newspapers around the world:

45 die in massacre in Mexican village

ACTEAL, Mexico (AP) — A column of gunmen descended on an Indian village, opened fire with AK-47s and hunted down those who tried to flee, including terrified mothers with babies. In all, 45 people were killed in southern Mexico's worst explosion of violence since a leftist uprising four years ago.

Word of the massacre, which occurred midday Monday, was spread Tuesday by survivors and peasant

174

groups, who said about 70 gunmen loyal to a local faction of Mexico's ruling Institutional Revolutionary Party — some of them wearing state police uniforms — marched through the village firing indiscriminately.

The attack came as villagers were in church, praying for an end to the violence that has festered in impoverished Chiapas state.

"We were in church praying when we heard the shots and everyone went running in every direction," said Juan Vazquez Luna, 15, whose mother, father and four sisters were killed. Three other siblings were wounded.

Villagers fled down the mountainside toward the river, they said. Women hauled babies in shawls, men carried toddlers by the waist. People tripped on the undergrowth as they rushed down the hill. The gunmen followed them, continuing to fire, witnesses said. Soon the packed earth along the river was covered in blood.

"They didn't respect anyone. Not old people, not children, nobody," said Ernesto Mendez Paciencia, an 18-year old coffee farmer whose two brothers, 8 and 11, were killed.

Forty-five people were killed and 11 were wounded Monday in the massacre, Chiapas state Gov. Julio Cesar Ruiz said, making it the deadliest attack since rebels of the Zapatista National Liberation Army rebelled Jan. 1, 1994 to demand rights for Indians. Before a cease-fire took hold, 135 people had died in the uprising.

Mauricio Rosas, director of the Red Cross office in San Cristobal, said the death toll was 42. He told a Mexico City radio station that the victims included 21 women, six men, 14 children and an infant.

The bodies — which were taken to Tuxtla Gutierrez, the state capital — had been shot and hacked with machetes, he said. The survivors were being cared for in San Cristobal, 12 miles south of Acteal.

In a nationally broadcast address Tuesday, President Ernesto Zedillo called the massacre "an absurd criminal act."

"There is no cause, no circumstance, that could justify this action," he said.

Zedillo called on the federal attorney general and the national human rights commission to investigate, and said no resource would be denied to them. He also said federal authorities would help the state government main-

tain order, tacitly acknowledging the state government's inability to do so.

Survivors of the massacre blamed peasants from surrounding villages loyal to Zedillo's ruling party, known as the PRI. Since the rebellion began, villagers have aligned themselves with, and received backing and weapons from, either the PRI-led government, or the rebels.

As I read the above story, I could not help but compare the similarities between the recent Mexican massacre and the one about which I had just written. I was also moved to recall the Trail of Tears, in which many of my own ancestors were relocated, and the Wounded Knee Massacre. The common thread to each is, obviously, mistreatment or deprivation of Indians. Similar in many ways, but so vastly different also. Those on the Trail of Tears had food and were not deprived of their clothing. Those victims at Wounded Knee were armed, and were fighting back. The Acteal Indians had the benefit of a global media to advertise their misfortune, and have used it effectively to garner local and world opinion against those who harmed them.

On November 12, 2000, the newspapers across the country published an article which stated that the Sand Creek site had just passed the last hurdle in Congress to be declared a national historic site. Through the sponsorship of Colorado Native American Congressman, Ben Nighthorse Campbell, the Sand Creek Bill has finally become reality. However, the Gnadenhutten Massacre occurred nearly 100 years earlier and is known to but a scant handful of Americans. I cried as I recalled the Trail of Tears, the Battle of Wounded Knee, and as I read this newspaper account, just as I cried while writing of the evil deeds which occurred at Gnadenhutten.

So far as I know, no one in the British government has ever acknowledged or apologized for the treatment of the Delaware converts and their Moravian missionaries. And no one in the federal government was ever charged in the executions at Gnadenhutten, or even accused. Nor has there ever been a formal apology from the United States Government. There are no planned national monuments for the Delaware victims.

There is no national marker or designation of any kind in any of the parks and restored villages in the Ohio Territory that were once the homes of the Moravians and their beloved and totally innocent Delaware brothers. I pledge to use a portion of the profits of this book to attempt to establish such a national marker, and I urge every American to join me in this effort. The savage and senseless indignities suffered by the poor Delaware converts executed at Gnadenhutten deserve that much.

In the more than two centuries following the Gnadenhutten massacre and the ordeals of David Zeisberger and the others, the Moravian Church has continued to grow. Now more than 720,000 members strong, the membership spans the entire globe, including more than 160 congregations in twenty states and Canada.

RJM

Note: For a much more accurate, detailed, and historically correct interpretation of the Moravian/Delaware relationship, I urge you to read *David Zeisberger: A Life among the Indians*, and also *Blackcoats among the Delaware: David Zeisberger on the Ohio Frontier*, both written by Earl P. Olmstead, president of the Tuscarawas County Historical Society, and curator of the Tusc-Kent Archives, Tuscarawas Campus of Kent State University.

APPENDIX

Ohio Territory 1772-1782

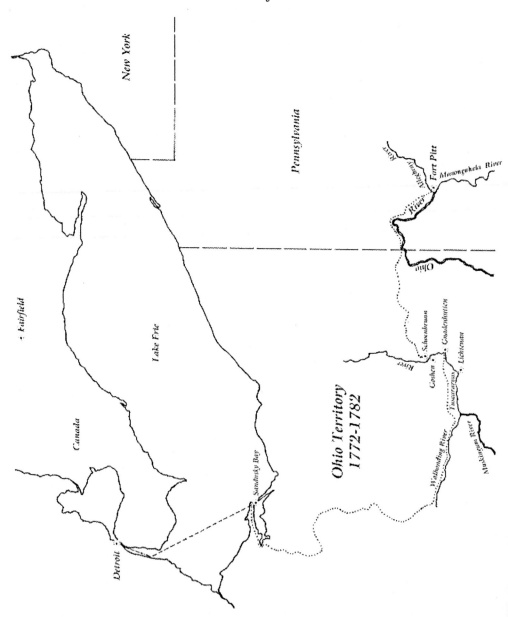

Treaty with the Delawares 1778
Sept. 17, 1778, 7 Stat., 13.

Articles of agreement and confederation, made and entered into by Andrew and Thomas Lewis, Esquires, Commissioners for, and in Behalf of the United States of North-America of the one Part, and Capt. White Eyes, Capt. John Kill Buck, Junior, and Capt. Pipe, Deputies and Chief Men of the Delaware Nation of the other Part.

ARTICLE 1. *That all offences or acts of hostilities by one, or either of the contracting parties against the other, be mutually forgiven, and buried in the depth of oblivion, never more to be had in remembrance.*

ARTICLE 2. *That a perpetual peace and friendship shall from henceforth take place, and subsist between the contracting parties aforesaid, through all succeeding generations: and if either of the parties are engaged in a just and necessary war with any other nation or nations, that each shall assist the other in due proportion to their abilities, till their enemies are brought to reasonable terms of accommodation: and that if either of them shall discover any hostile designs forming against the other, they shall give the earliest notice thereof that timeous measures may be taken to prevent their ill effect.*

ARTICLE 3. *And whereas the United States are engaged in a just and necessary war, in defence and support of life, liberty and independence, against the King of England and his adherents, and as said King is yet possessed of several posts and forts on the lakes and other places, the reduction of which is of great importance to the peace and security of the contracting parties, and as the most practicable way for the troops of the United States to some of the posts and forts is by passing through the country of the Delaware Nation, the aforesaid deputies, on behalf of themselves and their nation, do hereby stipulate and agree to give a free passage through their country to the troops aforesaid, and the same to conduct by the nearest and best ways to the posts, forts or towns of the enemies of the United States, affording to said troops such supplies of corn,eat, horses, or whatever may be in their power for the accommodation of such troops, on the commanding officer's, &c. paying, or engaging to pay the full value of whatever they can supply them with. And the said deputies, on the behalf of their nation, engage to Join the troops of the United States aforesaid, with such a number of their best and most expert warriors as they can spare, consistent with their own safety, and act in concert with them; and for the better security of the old men, women and children of the aforesaid nation, whilst their* *warriors are engaged against the common enemy, it is agreed on the part of the United States, that a fort Of sufficient strength and capacity be built at the expense of the said States, with such assistance as it may be in the power of the said Delaware Nation to give, in the most convenient place, and advantageous situation, as shall be agreed on by the commanding officer of the troops aforesaid, with the advice and concurrence of the deputies of the aforesaid Delaware Nation, which fort shall be garrisoned by such a number of the troops of the United States, as the commanding officer can spare for the present, and hereafter by such numbers, as the wise men of the United States in council, shall think most conducive to the common good. For the better security of the peace and friendship now entered into by the contracting parties, against all infractions of the same by the citizens of either party, to the prejudice of the other, neither party shall proceed to the infliction of punishments on the citizens of the other, otherwise than by securing the offender or offenders by imprisonment, or any other competent means, till a fair and impartial trial can be had by judges or juries of both parties, as near as can be to the laws, customs and usages of the contract parties and natural justice: The mode of such trials to be hereafter fixed by the wise men of the United States in Congress assembled, with the assistance of such deputies of the Delaware Nation, as may be appointed to act in concert with them in adjusting this matter to their mutual liking. And it is further agreed between the parties aforesaid, that neither shall entertain or give countenance to the enemies of the other, or protect in their respective states, criminal fugitives, servants or slaves, but the same to apprehend, and secure and deliver to the State or States, to which enemies, criminals, servants or slaves respectively belong.*

ARTICLE 5. *Whereas the confederation entered into by the Delaware Nation and the United States, renders the first dependent on the latter for all the clothing, utencils and implements of war, and it is judged not only reasonable, but indispensably necessary, that the aforesaid Nation be supplied with such articles from time to time, as far as the United States may have it in their power, by a well-regulated trade, under the conduct of an intelligent, candid agent, with an adequate salary, one more influenced by the love of his country, and a constant attention to the duties of his department by promoting the common interest, than the sinister purpose of converting and binding all the duties of his office to his private emolument: Convinced of the necessity of such measures, the Commissioners of the United States, at the earnest solicitation of the deputies oresaid, have engaged in behalf of the United States, that such a trade shall be afforded said nation, conducted on such principles of mutual interest as the wisdom of the United States in Congress assembled shall think most conducive to adopt for their mutual convenience.*

ARTICLE 6. *Whereas the enemies of the United States have endeavored, by every artifice in their power, to possess the Indians in general with an opinion, that it is the design of the States aforesaid, to extirpate the Indians and take possession of their country: to obviate such false suggestion, the United States do engage to guarantee to the aforesaid nation of Delawares, and their heirs, all their territorial rights in the   fullest and most ample manner, as it hath been bounded by former treaties, as long as they the said Delaware Nation shall abide by, and hold fast the chain of friendship now entered into. And it is further agreed on between the contracting parties should it for the future be found conducive for the mutual interest of both parties to invite any other   tribes who have been friends to the interest of the United States, to Join the present confederation, d to form a state whereof the Delaware Nation shall be the head, and havea representation in Congress: Provided, nothing contained in this article to be considered as conclusive until it meets with the approbation of Congress. And it is also the intent and meaning of this article, that no protection or countenance shall be afforded to any who are at present our enemies, by which they might escape the punishment they deserve.*

In witness whereof, the parties have hereunto interchangeably set their hands and seals, at Fort Pitt, September seventeenth, anno Domini one thousand seven hundred and seventy-eight.

s/
Andrew Lewis
Thomas Lewis
White Eyes, his x mark
The Pipe, his x markk John Kill Buck, his x mark
In the presence of
Lach'n McIntosh, brigadier-general, commander of the Western Department.
Daniel Brodhead, colonel Eighth Pennsylvania Regiment,
W. Crawford, colonel,
John Campbell,
John Stephenson,
John Gibson, colonel Thirteenth Virginia Regiment,
A. Graham, brigadier major,
Benjamin Mills,
Joseph L. Finley, captain Eighth Pennsylvania Regiment,
John Finley, captain Eighth Pennsylvania Regiment

Printed in the United States
2372

9 781588 270603